Louise Allen loves immersing herself in history. She finds landscapes and places evoke the past powerfully. Venice, Burgundy and the Greek islands are favourite destinations. Louise lives on the Norfolk coast and spends her spare time gardening, researching family history or travelling in search of inspiration. Visit her at louiseallenregency.co.uk, @LouiseRegency and janeaustenslondon.com.

D1077069

Also by Louise Allen

Once Upon a Regency Christmas
Marrying His Cinderella Countess

Brides of Waterloo miniseries

A Rose for Major Flint

Lords of Disgrace miniseries

His Housekeeper's Christmas Wish
His Christmas Countess
The Many Sins of Cris de Feaux
The Unexpected Marriage of Gabriel Stone

The Herriard Family miniseries

Forbidden Jewel of India
Tarnished Amongst the Ton
Surrender to the Marquess

Discover more at millsandboon.co.uk.

THE EARL'S PRACTICAL MARRIAGE

Louise Allen

MILLS & BOON

All rights reserved including the right of reproduction
in whole or in part in any form. This edition is published
by arrangement with Harlequin Books S.A.

This is a work of fiction. Names, characters, places, locations
and incidents are purely fictional and bear no relationship to
any real life individuals, living or dead, or to any actual places,
business establishments, locations, events or incidents.
Any resemblance is entirely coincidental.

This book is sold subject to the condition that it shall not,
by way of trade or otherwise, be lent, resold, hired out
or otherwise circulated without the prior consent of the publisher
in any form of binding or cover other than that in which it is published
and without a similar condition including this condition
being imposed on the subsequent purchaser.

® and TM are trademarks owned and used by the trademark owner
and/or its licensee. Trademarks marked with ® are registered with the
United Kingdom Patent Office and/or the Office for Harmonisation
in the Internal Market and in other countries.

First Published in Great Britain 2018
by Mills & Boon, an imprint of HarperCollins*Publishers*
1 London Bridge Street, London, SE1 9GF

© 2018 Melanie Hilton

ISBN: 978-0-263-93275-1

MIX
Paper from
responsible sources
FSC˙ C007454

This book is produced from independently certified FSC™ paper
to ensure responsible forest management.
For more information visit www.harpercollins.co.uk/green.

Printed and bound in Spain
by CPI, Barcelona

To the Pit Crew with all my love

Chapter One

Beckhampton on the Bath Road—June 1814

'This is completely unacceptable.'

'You are accustomed to the forces of nature observing your convenience, ma'am?'

She should have ignored the man, obviously. No lady fell into conversation with complete strangers at roadside inns and most certainly not with tall, raffish ones. And by definition, as this one had addressed her uninvited, he was not behaving as a gentleman should.

Laurel turned her head to give him a fleeting glance, although the fine mesh of her veil blurred his features a trifle. She had looked more directly earlier, of course, when she was certain she was unobserved. She was female after all and, at twenty-five, not quite a dried-up spinster on the shelf yet, whatever her stepmother liked to imply. She had a pair of perfectly good eyes and a functioning pulse and the stranger was a good looking man if you liked tall, broad-shouldered blonds with overlong hair. And a tan—another indication that he was not a gentleman, although to be fair she supposed he might be connected to the East India Company or have just arrived home from the West Indies.

She had been sitting at a table in the public room of the Beckhampton Inn sipping tea with her maid, Binham, primly silent at her side, when he had sauntered in. He ordered porter which he drank with one elbow propped negligently on the bar as though this were some common ale house and not a highly respectable posting house on the Bath Road.

'I am used to the postilions I hire knowing the way to circumnavigate obstacles, sir,' she said now. 'I do not expect them to throw up their hands and declare that they must make an exceedingly lengthy detour simply because a tree is down and blocking the road at Cherhill.'

They were now standing in the yard and it was becoming unpleasantly crowded with the stage just in and three other post-chaises beside her own jostling for space and changing horses. In the midst of the bustle the guard from the London Mail was standing, the post bags slung about him and the reins of one of the abandoned Mail's team in his hand, ordering a riding horse to take him on to London while fielding agitated queries as to just how bad the blockage was three miles ahead.

'As I told you, ma'am, we can go south to Devizes and then Melksham and get to Bath that way round.' The postilion who had brought her the unwelcome news shot her a resentful look. 'By all accounts the only thing that'll get round that big old oak is a rider on horseback. The Mail's stuck on the other side and if they can't get the Mail through, they can't get anything on wheels past.'

'And I explained to you when we set out that I require to call in at Pickwick on the way.' Laurel opened the route book that she had tucked in her reticule and ran one finger down the column for roads to Bath. 'As I thought. If we go via Melksham, which is what you are suggesting, then it is a significant detour to reach Pickwick.'

'No other way to do it, ma'am.' The wiry little man stood firm.

Laurel sighed, more at herself than at him. The past few weeks she had lost both her patience and her sense of humour and she knew it. None of this was life and death—nothing actually felt very important any more, if she was honest. If they had to make a long detour and were late reaching Aunt Phoebe's house, then that was the risk one took in making a journey. Stepmama was right, she was turning into an old maid before her time, crotchety and intolerant.

'Very well. I am sure you know best.'

'Or possibly not,' the stranger remarked, brazenly intervening in the conversation again. 'What about the old road by Shepherd's Shore and round over the flank of the Downs to Sandy Lane?'

'The turnpike trust gave up maintaining that road more than fifty years ago, sir.'

'It is still there, is it not?'

'Aye, sir, and I'm sure it is fit for farm carts and riders, but not for the likes of Quality in a chaise.'

'The ground is dry, there is little wind and you have a team of four.' The man turned to Laurel. 'I am on horseback, so I can lead the way. It will be rutted and it's a long pull, but it bypasses Cherhill and Calne and you will be able to re-join the road to Chippenham and Pickwick without having to turn back on yourself.'

Laurel studied him, wondering why he seemed vaguely familiar, but unable to pin down why. One man could hardly be a danger to her, she told herself. She had an escort of a maid and two postilions, albeit sulky ones. There was the risk of breaking a wheel or an axle and finding herself stranded on top of these godforsaken Downs, of course, but she wanted to get to Bath badly enough to take that chance.

'Thank you, sir. I am obliged.' She turned to the postilions. 'You heard the gentleman, we will follow him to Sandy Lane.'

They turned and went to the horses without comment, although if backs of heads could speak Laurel thought they would be saying, *You'll be sorry.* Or possibly, *Women!*

'Ma'am, excuse me, but have we met before?'

He feels it, too?

The stranger was staring as though he hoped to penetrate her veil. He had blue eyes and dark, dark lashes.

'I hardly think so, sir.' She did not trust blue eyes, however attractive, and it was unwise to be drawn into conversation which was doubtless a handy ploy for scoundrels. Before you knew where you were you were revealing information about acquaintances and locations that would give a confidence trickster or a seducer valuable insights. Not that she thought him either, but presumably if such people were obvious they would not be very successful.

'No, of course not.' He frowned. 'It was something in the way you tipped your head to one side when you were thinking. It reminded me of an old acquaintance.' Whoever it was, the memory did not appear to give him much pleasure.

Laurel nodded and walked away from him to the chaise. His face was intelligent and sensitive when he was serious, not merely handsome. That expression made up for the blue eyes—in fact, it was positively engaging. *Trust me*, it said.

'Hah!' she said under her breath as she climbed into the chaise and made room for Binham on the seat beside her. Men were not trustworthy, strangers or relatives, or friends. Life had taught her that.

'My lady?' Her new maid, a stickler for protocol, including being addressed by her surname by her employer and as Miss Binham by the lower servants, was radiating disapproval at the conversation with a strange man. Her stepmother thought well of Binham. Laurel had plans to find the lady's maid a new employer at the earliest opportunity unless she showed signs of developing a sense of humour.

'Nothing, Binham. Hold tight, this will be a bumpy ride, I fear.'

They turned south, then west, climbing steadily, paralleling the modern road two miles or so away to their right on the other side of the great rise of Downland. Almost immediately the metalled road turned into a chalk track, rutted and white with dust.

Binham gave a little shriek at the first lurch, clutched Laurel's dressing case to her bosom with one hand and grabbed for the strap with the other. Laurel held on tightly and looked forward, through the glass between the team of four and the postilions, to the horseman leading the way.

He was sitting relaxed on a big grey horse that had as much of a raffish air about it as its master, its tail ungroomed and long, its legs covered in the thick dust of the road. It was not some hired hack, that was for sure, not ridden on such a loose, trusting rein by a man who looked as though he had spent so long in the saddle that he was perfectly at home there.

Laurel pushed back her veil and narrowed her eyes at the broad shoulders, the comfortable slouch. It was most improbable, but there was still something familiar about the man.

No, it isn't familiarity, she thought. *It is as if someone rubbed out a faint pencil sketch of a young man and then drew this one on the same sheet of paper with the ghost of the original showing through.*

Which was ridiculous. The only person she had ever known with such lapis-blue eyes had been Giles Redmond and he had been an unprepossessing youth, his big feet and hands, large nose and ears all seeming to belong to someone else and not the mousey, scholarly young man. He had been thoughtful and sensitive though, always a loyal friend—and always failing to meet his father's expectations.

Gentle, kind, fun to be with and tolerant of the neighbours' daughter, two years younger than him: no one had suspected that sixteen-year-old Laurel Knighton could fall for such a plain and retiring youth, even if he was the heir to a great title. But kindness, humour and intelligence could be as attractive to an impressionable girl as good looks and confidence.

The Marquess of Thorncote, Giles's father, had wanted a son from the same mould as himself for his heir—active, noisy, enthusiastically confident, a man who would hunt all day and wench and drink all night. Instead he had Giles, nose in a book, secretive and more likely to shoot his own foot off than hit a pheasant.

Strange that he had so little idea of what his son was truly like, any more than she had known. It had almost been funny, the expression on the Marquess's face the day the worm turned and Giles showed his true colours and her friend had revealed himself for the treacherous, deceitful beast that he was.

But that was nine years in the past. The Marquess was ailing now, they said, not that there was any social interaction between Malden Grange, home of William Knighton, Earl of Palgrave, her late father, and Thorne Hall. Not since the day of the betrothal debacle.

Malden was not her home any longer, not now that she had no function beyond that of spinster stepdaughter. Laurel narrowed her eyes at the worn brown riding coat ahead as though its wearer was personally responsible for her change of circumstances and the move to Bath.

Which was unfair, she told herself.

Just let me get to Laura Place—the name so close to her own must surely be a good omen—*and I will learn to be contented and useful again. I refuse to become a sour old maid. I* will *be happy, find happiness in all the little things*.

She was simply resentful of the stranger triggering something in her memory of those long-ago days, she supposed.

They were still climbing, the horses labouring now as the wheels stuck in deep ruts or lost their grip on loose stones. Open grassland spread out on either side and Laurel dropped the window, filling the stuffy interior of the chaise with cool air and the sound of birdsong all around them.

'It feels like the roof of the world,' she said as they came to a halt and she realised the vehicle was on the level. Then she hastily adjusted her veil as the stranger brought his horse round and leaned down from the saddle to look through the open window.

'The team needs to rest a while after that pull and the view is spectacular.'

'I have been looking at it, thank you.'

Definitely not a gentleman if he persisted in talking to a lady to whom he had not been introduced.

'Not on that side, this way.' He gestured with his riding crop. 'Come and see.'

Outrageous, of course. She should snub him and raise the glass and sit demurely in the carriage until the horses were rested. She was thoroughly bored with that carriage.

I am looking for happiness in small things, Laurel reminded herself, looking at the froth of white cow parsley in the sunlight, smelling the fresh scent of growing things. 'Very well. Come along, Binham. Oh, do leave the dressing case. Who is going to steal it up here?'

With the maid's stare heating the spot between her shoulder blades Laurel picked her way along a side track and was suddenly not only on the roof of the world, but on its very edge. The close-cropped grass fell away at her feet, the valley of the Avon spread out before her. The face of the Downs was marked with deep, wide, dry valleys, as though a giant had pressed his fingers into the earth while it was still malleable, and the grass was starred with the white shapes of grazing sheep.

'Oh, how lovely.' She flipped back her veil to see better, the breeze a cool caress on her cheeks.

'Ouch! I've turned my ankle, my lady.'

Binham was glaring mutinously at the tussocky grass with its liberal sprinkling of sheep droppings. She had hardly taken a few steps, let alone enough to twist her foot. This was simply rebellion. Laurel was too weary of her to argue. 'Go back to the chaise then, Binham.'

Beside her the stranger watched the retreating maid, then turned back to Laurel, his gaze sharpening as he took in her unveiled face. Surely she had imagined the fleeting puzzlement in his expression, because it was not there now. 'Yes, it is lovely,' he agreed. 'I have missed England in the spring.' So she had been right, he had been abroad. 'Listen to the skylarks. See, there is one, so ridiculously high.' He pointed, leaning right back to look up at the tiny speck far above their heads.

Laurel leaned back, too, following the line of his pointing finger. 'So brave, singing its heart out, trying to touch the heavens.'

She lost her balance and stumbled. The man caught her, turned her and stood, his hands cupping the points of her shoulders. 'Dizzy? I have you.'

Yes, yes, you do.

There was something about him, something so familiar, so dear and yet so tinged with regret and sadness—and yet, surely she had never met this man before.

She stood there, looking deep into the blue depths of his eyes, stood far too close, too long, his palms warm even through the thickness of her pelisse and gown. Then he took his hands away, as though freeing a captured bird, and, very slowly, giving her all the time in the world to run, he bent forward until his mouth met hers.

It was the merest brush, a caress without pressure, without demand. He stood still, lips slightly parted as hers were, exchanging breath in a way so intimate she felt an ache of longing in her breast.

Then he stepped back abruptly, his face as neutral and guarded as if they had never stopped talking about birds and landscape. 'The horses will be rested sufficiently now. We had best be on our way.'

Laurel blinked at him, dazed, then caught herself. She was behaving like some bemused village maiden when she was a sophisticated, experienced lady who had been kissed dozens of times. Well, six at least, by partners at local Assemblies and once, embarrassingly, by the curate emboldened after three glasses of the New Year's Eve punch.

She lifted her chin and walked away towards the chaise without a word, lowering her veil as she went.

The postilions got up from beneath a hawthorn bush where they were sharing a clay pipe between them. Neither looked very happy at such a speedy return. Doubtless they thought she had disappeared for a prolonged period of dalliance, leaving them to their leisure, Laurel thought, thankful for the concealing veil.

Although who vanishes into the countryside to misbehave with a chance-met stranger with their maid on their heels?

It had been the merest chance that Binham had turned back in a sulk, the merest chance Laurel had almost fallen and he had caught her.

Or perhaps she was being naïve and he had lured her out and unbalanced her on purpose.

She certainly knew very little about dalliance, inside or in the open.

The track wound its way downhill, the carriage lurched and swayed, and Laurel, searching for something to take her thoughts from that magical moment on the hilltop, could appreciate why the turnpike trust had given up on maintaining it and opened up the longer, gentler route. They passed other lanes, a few farms, and then after perhaps twenty minutes drew up on the level in a small hamlet in front of an old inn, sprawling under a canopy of trees.

The horseman wheeled his mount and bent to speak to her through the window. 'Here you may try the famous Sandy Lane pudding at the Bear Inn, as favoured by none other than the late Beau Nash himself, or press directly on to Chippenham. The roads are metalled again from this point so your journey should be smooth.' He did not sound like a man who had just kissed a complete stranger on top of the Downs.

'Thank you, sir. I will press on, if you would be so good as to tell the postilions.' She did her best to sound as politely indifferent as he did. 'I appreciate your suggestion and your guidance, it has saved me a long detour.'

'My pleasure, ma'am.' He touched his whip to the brim of his hat, then called out instructions to the men before urging the grey horse forward.

'A small adventure,' Laurel commented to Binham, who pursed up her mouth in response. An adventure and a lesson not to be so suspicious and grumpy. The chance-met stranger had been a not-quite-harmless Samaritan and only slightly a dangerous rake. She had no excuse for regretting his departure, she told herself firmly, resisting the temptation to run her tongue over her lips.

The Earl of Revesby shifted in the saddle and thought longingly of sinking into a deep, hot tub at the Christopher Hotel. But first he was going to see where the discontented traveller with the mysterious deep brown eyes and the glossy dark hair and the cherry-sweet lips was bound for. He dug into the pocket of his greatcoat, found the worn lump of pewter inside and turned it between his fingers, the infallible remedy for impatience, restlessness, nerves.

Arthur, the big grey, named for the Duke whose nose resembled his, cocked up a rear hoof and relaxed, and his rider slapped his neck. 'We're both tired, a stable for you soon, boy.' He had waited for the chaise to pass him, as patient as any highwayman in the shelter of a copse, then had followed at a distance all the way to Bath, driven by curiosity, arousal and a nagging sense of familiarity.

What was he doing kissing a chance-met lady?

His head reminded him firmly that, besides any other considerations, that kind of thing led to consequences which could range from a slapped face to a marriage at the end of a shotgun wielded by a furious father. But there had been a compulsion, a spur-of-the-moment irresistible impulse far louder than the competing voice of common sense.

He'd had no difficulty ignoring the many lures thrown out to him on his way home from Portugal, yet now he had fallen victim to a pair of fine brown eyes. *Again*, he reminded himself savagely. He appeared to have developed a dangerous partiality for dark brown eyes and, given how much trouble simply smiling at the owner of a fine pair of them had got him into, it was madness to escalate to snatching kisses.

As he watched, a footman hurried out of the elegant house on Laura Place, followed by a grey-haired lady who embraced the passenger almost before she set a foot on the ground. Neither of them looked round as the horse walked past down Great Pulteney Street. The irritable lady with the sense of beauty and the tantalising gaze was safe and he knew where she was. That was quite enough for one day.

Chapter Two

'Darling Laurel, here you are at last! Welcome to your new home, my dear. I expect you would like to freshen up a little before we have some tea—Nicol, show Lady Laurel and her maid to her rooms—and then we can be cosy and talk.'

Aunt Phoebe, the widowed Lady Cary, spoke as rapidly as ever, Laurel thought. Slightly breathless after her first encounter in years with her mother's sister, she followed the butler up two flights of stairs. She had been given a suite of rooms, he told her and she found it took up the entire floor—on one side a bedchamber and dressing room overlooking the garden at the back and on the other a sitting room with a view of Laura Place with its fountain in the middle of a railing-encircled patch of grass and shrubs. Behind the sitting room was a bedchamber for Binham, who was pleased to give it a stately nod of approval. Laurel took off her bonnet, gloves and pelisse, washed her hands and face then went back down again, leaving Binham to unpack.

'Darling, is it all right?' Phoebe picked up the teapot and began to pour the moment Laurel stepped into the drawing room. 'I thought that apple green for the hangings in the bedchamber was appealing, but you must change it if you loathe it.'

'It is delightful. All the rooms are.' She took the cup and sat down. 'I am so grateful and I will do my very best to be a good companion for you. You must tell me exactly how you want things done and how you would like me to go on.'

'Laurel, what nonsense! I do not need a companion, not the kind I give orders to, that is. I am very happy to have your company and to give you a home, but I have more than enough to fill my life without having to take on a companion. What a ghastly thought, it makes me feel ancient. Although I suppose I am not quite a spring chick, although I don't feel it, at least I do not when I have a new hat or go dancing or… Yes, dear?'

'But Stepmama said that I could be of some use to you.' Laurel studied her aunt, who looked younger than her sixty-odd years, highly fashionable and very active and lively indeed. A severe critic might murmur something about *mutton dressed as lamb*, or *Chatterbox!*, but that would be unkind, Laurel decided. Her aunt was clearly amiable and well meaning. She certainly was not the elderly invalid Laurel had been expecting. Had this journey been in vain and there was nothing here for her usefully to do and no chance of a new life? 'She said that this was one place where I might be of some use to someone, in fact.'

'Have a ginger biscuit. My sister-in-law is an old cat. I cannot imagine what your father, Lord rest him, was thinking of when he married her. How old are you, Laurel dear? Twenty-six soon? And I suppose she tells you that you are on the shelf, simply because your father's dynastic plotting went awry nine years ago and now you are out of mourning she is too tight-fisted to give you a London Season and let you find a husband for yourself.' Phoebe snapped a ginger biscuit between small white teeth.

'I do not look for marriage, Aunt Phoebe. I had the chance, although I did not realise it at the time, and I made a mull of it.' She and Giles between them. 'He was in love—' or, more accurately, in lust '—with someone else and I… I made rather a fuss about it.'

That was putting it mildly. She had turned a family crisis into a full-scale district-wide scandal, ruined her own chances and drove Giles into exile in Portugal, of all things. And, inevitably, into disgrace with his father. 'I expect Papa told you all about it at the time.'

'Your father sent me an absolute rant of a letter about undutiful daughters, idiot youths and lamentations about the failure of his scheme to join the two estates. I could not make head nor tail of most of it. I was going to invite you to stay with me in town to get away from the fuss and botheration, but then your dear mother died and then my poor Cary and when we were all over the worst of that your father wrote to say he needed you to look after young Jamie… Oh, dear, I *knew* I should have insisted that you come to me.'

'Jamie did need me. He was so devastated when Mama died—he was only five. And then Papa married again and… It was all rather difficult. Jamie did not take to Stepmama and she found him difficult to accept. I do not think she ever came to terms with him being illegitimate. I could not understand at first, but now I suppose she thought that if Papa could raise his late cousin's son, then he might have a tolerant attitude towards infidelity, when of course, it was quite the opposite. He and Mama deplored Cousin Isabella's actions, but they believed an innocent child should not suffer for them.'

Not many people could, to be fair. It was a good thing Jamie had gone away to sea now he was old enough to be hurt by snubs and chance remarks about his mama, who had run off with her groom and who had died giving birth to their son. 'It was all too much for a little boy,' she explained. 'He needed the stability of someone familiar to care for him. And then with Papa dying a year ago…'

'He needed you for nine years? After a few months you could surely have employed a governess and then some tutors and freed yourself to live your own life. You could have married, dear.'

'Jamie needed me. He was—is—very much attached to me,' Laurel flared, on the defensive. Was this going to be like living at home all over again? Who would she marry when the whispers all around the area were that years ago Lady Laurel had driven away her suitor—a young man much liked in the district—and that her father had decimated her dowry in fury at having his plans thwarted?

'Oh, bless him. So young to be leaving home to become a midshipman. It must have been a terrible wrench for him, poor little lad.' Phoebe fumbled for a tiny lace-edged handkerchief and dabbed at her eyes.

'Yes. Yes, of course it was.' The 'poor little

lad' had scrambled up into the gig, all five foot six of lanky fourteen-year-old, his precious new telescope clutched under his arm. He had immediately begun chattering to Sykes, the groom whose son was a second mate on a cutter, about life at sea and his ambitions and his new ship and how well he had done in his midshipman's examinations.

'...third in the geometry paper and second in...' His voice had floated back down the driveway to where his stepmother Dorothy and Laurel, her handkerchief scrunched in her hand and a brave, determined smile on her face so he would not turn around and see her weeping, stood on the steps to wave him goodbye. But Jamie had not turned round, not for a second.

His letter home, sent from Portsmouth just before he boarded his ship, was blotted, scrawled and bubbling with excitement. He'd met some of the other midshipmen—great guns all—and seen the captain, trailing clouds of glory behind him from his last engagement with the French, and as for the ship, at anchor in the bay, well, the *Hecate* was the finest thing afloat. It was capital not being tied down with boring lessons any more and having all the other fellows to talk to, Jamie wrote before signing his name. And that was the only reference to her.

'I expect he is homesick and perhaps seasick,' Laurel said, fixing her smile in place securely. 'But I am sure he will recover from both soon enough.'

Stepmama had been right. Jamie had not needed her, had not needed her for years. It was she who had used him as a shield behind which she could do more or less as she pleased, provided that did not involve straying more than five miles from home. And now she was not needed at Malden Grange at all. Her stepmother had the domestic situation firmly under control and did not welcome another woman's finger in her pies— literally or metaphorically. And she had begun to make snide remarks about Laurel's allowance now Jamie required fitting out and would doubtless need more financial support as he climbed the ladder of his new career.

Her second cousin Anthony, now Earl of Palgrave, had been most gracious in allowing them to remain at home and not requiring them to move out to the Dower House immediately. He apparently enjoyed living at the original seat of the earldom, Palgrave Castle, on the other side of the county, but surely he would marry soon and might well want to move his bride into the more modern and convenient Malden Grange that her father had always used.

'I only want to be of use,' she had said and her stepmother had pointed out tartly that no help was needed and that if she thought she was going to turn into one of those do-gooding spinsters, setting up schools for dirty orphans or homes for fallen women, then she was not doing it at Dorothy's expense or from under her roof.

At which point it had occurred to Stepmama that Laurel had a widowed aunt in Bath. Bath was full of old maids, widows and invalids, therefore Aunt Phoebe, who was certainly widowed, was probably also an invalid. Laurel could go and be useful looking after her, she had declared. Lady Cary could well afford a companion, as it was common knowledge that both her father and her husband had left her well provided for.

'And I do not want a husband,' Laurel added firmly. She was too old and cynical now to be starry-eyed about men and she was approaching the age when no one would expect her to find a spouse. She would be that creature of pity, a failure, an unmarried woman, and she would be happy to be so, she told herself. Her judgement of character had proved disastrously faulty, now she had no wish to risk her heart and her future happiness. She had managed to hide away while she was at the dangerous age when everyone expected her to marry—now, surely, at almost twenty-six she was safe from matchmakers?

'Really, dear? You do not want to marry? But you are so pretty and intelligent and eligible: it is such a waste. I will not despair and I will be very glad to have your company, of course, until some sensible man comes along and snaps you up.' She leaned forward and patted Laurel's hand. 'Your home is here, dear, for as long as you want it.'

'Thank you,' Laurel said with some feeling. It was reassuring to have someone who wanted her. 'But I cannot live off your charity, Aunt Phoebe. If you required a companion, then of course, board and lodging in return would be fair, I suppose. But I do have my allowance from Papa's estate and what Mama left me, so I can pay my way and share expenses.'

'Bless you, child.' Phoebe waved a beringed hand at the cake stand. 'And eat, Laurel, you look ready to fade away.' She cocked her head to one side and Laurel tried to return the beady look calmly. 'You are too pale and with that dark brown hair and eyes you need more colour in your cheeks. I expect a year in mourning has not helped matters. I have no children,' she added with an abrupt change of subject. 'My poor dear Cary always felt that very much, but he never reproached me. You, my dear, are as welcome here as my own daughter would have been.'

'I am? But, Aunt… Phoebe, I do not know what to say. Except, if you are certain, thank you. I hardly know—' It was impossibly good news. Welcome, a new home where, it seemed, she could be free to be herself. Whoever that was.

'There is no need to thank me,' Phoebe said with her sweet smile. 'I am being a perfectly selfish creature about this. I have no expectation of keeping you long, whatever you say—there are too many men in Bath with eyes in their heads and good taste for that!—but I will very much enjoy your company until the right one comes along and finds you.'

'Our best suite, my lord.' The proprietor of the Christopher Hotel bowed Giles Redmond, Earl of Revesby, into a pleasant sitting room overlooking the High Street. A glance to the right through the wide sash windows revealed the Abbey, basking golden in the early evening light. To the left the bustle of the High Street was beginning to calm down.

'Thank you. This will do very well. Have bathwater sent up directly, if you please.'

'Certainly, my lord. Your lordship is without a valet? I can send a man to assist with unpacking. Your heavy luggage came with the carrier this morning and has been brought up.'

'My man will be arriving shortly.' Dryden was with Bridge, his groom, bringing the curricle and team on in easy stages from Marlborough where they had all spent the previous night.

The man bowed himself out leaving Giles to contemplate the unfamiliar English street scene below. The family had always stayed at the Royal York Hotel, higher in the city on George Street, but now that felt too much like coming to Bath as a child. Then he had been with his father on their visits to Grandmama on her annual pilgrimage to take the waters.

He would not have found his father at the Royal York on this occasion in any case. Giles's letter informing the Marquess that he was returning to England had been countered by a reply from his sire telling him that he was in Bath in a greatly decayed state of health. It was not quite a summons to a deathbed, but was not far short of that in tone.

The Marquess was residing at exclusive lodgings where invalids of the highest rank could be accommodated, so presumably he genuinely was unwell, but from the vigour of the handwriting and the forceful slash of the signature it seemed highly unlikely that his demanding parent was being measured for his coffin yet.

It would be childish to ignore the summons and continue with his plans for establishing himself in London before returning to Thorne Hall, Giles had thought.

Nine years ago he had left home and shaken the dust of England off his boots with the impetus of a monumental row at his back. Since then he had managed to live his life to his own quiet satisfaction and greatly to his father's displeasure. Gradually the anger had melted into grudging acceptance and, now Giles was ready to come back to England, a strong hint of welcome.

Life as a civilian during the Peninsular War had been stimulating, especially when he had found himself involved in intelligence gathering, but peacetime Portugal was less appealing, especially in the final few months after he had encountered the very lovely Beatriz do Cardosa, daughter of Dom Frederico do Cardosa, high-placed diplomat and distant relative of the royal family. Beatriz, spoilt, indulged, sheltered and innocent, had been betrothed to a minor princeling from the age of five.

Not that he had known this until he had made the mistake of smiling at her, charmed by her beauty, mesmerised by eyes the colour of dark

Louise Allen

35

chocolate. Beatriz had smiled back across the dinner table and from then on he had found himself encountering her everywhere he went.

She was rather young, he discovered, and not the most intellectual of young ladies. In fact, a lovely little peahen. But she was pretty and she was enjoying trying out her powers by flirting with him, which was all highly enjoyable until the ghastly evening when they had encountered each other in a temporarily deserted conservatory and she had flung herself on to his chest, weeping.

Giles, who was, as he told himself bitterly afterwards, neither a saint nor a eunuch, had gathered her efficiently into his arms, patted those parts that he could with propriety and murmured soothing nonsense while mentally wincing at the damage to the shoulder of his evening coat.

Beatriz, it turned out, had just been introduced for the first time to the princeling she was destined to marry. He was, according to the sobbing Beatriz, old—thirty-five—fat, short and ugly—plump, medium height and somewhat plain, as Giles discovered later—and had fat, wet lips. Untrue, although Giles was not inclined to approach very close to check that.

He had produced a large, clean handkerchief and had done his best to calm her down, with such success that when Dom Frederico had entered the conservatory there was no sign of tears and his grateful daughter had both arms around the neck of Lord Revesby.

In the course of the painful subsequent discussion Giles could only give thanks for his recent training in diplomacy. Somehow he had managed to convince Dom Frederico that he had no designs on his daughter, that Beatriz was quite innocent of any misbehaviour, and that he had found her weeping and had been foolish enough to offer comfort rather than seeking out her *duenna*. When he subsequently met the princeling that Beatriz was destined for he could sympathise with her tears, for the man was definitely self-important and not very intelligent, but that was the fate of well-connected young ladies, to marry where their family's interests lay.

It was time to reach an accommodation with his ailing father, if that was possible without them strangling each other within days. And it was time to take over what parts of the business of the marquessate that his father was inclined to relinquish. To do that he must settle down. He needed to find a wife, he knew, and, as he was not as demanding as a plump Portuguese princeling, English society must be awash with suitable young ladies only too happy to wed his title.

A flicker of blue skirts caught his attention for a moment, but of course it was not the mystery lady from Laura Place. The woman passing on the other side of the street was a small and buxom blonde in a highly fashionable ensemble and the short-tempered passenger in the chaise had been taller. When she had emerged from beneath that frightful veil she had been dark haired and dark eyed, like Beatriz, which had taken him aback for a second.

The rest of the encounter was a blur and Giles had had his eyes closed for most of that strange, impulsive kiss. He could not account for it. Flirting with Beatriz had been entertaining, but he had never felt the urge to do anything as rash as kiss her. Not that he had lived like a monk for the past few years, but occasional discreet liaisons with attractive widows had not involved snatched kisses with total strangers either.

The brunette in the chaise had been wearing a blue walking dress, plain but good and not unfashionable. A very superior governess, perhaps. He did not envy her students if they tried her patience. She had a tightly reined temper and that momentary loss of control had surely been as unfamiliar to her as it was unexpected for him. And yet there had been something about her, something familiar, which was unlikely. He knew no governesses, nor did he have to tolerate ladies of uncertain temper. Why he hadn't had his face slapped for his presumption on the hilltop he had no idea. Possibly she had been completely taken aback, because she was most certainly not a lady given to promiscuous kissing, that was plain enough.

Chapter Three

He would call at Laura Place tomorrow, Giles thought, moving back from the window as he shrugged out of his comfortable old riding coat.

But, no, damn it, he realised, one hand at the knot of his neckcloth. *I can't very well do that without revealing that I followed her home, which might be enough to alarm any right-thinking female.*

He unwound the now-crumpled muslin from around his neck as he considered the problem. This would take some thought if he were to satisfy his mysteriously insistent curiosity about who she was and why kissing her had made him feel he had...had come home, of all the bizarre impressions. But he could manage it with a discreet enquiry of Bath's Master of Ceremonies at the Assembly Rooms who would have all the well-bred residents and visitors in the city at his fingertips. After all, how difficult could securing an introduction to the Laura Place ladies be, compared to identifying French spies in the Portuguese court or riding through Spain behind enemy lines?

A knock at the door heralded the arrival of porters with cans of hot water and, on their heels, Dryden, pin neat as usual, despite a day spent in an open vehicle. 'My apologies for my tardiness, my lord. There was a tree across the road at Cherhill, as no doubt you encountered for yourself. I will lay out your evening clothes directly.'

'I will be dining here in my room and not going out, Dryden. A clean shirt and my banyan will do.' He had been in the country for only two weeks, but the volume of correspondence was threatening to take over his life. He would need a secretary soon, but for now he would have to tackle the most urgent matters himself. 'However, I will need your very best work tomorrow morning, Dryden.'

'The Marquess? Of course, my lord. The new waistcoat, I presume?'

Father, secretary, correspondence, Laura Place ladies.

Giles made a mental list as he began to strip off his dusty riding clothes. Not the most thrilling of programmes and, in places, downright difficult, but time enough to discover how to make England interesting.

He added, *Clubs, mistress, decide where to live.* Then, *A wife.*

Giles grimaced. He was not looking forward to the Marriage Mart.

'I am certain that taking the waters does me a great deal of good, you know.' Aunt Phoebe lowered her voice and murmured, 'It keeps one so regular! And I meet all my friends and acquaintances here every day.' She fluttered her fingers at a pair of mature ladies on the far side of the room. 'The Misses Prescott. And of course it is the perfect excuse for seeing who has come to town and for exchanging the latest news. I come almost every morning.'

Oh, dear, Laurel thought. *That might become rather tedious.*

But she smiled and nodded politely to the Misses Prescott and reminded herself that a little boring routine was well worthwhile for such a change of scene and her aunt's kindness.

Phoebe settled herself at one of the little tables in the Pump Room and signalled to a waiter for two glasses of the water. 'And you may save yourself the effort of tactfully not telling me that I am a shallow and frivolous creature, for I have a full hand of excuses,' she said, straightening her bonnet. 'And the strongest is that this is quite the best way of judging the new company before one finds oneself on nodding terms with some vulgarian or a crashing bore.

'Look at that woman, for example,' she added with a discreet gesture towards a slender brunette accompanied by a maid and a young woman who might be her daughter. 'I saw her yesterday and thought what style and elegance she has. But she treats her unfortunate maid as though the girl is a drudge, and a foolish one at that, however charming and caressing her manner is to her daughter and other ladies.'

Laurel took an incautious gulp of water and almost spluttered it back out again. 'This is disgusting,' she whispered.

'I know,' Phoebe agreed. 'But it does one so much good. Apparently it is full of the most wonderful minerals and salts. You should drink a glass a day.'

The benefit she derived was probably from the exercise involved in walking to the Pump Room and back daily and the stimulation of seeing all the new arrivals, Laurel decided, but kept the thought to herself.

Phoebe was still looking around the room, nodding greetings to old acquaintances. She gave Laurel a discreet nudge in the ribs. 'Oh, my goodness, now *there* is a handsome creature just come in! And half the age of most of the gentlemen.'

Ouch. Phoebe's elbows were sharp. 'Who? Where? Oh.' Goodness, indeed. The man who had just strolled into the room was tall, blond, tanned, beautifully barbered and elegantly attired—and all too familiar, despite his changed appearance. Laurel could not decide whether her blood was rushing to her face in a blush or draining to her toes in embarrassed alarm. Or possibly simply overheating with a dismaying and inconvenient physical attraction.

'Why, that is the gentleman I told you about, the one who showed me the way over the Downs when the tree had blocked the road. Only then he looked as though he could scarcely afford a decent coat, let alone a pair of boots like that,' she managed. 'And he has had his hair cut. Phoebe? What is it?'

Her aunt was staring at the man as he came closer, her expression one of complete dismay. 'The last person I would have expected to see in Bath... It must be him because, good heavens, he is the perfect image of his grandfather. I had no idea he was in the country. Of all the unfortunate things to have happened, I cannot believe you did not recognise him. Or perhaps not, if you had never met his grandfather because he has changed so much… With any luck he will not notice us.'

'Phoebe, what are you talking about? That is not someone we know. Is it?' The gentleman had seen them, she realised, and must have recognised her from yesterday. He began to make his way across the room towards them, this time with obvious intent. He kept his expression politely neutral, although as he came closer she saw a crease developing between his brows, so dark in contrast to his sun-bleached hair.

Phoebe made an abrupt gesture with her hand as though to ward him off. 'Oh, dear, I wonder what is the right thing to do—'

'Madam.' He arrived in front of them before she could finish and made a slight bow. 'Forgive me for approaching you without an introduction, but I believe I had the honour of being of some slight assistance to this lady yesterday and wished to enquire if she is quite recovered from her journey.'

'You are Lord Revesby,' Phoebe said, peering up at him like a flustered little bantam hen, not at all sure whether to ruffle her feathers at this fox in her hen coop or simply fly away cackling in alarm. 'But why did you not introduce yourself to my niece when you met her yesterday, instead of waiting until now?'

'Yes, I am Revesby, but I fear you have the advantage of me, madam. I did not introduce myself as she was alone save for the presence of her maid and I did not think it appropriate to make myself known to her.' He seemed puzzled by Phoebe's question, but Laurel could only admire the way he kept his tone polite and any sign of irritation hidden. He obviously had breeding. 'I could not introduce myself to a lady with whom I had merely a chance encounter on the road.'

You could kiss her though.

Then she realised what Phoebe had called him. 'Revesby? *You* are Giles Redmond?' No wonder that hint of familiarity had been teasing at her. This was Giles. Her friend. Her nemesis. So changed. *All grown up.*

'Yes,' he agreed, looking squarely at her for the first time. She saw the recognition dawn on him even as she felt the dizziness of shock take her. He had not recognised her, any more than she had him. 'Laurel? *You* are Lady Laurel Knighton?'

'I am. What are you doing here?' She would not faint and she would not raise her voice, even if the man who had ruined her life was standing in front of her. Why had she not recognised him yesterday? Laurel made herself focus. Stupid question. This was a man, not a boy. A man who had grown into those ears and feet and the nose. A man who had lost the scrawniness of youth to muscle and bone. Heavens only knew where the diffidence and the shyness had vanished to. But then those had been only the outward appearance—underneath it he had been someone different all the time, a juvenile libertine, a deceiver and a false friend.

'I have private business here. You were the cause of my leaving the country once, Lady Laurel. Now, I am glad to say, I go where I wish, when I wish.'

'And you wish to be in Bath, of all places?' She knew she sounded scornful. It was a beautiful city, but there was no getting past the fact that these days it was true to its reputation as the resort of the infirm and the elderly.

'I can assure you, my presence in the same town as yourself is in no way intentional.' He looked as though he would rather chew wasps. 'My father is unwell and undergoing treatment here.'

Phoebe cleared her throat and he turned, unsmiling. 'I beg your pardon, ma'am. I am aware we have not been introduced.'

'But we have, Lord Revesby.' Despite the

crackling antagonism between Laurel and the Earl, Phoebe sounded absolutely delighted with his presence now and her cheeks were flushed becomingly with pink. 'You will not recall it because I last saw you when you were the merest child. Why, I dandled you on my knee. I am Lady Cary, Lady Laurel's aunt.' She frowned slightly. 'But how did you identify her just now, know to cross the room to us? My niece was travelling veiled.'

Laurel knew the heat was definitely a blush this time. Would Giles reveal that she had removed her veil for a few incautious minutes and that he had taken advantage of that? Although to do so would expose him, once again, as a libertine.

'It was you I recognised, Lady Cary, although not from my childhood. I must confess that I followed the chaise. After all, I too was coming to Bath and I wanted to make certain that the chance-met lady arrived safely.' Giles glanced, unsmiling, at Laurel, then back to Phoebe. 'I would not have recognised you today, ma'am, but I was close enough to glimpse you in Laura Place greeting your guest. When I saw you across the room just now I came over to enquire.'

'You followed me? Why on earth would you do that? Perhaps your rakish propensities have not improved with age, my lord,' Laurel said sharply. Her own behaviour the day before had been decidedly improper and knowing that added vinegar to her tone.

'My *what*?' Several heads turned and he lowered his voice. 'You were an hysterical girl nine years ago, Laurel, and, it appears, you are as poor a judge of men now as you were then,' Giles said, his voice silky with suppressed anger. 'I assisted you yesterday out of a disinterested desire to help a stranger.' In the look he gave her she read the message that he was not going to mention that kiss unless she did, but that was as far as any truce between them would go. 'I followed because I was certain I knew you from somewhere. If I had realised who you were, I would have ridden in the opposite direction, believe me.'

Let alone have kissed me, no doubt.

That behaviour was all of a piece with what she knew of his true character.

'Lord Revesby!' Phoebe was all of a flutter at their hostility. Laurel realised that she had been paying no attention to where they were or who might overhear. Certainly the tension was too blatant for even good-natured Phoebe to ignore. 'Laurel! Please, both of you—whatever is the matter? Surely not that old business? Oh, dear, I beg of you, do not make a scene in here, Laurel, it would be *fatal* to your prospects.'

'We could always summon a porter to have Lord Revesby removed,' Laurel added. 'We did not desire his presence, after all.'

Giles's smile, if that was what it was, conveyed disbelief that anyone would be capable of ejecting him forcibly. Laurel's fingers twitched with the desire to box his ears, but she kept her hands clasped in her lap, merely looking pointedly away as he sketched a bow and strolled away to the entrance.

'I do not think anyone noticed.' Phoebe cast a glance around the room and sat down again. 'Of all the unfortunate encounters. Are you all right, my dear? You were positively bristling and I had thought… It is such a long time ago…'

'I am perfectly all right, Aunt, thank you. After all, as you say, it is nine years since I saw Giles—Lord Revesby—last. The wretched man might still annoy me, but he hardly has the power to upset me, not after all this time.'

Giles had hurt her, betrayed her friendship and, she had realised afterwards with a shock, broken her heart, as well as causing a scandal, confounding their fathers' mutual plans for their future and, incidentally, sending her godfather's daughter into an hysterical decline that lasted almost an entire summer.

'Would you like to leave, Laurel? I think he has gone. We should return home—I could call a chair for you. Or would the walk be soothing?'

'I am certainly not adjusting my movements in order to avoid one man. I will *not* be driven out of anywhere by Giles Redmond. Besides, if he is staying while his father is in Bath taking treatments, we might encounter him at any time and I refuse to run away whenever we encounter him.' She sent a sidelong glance at her aunt. 'How much do you know about what happened?'

'Not a great deal, your father's letter was such a tirade I could hardly make sense of it. But we cannot discuss it here, can we?' Phoebe fanned herself vigorously with her hand. 'I know—let us drink our water and then we may stroll back by way of Miss Pringles's haberdashery shop for that braid I need. We will both find the walk beneficial and then when we get home you can tell me all about it in the privacy of our own drawing room over a nice cup of tea.'

'Of course. What I can remember of it. After all, it was so many years ago and I was only just sixteen,' Laurel said with a smile that was intended to betray nothing but rueful regret about an unfortunate incident that was virtually ancient history now.

The smile was very successful, she thought, catching a glimpse of herself in one of the mirrors lining the walls above the dado rail. Especially as she had just lied. Every word that had been spoken that day, every expression on Giles's face, every stab of anguish she had felt, were still crystal clear. She had lost more than a friend and a neighbour, she had lost the young man she had fallen in love with without realising it.

How very fortunate that she had not married him after all, considering how objectionably he had turned out.

Hell and damnation.

Giles stalked along the High Street from the Pump Room and turned left into Bond Street, welcoming the stretch to his leg muscles as he climbed towards Queen's Square and his father's lodgings. If the old man discovered that Laurel Knighton was in Bath at the same time as his prodigal son it would probably give him a seizure. It was enough to give Giles a seizure, come to that, and *his* constitution was perfectly sound.

Neither of them had ever discussed Laurel directly in their punctilious, cautious, correspondence. It had taken his father a good month to recover from the worst of his fury over the collapse of his plans to marry his heir to the well-dowered girl next door. Then there had been the scandal over Giles's flat refusal to do the decent thing and marry Miss Patterson instead, even after he had so gravely insulted her in the midst of the hideous row with Laurel.

Eventually the Marquess of Thorncote had simmered down sufficiently to write in response to Giles's formal and polite letter informing his sire that he had removed his person—as instructed— as far as possible from the Marquess's sight. That had taken a while to reach home as, to his father's indignation, Giles had attached himself to his cousin Theobald's entourage sailing for Portugal and Theobald's new diplomatic post with the Court at Lisbon.

His father had replied, acidly, that his instruction to 'remove' himself had meant relocating to one of the family's other country estates. Anyone but a stiff-necked ingrate would not interpret it as a direction to take himself off into a war zone at the age of barely eighteen. Giles would kindly bring himself back immediately if he wished to avoid falling even further into the Marquess's ill favour. If there was any deeper hole to fall into.

But Giles found he had no desire whatso-ever to go home and that had nothing to do with ghastly embarrassment, torrid gossip, furious or fainting young ladies, or fathers demanding satisfaction and reaching for their horsewhips. He wrote a temperate letter of refusal to his parent and made himself at home in Lisbon.

It had been, as Giles was fully prepared to admit, a young man's over-dramatic solution to a monumentally unpleasant situation. But he soon found that life in Lisbon suited him down to the ground. He grew up fast and hardened up as quickly. Then the quiet gentleman who was believed generally to be the British army officer attached as liaison to the diplomatic corps revealed himself to be rather more than that and recruited Giles into his intelligence organisation. Giles had never imagined himself involved in spying, let alone risking his neck behind enemy lines, but he discovered that it was something he enjoyed and was good at into the bargain.

Now he was furious. He recognised that it was as much with himself for being thrown off balance as with Laurel, the infuriating female. The fact that the gangly, plain, awkward fledgling of a girl had turned into a lovely young woman—at least, she was lovely when she was not glaring at him—only fuelled his own bad temper, for some inexplicable reason.

He arrived at the doorstep of the elegant lodging house and spent a good half-minute getting his breathing under control before he rapped the knocker.

The man who answered was clad in a respectable suit of dark superfine with crisp white linen and had the unmistakable air of being a retired gentleman's gentleman. He ushered Giles in and escorted him upstairs with a few unexceptional remarks about the weather. At the top he paused. 'The Marquess has taken all of this floor for his accommodation,' he said, low-voiced. 'He is having a good day today, I am happy to say, my lord. His gout has eased considerably and I believe the anticipation of your visit has raised his spirits.'

'How bad is his health?' Giles asked bluntly. 'I would rather have the truth with the bark on, if you please.'

'You will wish to speak to the medical practitioner who attends your father, my lord, to satisfy yourself. I would only venture to say that the Marquess's condition is always vastly improved when his mood is good.'

In other words the gout was thoroughly unpleasant, but everything else was in his head, Giles mentally translated. Whether his father was looking forward to taking the prodigal to his bosom in an excess of forgiveness or was pleasurably anticipating giving vent to nine years' accumulated disapproval remained to be seen.

'This way, my lord.' The landlord tapped on a door, then opened it. 'Lord Revesby, my lord.'

Chapter Four

Giles stepped into a spacious sitting room with a pair of windows overlooking the square. His father was seated in a large winged chair with his left foot, heavily bandaged, resting on a gout stool and as Giles entered he turned to scowl at him from under heavy brows that had turned almost white.

But despite the grey in his hair and the white brows and the footstool this was not an old man, far from it.

He's only sixty, Giles reminded himself. *It must be maddening to find himself crippled like this, no wonder he is turning into a hypochondriac. He should be rampaging about the estate giving everyone hell and persecuting foxes and pheasants as he always did.*

'My lord,' he said formally as he approached. 'I am sorry to find you not in the best of health.'

To his alarm the Marquess lurched to his feet and pulled him into an embrace. 'Giles. My God, it is good to see you again, my boy.'

When the grip on Giles's shoulders relaxed he eased his father back down into the chair, restored his foot cautiously to the gout stool and sat down opposite, unbidden. He spent an unnecessary moment fussing over the cushion at his back so his father could deal with the tears on his cheeks. He had not seen his father weep since that awful day more than twenty years ago when both his mother and his just-born sister had died. 'Sir, you should take care.'

'Hah! I should indeed take care. Too late for that now,' he added.

'Surely not?' Now Giles was here he realised how much he had missed his father, even at his blustering, noisy worst. He had loved him and hadn't known it. 'Father, your gout is obviously bad, but you are a young man still, in your prime. Nothing is too late.' Even as he said it a superstitious chill ran through him. 'Or is there something else, some disease you haven't mentioned in your letters?'

'No, there's not a damn thing wrong with my health, only this hell-bitten foot and a lack of exercise giving me the blue devils.' The older man shook his head, his expression strangely rueful.

'Let me look at you. I cannot believe how you have changed, which is foolish of me. You're a grown man now and you've the look of your mother's family about you, and that is no bad thing—fine-looking men, the lot of them.'

'I should have come home sooner,' Giles admitted.

'I do not think so. I can read between the lines, and your cousin Theobald dropped me a few discreet hints. You've been involved in more than Court affairs in Lisbon, I would guess. Scouting into Spain? Intelligence work?' When Giles shrugged and smiled, his father nodded. 'I thought as much. You would have probably been safer in a regular regiment, in uniform, damn it, than risking your neck without its protection, but you've been doing your duty for your country and I am proud of you.'

Giles could find no reply. His father had never said anything before to suggest that his only son was not a grave disappointment, a bookish, clumsy, serious boy. When he was younger, before he realised the implications of primogeniture, he had wondered why his father did not remarry and sire another son, a satisfactory one to inherit.

Now that had changed, it seemed. He sensed that it was not simply that he had somehow proved himself to his father with his activities in the Peninsula, but that there had been something in their exchange of letters, stilted though they had been, that had gradually built a bridge of understanding, of sympathy, between them. Perhaps that link would never have been constructed when they had been close enough to irritate each other in person.

Giles cleared his throat. 'So is Bath proving helpful with your gout?'

'The damn quack has me on a reducing diet and has ordered my man Latham to hide the port and it seems to be working, confound it, so I suppose I must admit he has the right of it, the arrogant, expensive, devil. But the gout's neither here nor there. I wanted to see you urgently and thank the Lord—or more probably Wellesley, or Wellington as he is now—for ending the war and bringing you home, otherwise I would have had to send for you.'

The warm feeling inside him, the pleasure at his father's pride and the relief that this encounter was not going to be the fraught affair he had been steeling himself to deal with, drained away. There was trouble brewing or, judging by the bleak look in his father's eyes, it was already brewed, thick and dark. 'What is wrong, Father?'

The older man shifted in his chair and when

he did answer, it was oblique. 'It was a bad thing that the marriage to Palgrave's chit fell through.'

That old history, coming so close on his encounter with Laurel that morning? The sensation of a chilly finger on his spine was back. 'Father, it is nine years in the past. She was far too young to think of marriage. So was I, come to that. Even without that misunderstanding we might well have grown to find we were incompatible.' They certainly would be from the evidence of that morning's encounter. Although the memory of Laurel's lips persisted. 'I will set about finding myself a suitable bride as soon as possible, I promise you.' Giles put as much energy and commitment into the promise as he could muster.

The Marquess shook his head. 'You know her father and I had planned that marriage between you for years, ever since you were children. It would have united the two estates. Even after everything went wrong and you left the country and there was a coolness between the two households, it seems that Laurel's father still cared a great deal about that alliance. And now, I find, I care about it again, too. It would solve everything.'

Why bring this up now? Surely he doesn't think himself in such bad health that he is worrying about the next generation of heirs?

And if his father really was becoming agitated on the subject, then surely he knew as well as Giles that a marquess's heir should have no difficulty securing an eligible match?

Giles found he was on his feet. He paced to the window and turned, his back to the light, so the irritation on his face would be hard to read. Even so, the words that escaped him were harsh. 'Why the devil are we still talking about this? That fiasco is cold news, no one gives a damn about it.' Except, apparently, him, judging by that sudden loss of control. That was an uncomfortable insight. At the time it had been infuriating and deeply embarrassing, but surely he had got over that by now? His duty now was to find a suitable bride and he certainly had no intention of being distracted by nonsense about Laurel.

'Giles, sit down and listen to me. You have to do something within a few months or we risk ruin.'

Perhaps he had drunk too much last night, or had hit his head and was concussed, or this was all some kind of anxiety dream brought on by travel weariness and frustrated desire and worry about this meeting. Giles resisted the urge to pinch himself. 'Ruin? How can we be facing ruin? This is ridiculous.' He sat down. '*I* have to do something? Tell me.'

This time his father did not hesitate, just plunged in. 'Five years ago I started to speculate. It seemed I had the knack for it. I made money.'

Giles had the strange sensation that the blood was draining out of his head towards his feet. 'Yes?'

'I went on investing, speculating.' Now that his father had started confessing the words poured out. 'What I should have done, of course, was to keep back my initial stake, put it into land or government bonds, kept adding a proportion of my gains to it as I went along. But I kept investing it all, making it work, or so I thought.'

He sighed and rubbed one hand over his face as though intolerably weary. 'Then I lost, heavily. Cornish tin mines failed to produce silver, a Brazilian scheme fell through. It was one disaster after another. I put in more, tried to make up the losses. Before I knew where I was, everything had gone, Giles. Everything except the entailed lands.'

Everything. The title had never been a very wealthy one. An ancestor had been granted the spectacular honour of a marquessate for a very murky piece of assistance to the first King George. He had risen from a minor rural earldom to the upper branches of the aristocratic tree without the generations of slow accumulation of wealth that most of the great noble families had behind them. There were no estates dotting the length of the land, no great hoard of jewels dating back to the Tudors, just Thorne Hall, its lands and the trappings of a very comfortable lifestyle.

'So, what did you do?' Incredibly Giles was keeping his voice steady.

'I sold off all the unentailed land to Palgrave, which met some of the debt. Then I borrowed the rest from him.'

'How much do we still owe?' This was a nightmare, had to be. He was going to wake up in a minute, sweating, in his bed in Lisbon...

His father told him, then into the appalled silence added, 'The estate earns enough to service the loan, but not to clear it.'

All right, he was not, apparently, going to wake up. 'Palgrave died just over a year ago, yes?' Laurel had been out of mourning when he saw her, he realised.

'He left letters for me and for his heir. Malden Grange and the land he bought from me are in trust to Laurel, with the new Earl as trustee. Malden was never the main house, so its land is not entailed. This man prefers the old place on the other side of the county, along with its mouldering castle ruins—he's something of an antiquary, it seems—and he has his own properties anyway.'

The Marquess shifted uncomfortably in his chair. 'He's been damn reasonable about the whole thing and he's been discreet, which is more important. Nothing has been said to Laurel and her stepmother, so they think he is simply being generous in allowing them to remain in the main house rather than moving to the Dower House.'

'Forgive me, but I fail to see how this affects anything. The Earl's tact is appreciated, but the debt is still to be paid off and the land is gone.' Somehow he was holding on to his temper. He hadn't been in England at his father's side, where he should have been. If he had, then this probably would not have happened. But he had not been here. Another painful reality that must be lived with, dealt with.

'In those letters Palgrave set out his intention for Laurel to inherit the land and property that is in trust, provided she marries within eighteen months of Palgrave's death in accordance with the terms he set out. The balance of my debt to the estate would also transfer to her on her marriage—or, rather, to her husband. If she does not marry as directed then everything falls to the new Earl, with the exception of a generous dowry or allowance for Laurel, depending on whether she marries or not.'

Giles sat back, took a breath and summarised. He might as well have this clear in his head in all its horror. 'So we are at the mercy of whoever Laurel decides to marry if we are unable to raise the money to buy back the land. Or if her marriage does not fulfil the requirements, then we are in debt to the new Earl.' And at his mercy, or the husband's, if either decided to call in the balance of the debt early. He kept that observation to himself.

'Not exactly.' His father looked at him with what Giles could have sworn was apprehension. 'Laurel only gets the land and the debt if she marries the Earl of Revesby in the next five months.'

'But I am the Earl of Revesby.'

'Precisely.'

'We are rather thin of company tonight,' Phoebe complained after one sweeping assessment of the crowded room. 'I had hoped for a greater variety of partners, and certainly more nearer your age for your first ball at the Assembly Rooms. Oh, dear, I *am* disappointed.'

'It looks very well attended to me.' Laurel suppressed a nervous qualm at the sight of so many people, all of them strangers and many of them discreetly curious. Because of being in mourning for her father it was over a year since she had attended even a small neighbourhood Assembly, one where she knew everyone. She never expected to be the local belle of the ball, she was too old for that and known to be devoted to raising Jamie, and she had not expected to be very conspicuous here. The veiled assessment, the polite curiosity and the more open interest of some of the younger gentlemen who were in attendance came as a surprise.

'I do wish people would not gape so,' she murmured, taking refuge behind her fan.

'Whatever did you expect, dear?' Phoebe was arch. 'You are very attractive, your gown is elegant, if not perhaps in the very first stare of fashion, and you are a new young face where that is always welcome. As I said, the company is thin of many eligible gentlemen tonight, but we must not despair, I have every hope of finding just the man for you.'

'I am not so young—and I meant it when I said I did not want to marry.'

'Tish tosh! I cannot imagine why you believe yourself to be on the shelf, Laurel, or feel you have to be a recluse. I blame your stepmother entirely for putting such nonsense into your head.'

'It is not that I do not want to be sociable, only that I am past the age—'

'Look, dear, there are some chairs, right in the middle of the long wall. I will hurry and secure them. We will have an excellent view from there.'

And be most excellently on display ourselves, Laurel thought, reluctantly making her way through the throng.

Phoebe swept on and secured the chairs under the noses of two ladies wearing alarming toques, nodding with plumes.

'Should I not give up my chair to one of them?' Laurel whispered.

'Certainly not. Those are the Pershing sisters and a more disobliging pair I have never met. Now, let me see who is here.' She looked around, tutting when she failed to locate who she wanted. 'I must find the Master of Ceremonies and introduce you so that he is certain to include you in all the invitations. And there is Lady Bessant.' She waved. 'She will come over soon, I have no doubt. Her son was widowed nine months ago. Such a nice man, so suitable. A trifle stolid, to be sure, but— Oh, and Mrs Terrington, who has three grandsons and two of them are passably intelligent. And over there—'

Laurel ignored the remarks about available men and tried to pay attention to everything else:

this would be her new world and she must learn names and faces quickly. As she glanced around several of the younger ladies looked towards the door and some of the mamas came, very subtly, to attention.

An eligible gentleman is coming, Laurel thought with amusement. And then Giles entered, talking to a shorter man.

'Ah, now *there* is Mr Gorridge, the Master of Ceremonies, just coming in with—oh, no, it is Lord Revesby again.'

'And they are coming this way,' Laurel said, with a sinking certainty that she was their objective.

'My dear Lady Cary, you must forgive me for not calling earlier. I have only just heard of the arrival of Lady Laurel.' The Master of Ceremonies was effusive, bowing over her hand, assuring her of his attention if he could be of the slightest service to such a distinguished new arrival in Bath.

Laurel murmured all the right things, agreed that she would certainly wish to subscribe to the concert programme, admitted to enjoying balls, confessed that she was not at all attracted by card play and made him laugh indulgently when she wrinkled her nose when he asked if she had tried the waters yet. And all the time she was aware of

Giles seeming to fill her vision while he waited silently, a pace behind Mr Gorridge.

'And you must allow me to introduce to you the Earl of Revesby, newly arrived in Bath, just as you are, Lady Laurel.'

'Lord Revesby made himself known to me this morning,' Laurel said with the coolest smile compatible with good manners. Whatever happened she must not make a scene, not here with all of Bath society watching. 'We were childhood…acquaintances.'

'Neighbours, of course.' Mr Gorridge would have acquired an encyclopaedic knowledge of the aristocracy and gentry in order to perform his office, she realised. 'But it has been some time, I think, since you last met, given that his lordship has been nobly and courageously serving his country in the Peninsula.'

'Really? Nobly *and* courageously serving?' Laurel arched her brows in polite surprise. 'I understood that Lord Revesby had been ornamenting the Court at Lisbon. But perhaps that is more onerous than I had imagined. Possibly one had to wear a dangerous wig? Or elaborate Court livery?'

'It had its moments, to say nothing of lethal wigs,' Giles murmured. The Master of Ceremonies gave them both a nervous glance, apparently unsure whether these were witticisms, and bowed himself off to attend on a querulous dowager countess who was gesturing at him impatiently with her fan. 'May I?' Giles asked to join them.

Chapter Five

'There is nowhere to sit,' Laurel began.

Of course, with his luck, just then a chair beside them was vacated by a gentleman who was announcing to his wife that he was off to the card room before the orchestra began its infernal caterwauling.

Giles sat down without waiting for Laurel's assent. On her far side Phoebe was clearly flustered at the sparking hostility. She said nothing though, perhaps as much at a loss as Laurel to know how to snub a perfectly respectable member of the *ton* in the middle of a Bath Assembly. A perfectly respectable, exceedingly handsome war hero, if Mr Gorridge's remarks were to be believed.

'We began on entirely the wrong foot this morning,' Giles said, leaning forward so that he could address Phoebe across Laurel.

It gave the younger woman an excellent opportunity to admire the breadth of his shoulders and the crisp line of his recent haircut across the tanned skin of his nape. She told herself she could hardly avoid looking, not without turning away very rudely.

'Ladies, I must apologise for approaching you directly the other day, and without an introduction. I imagine it must have been disconcerting to receive the impression that you were being, perhaps, stalked, Laurel.' The expression in those blue eyes was perfectly serious.

Why is he being conciliatory? Laurel wondered. *Why is he here at all? He could avoid me perfectly easily and that would be more comfortable for both of us.*

When Phoebe uttered incoherent phrases about *quite understanding* and *doubtless the best of motives* and Laurel maintained her chilly silence, Giles added, 'I can only excuse it because of the sense I had at that first meeting at Beckhampton that we were already acquainted, Lady Laurel.'

'Acquainted? Certainly we were. I was apparently a hysterical girl and you... Words fail me.'

'Oh, thank heavens for small mercies,' Phoebe murmured beside her.

'We must discuss that disaster in private,'

Giles said. 'Neither of us can afford the appearance of a disagreement in public.'

'We have no reason to discuss anything.' Laurel wondered where the feeling of panic was coming from. She should send him on his way, firmly and coldly. They had nothing to discuss. *Nothing.* 'We have no reason to meet, in public or in private.'

If only he wasn't such a stranger and yet so familiar. The more she was close to him the more she heard the echoes of the past in his voice, saw it in those compelling eyes. And if only he wasn't such an assertively male creature. Yet he was not behaving like his own father always had—loud, cheerfully dominating the world around him. Giles's manner was perfectly controlled, his voice even, his movements elegant. He was being the perfect gentleman—or perhaps the perfect courtier she had assumed he had spent his time being in Lisbon. Only, perhaps not…

What had Mr Gorridge meant? *Noble and courageous.* Had Giles fought? But he hadn't been in the army… Why was he even *speaking* to her?

'I beg to differ, Laurel. We are both going to be in Bath for the foreseeable future. I imagine neither of us wishes to lock ourselves away for fear of encountering the other and if our relationship appears strained when we do meet it will cause comment. People will begin to recall the whispers of an old scandal and that can do your standing in Bath no good. Neither would I relish it. It would interfere with my own plans.'

'Lady Laurel, to you, my lord,' she retorted and got a faint, mocking smile in return. It would serve him right, him *and* his plans, if she slapped his face as he deserved.

'And might I enquire what those plans are, Lord Revesby?' Phoebe, who had apparently got a grip on her flustered nerves, gave Laurel a reproving look. *Not in public*, it said.

'Marriage, Lady Cary. One of the things that will assist my father's recovery is my making a suitable match. He has been alone too long and he will enjoy having a family around him.'

'You will be in London for the next Season, I imagine,' Phoebe remarked.

Laurel wondered where her stomach had dropped to and why it should. Why did she care who Giles married? He was no longer the man she had thought him, if he ever had been. But *a family*? A brood of small Gileses.

'Perhaps, Lady Cary, if it takes me so long to find the right bride. But this is June, the Season is over for this year and Bath has its charms, I find.' He was not looking at the dance floor where quite a number of ladies of marriageable age were being led out by their partners for the opening set.

He was looking at her, Laurel realised. *What? No!*

Beside her Phoebe made a small sound. Before either of them could say anything a gentleman in his late forties stopped and bowed slightly. 'Lady Cary, good evening. Might I crave the favour of an introduction to your companion?'

'Of course, Sir Hugh. Laurel, my dear, Sir Hugh Troughton. Sir Hugh, my niece, Lady Laurel Knighton, who has given me the great pleasure of coming to share my house with me. Laurel, Sir Hugh was a colleague of my late husband's in the War Office and is in Bath to accompany his sister who has been unwell. I do hope Miss Troughton is feeling a little better, sir.'

'A very junior colleague,' he said, bowing over Laurel's hand. She rather liked his smile and the openness of his plain face under a thatch of brown hair just greying at the temples. 'Thank you, Lady Cary, my sister is finding the fresh air and the waters very helpful. I expect we will be returning to town next week. And...' He looked enquiringly at Giles.

'Revesby.' Giles stood up and offered his hand.

'Delighted.' Sir Hugh shook it energetically. 'I had heard you were coming home.' He lowered his voice. 'I have had the pleasure of reading many of your despatches. Very useful indeed, as I am sure you are aware. I think there is a letter on its way asking you to come in to Whitehall for a debriefing at your earliest convenience.'

'I am attending my father who is unwell, but I will give whatever help I can, naturally.' Giles spoke equally quietly. 'You will doubtless let me know if there is anything more urgent.'

'Excellent. Now, mustn't bore the ladies with this, er, diplomatic talk. Lady Cary, I do hope you will do me the honour of the second set? And Lady Laurel, the third?'

When they both agreed Giles said, 'And perhaps I can hope for the reverse? Lady Laurel, the next set? And Lady Cary, the third?'

His tactics are excellent, Laurel thought, irritation vying with admiration. *I have already accepted an offer to dance and therefore etiquette forbids me from refusing another gentleman, whoever he may be. If I wish to claim a strained ankle or exhaustion, I will have to wait until I have partnered him for at least one dance.*

'I would be delighted,' she said, smiling at him.

'Such sharp teeth you have, Laurel,' he murmured. 'I still have the scars.'

'Where?' she asked, startled. Beside her Phoebe

and Sir Hugh were in earnest discussion of the best choice of physician for his sister.

'On my right calf. Surely you recall. You must have been about ten and you were furious with me because I had climbed the apple tree at the Home Farm to fetch my kite and refused to pick apples for you. You bit the only part of me you could reach.'

'Goodness, yes.' A chuckle escaped her at the memory. 'How I made you yell.'

'You were a little savage.' The way he said it sounded almost approving.

'You were most disobliging. "It isn't our tree. It would be theft,"' she quoted. 'Scrumping isn't theft.'

'Try telling that to Farmer Goodyear.'

A discordant note from a tuning violin jerked her out of the happy childhood memories back to the present. This was becoming far too cosy. Why Giles should be so amiable she could not imagine, not after those gritted-teeth remarks in the Pump Room. And surely that significant look when he had been speaking about marriage to Phoebe had only been to provoke her?

'As Mr Goodyear went to his just reward eight years ago, that is unfortunately not pos-sible,' Laurel said, deliberately sounding both pious and humourless. She needed to stop being charmed by reminiscence into relaxing, because the man was after something, she was certain. Or up to no good. Vengeance served very, very cold, perhaps.

From the way his mouth twitched she was not convinced that Giles took her remark at face value, but he sat back and watched the dancers, leaving her to recover her equilibrium. She shifted a little in her seat so that she could watch his profile covertly. Now she was over the first shock of seeing him again she was able to find more traces of the youth she had known beneath the handsome skin of the man he had become. The shape of his jaw and his nose and the arch of his brows were recognisable as she studied him. His hair had lightened from a honey-brown into blond, perhaps from the sun, because his brows were darker, as were his lashes. Those blue eyes, of course…

But the sensual curve of his mouth, the way his skin was tight over the bones of his face, his height and the breadth of his shoulders… Where had they come from? He must top his father by four inches and he looked hard and fit without a surplus ounce on his body. That might be expert tailoring, of course, but she very much doubted it.

She had the sudden urge to reach out and touch those shoulders. She had not touched him on the

Downs. There he had only brushed her lips with his as they shared a few fleeting breaths…

'Have I a smudge on the end of my nose?' Giles enquired without turning his head.

'No. As you are very well aware I was studying how you have changed in appearance,' she said calmly, refusing to blush over staring at a man. At this man. 'I doubt your character has changed as much as your looks.'

'You think not? Over nine years, in a foreign country and on the edge of a war?' He did turn his head to look at her then. 'Forgive me, but I think experience and life create many changes.'

'Not in fundamental character,' Laurel said firmly.

'So you judge me to be as fundamentally unsatisfactory as the last time we met, despite having barely exchanged a dozen sentences with me?'

'Undoubtedly you are. And older and more experienced, which makes it only worse.'

'That is sauce for the goose, as well as for the gander,' he murmured as the music for the last dance in the first set ended and a smattering of applause broke out. The dancers walked off the floor and Giles stood. 'Our set, I think.'

It was surprisingly difficult to rise gracefully to her feet and take Giles's outstretched hand.

Her knees seemed to have turned to jelly, as though all the nerves she had been keeping out of her voice and her gestures had fled to the back of her legs. She managed it somehow without stumbling and placed her kid-gloved hand in his.

'I did not look to see what this set is,' she confessed for something to say as they took their places at the end of a long line of couples. However she felt about him she was a lady and she knew how to behave in public. It would embarrass and distress Aunt Phoebe if her antagonism was obvious to onlookers. Some kind of small talk had to be found.

'It is various country dances, I think.'

The music began and Laurel recognised it as a severely modified version of an old tune, slowed down and with all the bounce taken out of it. The measures that had been put to it were unfamiliar, but it was slow enough to be able to follow easily.

'Whoever set this has a cloth ear for music,' Giles observed after a few minutes as they paused, waiting their turn to promenade down the line. 'And it is slow enough to be a funeral dirge.'

When they came together after a few more measures Laurel remarked, 'I would have thought that dancing at the Lisbon Court would have involved any number of very stately measures.'

Giles was striking enough in ordinary evening dress—black-silk breeches, white stockings, midnight-blue superfine tailcoat—but if the diplomatic corps wore full Court uniform at the Portuguese Court as they did at St James's then he would have looked even more magnificent with heavy silver lace on his coat. He was also a graceful dancer with the muscular control to move well through slow turns and promenades. She had often noticed that the slower the dance the more a clumsy dancer was caught out.

'You are correct. Court dances there are rather slow and old fashioned, unfortunately. Very mannered with much posturing. At first it was hard not to laugh at the sight of us all peacocking about. But Wellington wintered in Portugal and he liked to throw a ball at the drop of a cannonball. He expected all his young gentlemen to dance and he liked things lively.'

'And you were one of his young gentlemen, were you?' The more she heard the more she was convinced he had spent the past years in the thick of the Peninsular conflict, not lounging around at the Court exchanging pleasantries and diplomatic chit chat in the intervals between minuets. Which was both admirable and infuriating, because now she would have to admire him for it and, she acknowledged, she did not want to have to discover any good in him.

Not one scrap.

'I would drop by, on occasion.' His face was shuttered now, the smile simply a reflex on his lips. 'I was not in the army, Laurel. I was attached to the diplomatic corps.'

And something else, he cannot deceive me with that offhand manner. Intelligence work, perhaps? Interesting that he does not want to talk about that time, let alone boast about it. Oh, dear, another admirable trait.

'Thank goodness that is over,' Laurel said as the violins scraped their last mournful note and the dancers exchanged courtesies. 'Ah, this one is much better.' It was a proper country dance with vigorous, cheerful music. 'It is familiar,' Laurel said as Giles caught her hands and spun her around. 'But I cannot place it.'

'Neither can I.' They stood aside for the next couple to spin. 'Yet somehow I associate it with you.'

'With me?' And suddenly, as Giles joined hands across the circle and spun another of the ladies, it came back to her. The smell of lush green spring grass crushed under dancing feet, the scent of the blackthorn blossom in the hedgerows glinting in the torchlight, the cold white light of the moon and everywhere laughter and the scrape of a fiddle, the thud of the tabor and the squeak of a penny whistle.

'The village May Day fête,' she blurted out as he came back to her side and she was whirled into the circle away from him.

She had been what? Fourteen? They had all gone to the fête during the day which had been delightful, even though Stepmama had not allowed her to buy the gilded trinket she wanted because it was 'vulgar trash'. And equally she had forbidden Laurel to go to the dance in the evening. It would be an unseemly rustic romp, quite unsuitable for any young lady, even one who had not yet let down her hems and put up her hair. Laurel had bitten her lip against the tears of disappointment and nodded obediently, but she had opened her window wide that evening, had put on her nicest dress and had danced by herself in her room to the distant music on the warm air.

And then there had been a scraping sound against the sill and Giles's head had risen slowly into view. 'I say, are you decent, Laurel? Still dressed? Good. Come on, I've got the orchard ladder. We can go to the dance.'

She had not needed asking twice. They had scrambled down the rough rungs and run across the meadows, somehow hand in hand, although there was no reason for her to need any help. They danced all evening with other people, Laurel mainly with the other village girls of her age because none of the sons of tenants would risk the consequences of being found romping with the daughter of the big house.

And at the stalls set up around the green Giles had bought her the trinket she had yearned for. He slipped it in his pocket for safekeeping just as the musicians had struck up with the tune they were dancing to now and he caught her hands and pulled her into the measure. They had danced until they were breathless and, at the end, when all the lads pulled their partners into their arms and kissed them, he had kissed her, too. Just the innocent, friendly brush of his lips over hers for a fleeting second.

They had run back as the clock struck midnight like the best of fairy tales, still hand in hand, and when she put one foot on the first rung of the ladder Giles had kissed her again, just that same harmless, laughing caress, and she had laughed back and kissed the tip of his nose.

'Your charm,' he said, digging in his pocket.

'Look after it for me,' she had replied. 'If Stepmama sees it she will know I have been to the fair.' Then she had scrambled up the ladder and arrived in the bedchamber breathless. And in love.

Looking back on it now, Laurel knew her feelings had been entirely innocent of any physical desire. There had simply been the certainty that she was Giles's and he was hers and that this was an entirely satisfactory and inevitable state of affairs. Instinctively she had known that this truth did not need to be put into words or expressed in any way, any more than one needed to comment that rain was wet or that sheep were woolly. And, of course, Giles understood it, too, that went without saying as well. One day, when she was older, the words would be said...

It had not been until two years later, when Giles had left England and she was in disgrace, that it had occurred to her to look properly at herself in the mirror, to look and see a gangly, skinny girl with a mass of unruly brown hair and eyes that seemed too big for a face that had the odd freckle and a threatening pimple and no discernible beauty whatsoever.

Why would Giles have thought me anything but a plain child? she asked herself then. *I have no looks, not like Portia whom he* does *want. He was kind to me, that was all it ever was.*

She had grown up, of course, and found her looks—not conventional beauty, but something that was not so far from it—but by then it was too late, Giles had gone. And besides, better to learn early the lesson that all men are interested in is the externals, in beauty, dowry, breeding. Sex. Giles had kindly tolerated an awkward fledgling of a girl child several years his junior and she had not understood that until it was too late.

'Yes, the fête,' he said now. 'Lord, I had forgotten that. It was good fun, was it not?'

'Certainly it was,' Laurel agreed, getting her smile firmly fixed in place. 'Such fun.' The most magical hours of her life and, for him, a long-forgotten piece of *fun*.

He walked her off the floor when the set ended to deliver her to Sir Hugh for the next. 'Who would have thought it?' he said, almost as though to himself.

'Thought what?'

His attention focused on her as though he had come back from a great distance. 'That you would have turned into such a beauty.'

'Sauce for the goose, sauce for the gander,' she echoed his jibe of earlier as she took Sir Hugh's hand and sailed off to tackle the intricacies of the quadrille.

Chapter Six

He had deserved that and Laurel was as sharp as she had been as a child. He had been an unprepossessing youth who needed activity and excitement to provoke that last growth spurt into manhood.

Now the man had to marry the woman who had been that plain, gawky girl. Her adult beauty sugared the pill considerably, although it was an unconventional variety of attractiveness, more the charm of great dark eyes, the gloss of deep brown hair, the mobility of a wide, sensually expressive mouth and a deliciously curved, lithe figure.

She was not quite a classical beauty like Beatriz, who was superficially similar to Laurel, Giles thought as he led out Lady Cary to take their places in the forming sets. Laurel's looks relied on her expression, her mercurial changes of mood, the hint of deep sadness in those eyes that promised to reveal so much and yet hid her secrets safe inside. It would last longer than conventional loveliness though, persisting when others faded.

Her character was another matter and their encounters so far did nothing to reassure him that the temper and the unpredictability that had resulted in that disastrous row had moderated to make her the gracious wife that he should be seeking. She had eavesdropped, she had told tales about things she knew nothing about, she had caused his estrangement from his father and a rift between their families, and she was still holding a grudge against him for it.

On the other hand...

He changed hands as he thought it, turning Lady Cary in a complicated move that he could carry out without conscious thought. On the other hand, he did not have much choice. The options were to marry Lady Laurel Knighton to restore the Thorne Hall lands and remove the burden of debt, or to struggle for the rest of his days to repay the money and make something of the estate that was left to him. And see his father fret himself into an early grave with the worry and shame of it.

Put like that, there really was no choice. He

had left home an undutiful son, had spent nine years learning to do his duty in a hard school and now all he had to do to make his father happy, save his health, save the marquessate for generations to come, was to marry this rather beautiful lady of good breeding. Such a marriage was as he had always intended, only the bride was one he had not imagined. Men of his class were wise to wed with their heads, not their hearts, and this match truly would be a marriage of practicality.

He could cope with Laurel's quick temper and her resentments by ignoring them, he decided. He could take himself off to one of the other estates if she became difficult to live with—or send her to one. He had to get her with child, of course...

He turned and saw Laurel watching him for a moment as a gap opened up between the dancers. Did she know about the provisions of the will? His father said not and he could imagine that Laurel would throw the circumstances in his face if she knew them—and enjoy doing so, enjoy refusing him.

Best if she never knows, he thought. Let her believe he was taken with her just for herself, however surprised she would be. Although she was still bristling with suspicion and hostility, he could see hope that shared memories of happier times and old friendship would soften her, allow him to court her. That village dance so long ago came back to him now with surprising clarity for something he had not thought about for so very long. There had been a kind of enchantment about that night, an innocence that held within it the potential of the future. His fingers reached instinctively for his worry piece and he remembered that he had left it on the dresser so as not to spoil the line of his evening coat.

How old was Laurel now? Twenty-five, he calculated. Or twenty-six? If she had wanted marriage then she would have had plenty of opportunities, because surely she would have had a London Season or three by now and it was strange that she had not been snapped up. Bath was certainly not the place to find a husband unless she was deliberately looking for an older man, a widower perhaps. And why would she be doing that? Was her temper so shrewish still that she had driven away all her suitors?

Then he realised that he had no idea whether Laurel had had one or half-a-dozen London Seasons. With amazing tact his father had simply not mentioned their neighbours and their activities in his letters. His close friend from boyhood and in the Peninsula, Colonel Lord Nathaniel Graystone, had married Portia, Laurel's cousin. That marriage had ended with her death in childbed and, as both Portia and Gray had been at the heart of the 'Situation', as his father referred to it, Gray never mentioned Laurel and her kin to him either.

The music stopped and Giles offered his arm to Lady Cary to escort her back to her seat. 'And what are your plans, once your mind is at rest about your father, Lord Revesby?' she asked in her chatty manner.

'To get to know London and establish myself in society, look up friends, join some clubs, find a wife. I must spend a good deal of time at Thorne Hall supporting my father, of course.'

'Oh, yes, you said earlier about seeking a bride. I am sure you will find yourself invited to any number of house parties for the summer once it becomes generally known that you have returned.'

She beamed at him, a sweet, rather dithery lady, he thought, smiling back.

'You may not have to rely on the Season to find the right young lady after all,' she added, sounding suddenly not at all dithery.

Does she mean what I think she means?

'You do not think that Bath might prove…productive?' Giles did not turn to look for Laurel, but it took a conscious effort.

'Oh, Lord Revesby… I hardly know what to

say…' The wretched female was back to dithering and fluttering. He looked at her, not speaking, waiting for her to come to the point. He was not certain whether she was playing games with him or was thrown into confusion when she had to articulate perfectly rational thought processes. Lady Cary gestured towards the dance floor. 'Generally Bath is not much valued as a Marriage Mart. There are young ladies here, of course, but many of them do not have the connections I imagine you require in a bride, or they have reason of their own for not wishing for matrimony.'

'Novice nuns?' he asked lightly.

Lady Cary tittered. 'Many are young ladies devoted to an invalid relative. Of course, there are those who find themselves disinclined to marry. Dear Laurel…'

'You are not serious, ma'am? Laurel does not wish to marry?' He could understand that she would not want to marry *him*, or that her prospects had been limited by living in the country, but to discover that she might be irrevocably against marriage was a serious facer.

They had reached their seats and Lady Cary settled herself, unfurled her fan, fussed with her skirts and took her time about answering him. 'So she says.' She wafted the painted crescent back and forth briskly, the breeze welcome as he caught the tail of it on his heated skin. 'She seems sincere, but her experience with men is, I believe, limited, the dear girl.' She turned to face him fully, her cheeks pink, a look of determination on her face. 'But if she does not know her own mind, I think that you, of all people, are the man to direct it, Lord Revesby. After all, you know her so well and it would be *such* a suitable match.'

'We have flowers.' Phoebe stood back to admire the half-dozen bouquets arranged on the dining-room table the next morning. 'Some quite lovely bouquets. One for each of us from Sir Hugh.'

'Of which yours is somewhat the finer,' Laurel teased, inspecting them.

Phoebe tutted and shook her head in reproof. 'This one is for me from General Mitchell, which is probably in gratitude for saving him from the clutches of Mrs Winbourne who is determined to make him husband number four. Dreadful, encroaching woman. One for you from Mr Pittock, the rural dean. I do not think him an eligible suitor in any way, dearest.'

'He is very odd,' Laurel agreed. 'I fear that my remaining awake during his interminable lecture on medieval font covers, when we were sitting out and he trapped us in the corner, may have overexcited him.' She prodded the sheaf of flowers with one finger. 'I do feel that evergreens and white lilies gives a most funereal effect.'

'And the remaining bouquets?' Phoebe turned over the cards attached. 'One for each of us from Lord Revesby. How kind.'

They were charming, but modest, arrangements, exactly right as a gesture of thanks for the dances the night before, Laurel thought, grudgingly granting Giles approval for good taste.

And another good point, bother him.

'Shall I arrange them all? I can spread the funereal arrangement about amongst the other flowers which should cheer it up.'

She rang the bell for vases. 'I had best write notes of thanks. I do hope that does not encourage Mr Pittock. I really cannot see me as an ornament to the deanery!'

Phoebe turned from the window where she had been looking out on to the passing traffic in Laura Place. 'There is no need to write to Lord Revesby, Laurel.'

'No? But would that not be rather rude? However little I like him, I have no excuse for a snub.'

Or to give him cause to think I care enough to attempt one.

'I only meant that he is walking towards the front door this minute. We can thank him in person.' Phoebe sounded delighted. Whatever conversation she and Giles had had last night, it certainly seemed to have removed any lingering prejudices about him, despite Laurel telling her all about the reason for his absence from the country for nine years.

Which is more than I can say half an hour on the dance floor did for my prejudices.

Finding some things to admire in the adult Giles was more than infuriating, she found. She wanted to dislike him comprehensively, to tell herself that, after all, she had had a lucky escape in not marrying him.

What did Giles want now? They had exchanged some rather prickly conversation and a set of dances, had met without an exchange of blows, actual or verbal: there seemed to be a truce, in other words. Surely the thing now would be to avoid each other as much as possible and be coolly civil if circumstances forced them to meet. But Giles was rapping the door knocker this minute, not politely raising his hat from the far side of the street, so a meeting was imminent and must be dealt with. At least they were not in public.

'Lord Revesby, my lady.' Nicol, Phoebe's butler,

apparently saw no need to enquire first whether his mistress was at home to the Earl—or whether Laurel needed some time to compose herself before facing him.

'Lord Revesby, how good of you to call.' Phoebe was positively beaming at him for some reason. 'We were about to write to thank you for our delightful bouquets. So thoughtful.' She sent Laurel a look that plainly said, *Say something!* and gestured to a chair. 'Please, do sit down. May I offer you tea? Or coffee, perhaps?'

'Neither, thank you, Lady Cary. I called hoping that Lady Laurel might join me for a stroll through Sydney Gardens.' He gestured towards the window. 'It is very pleasantly warm.'

Any young lady in her right mind would be delighted to stroll with such a handsome, intelligent and altogether pleasing gentleman. Which presumably meant that she was not in her right mind because the very idea of being alone with Giles produced a strong feeling of panic. Which was unfortunate, because blind panic stopped what little was functioning in her brain from coming up with a single excuse for declining.

'I—er...'

'You will? Excellent.' Giles's smile was polite, but she could remember that look all too well. It meant trouble.

'I will not be long, Lord Revesby,' she managed with dignity. At least she had got the use of her tongue again. Laurel scolded herself silently all the way upstairs to the bedchamber for failing to come up with a convincing pretext. What could he want with her company? Presumably he would enjoy twitting her about her unmarried state because it seemed he was suffering from the delusion that his exile had been all her fault. 'Binham! I need to— Oh, you are here already.'

Her maid was laying out a pelisse and bonnet on the bed. 'Yes, my lady. I saw his lordship approaching on foot and I assumed he was calling to take you walking, it being such a lovely day.'

Did you, indeed? And what do you know about Lord Revesby?

It seemed as though everyone was conspiring to throw her together with Giles—Nicol and Binham and even her aunt, who could surely have produced some acceptable reason why Laurel was not free that morning.

She came downstairs with her best society smile, the one she produced when her stepmother had dragged her away from the schoolroom and Jamie's lessons, or the library and the company of a good book, in order to make stilted conversation with callers.

'Charming. You look like a sprig of spring

foliage.' Giles was at the foot of the stairs, waiting for her.

'Does that mean that you consider this outfit too green?' she demanded, society smile slipping. Compliments from Giles had always needed examining with care and now she was not prepared to believe a single flattering word he uttered.

'Not at all.' He was suspiciously straight-faced. 'If the hat had been green itself and not simply cream straw trimmed with matching ribbons, you might have looked rather like a topiary figure, but as it is, you hardly resemble one at all.'

'I knew Stepmama was wrong about making the entire pelisse green and not just the bodice,' she confided before she recalled that she did not like him or trust him and that he had just insulted her, even if she did agree with him.

Nicol was holding the front door open with what, in a butler, was a positive smirk. He obviously saw himself as matchmaking now he had a young lady in the house, or perhaps he was hoping for lavish tips from a host of gentlemen callers. Laurel thanked him frostily.

You should be on my side, she thought. Then told herself to be fair because he doubtless thought he was.

One of the attractions of Laura Place was that it was so close to the Sydney Gardens, a short stroll away along Great Pulteney Street. Laurel had heard of them, of course, famously the largest pleasure gardens outside London, and Phoebe had promised that there would be an eligible programme of evening entertainments for them to attend. For daytime, she had explained, the hexagonal grounds held walks, a labyrinth, a sham castle and grottos.

Giles offered his arm and Laurel reluctantly slipped her hand into the crook of his elbow, put up her parasol—green again, although by some miracle he refrained from commenting on it—and allowed herself to be guided up the incline towards the Sydney Hotel, through which one gained admittance to the grounds.

'Why have you called?' she asked abruptly, cutting through Giles's polite small talk about the weather. 'Why have you asked me to walk with you?'

'For the pleasure of your company?' he suggested.

'Giles, we last met nine years ago in the midst of an appalling family row when I refused to marry you because I found out that I had been grievously misled in my opinion of your character.'

'Grievously misled? You sound like a maiden in a melodrama, Laurel. You discovered no such thing, simply misunderstood something that you had no business overhearing. Instead of finding out the truth you promptly threw a tantrum and caused chaos. It was a miracle that your godfather or your father didn't end up putting a bullet in me and that my father did not have a seizure. No, let me finish.' She almost recoiled at the sudden hardening of his voice. 'We need to discuss it and clear the air, certainly, but I am not going to do that either in your aunt's house where you can storm off and leave me, or here and now on the street.'

I could storm off and leave you here, halfway down Great Pulteney Street.

She almost said it, but curiosity and a sense of fairness, admittedly deep-buried where Giles was concerned, stopped her. Matters had deteriorated into a shouting match almost immediately so she had never heard an explanation—or an excuse—from him. It might help her to hear what he had to say. In fact, hearing him flail about trying to find an excuse for his behaviour might be positively amusing, she told herself, struggling to keep her brittle defences up.

They passed through the entrance to the Sydney Hotel where Giles paid their admission and into the foyer which opened into the gravelled area surrounded by pavilions and booths that would, Laurel supposed, be packed during the evening entertainments. Now, mid-morning, a couple strolling in the distance and a gardener sweeping the grass with a besom broom seemed the only inhabitants.

'There, I think.' He pointed to a rustic seat in the dappled shade under a spreading lime tree. 'We should be undisturbed.'

Speak for yourself, Lord Revesby. I am already exceedingly disturbed.

She kept reminding herself that this physically attractive man, whose body heat she could feel where their arms rested together, was Giles, her childhood friend, the young man who should have grown up to be her husband, the young man who had broken her heart.

Had he?

She caught the thought. No, it had not been a broken heart. She had loved him, but not as an adult woman with a heart to lose, with a mature understanding of what marriage might be. This had been a betrayal of something much purer and simpler—friendship. Perhaps that was why it was so difficult to forgive and forget.

Chapter Seven

'It was all because of what you overheard, eavesdropping that afternoon in the barn,' Giles said as soon as they had sat down on the bench.

So, he was going to attack this head on, was he? 'Of course it was.' There had been nothing before, nothing that had sullied her perfect trust and faith in him. 'I was not eavesdropping,' Laurel said, defensive. 'It was hot and I went in to find some shade and to see if the stable-yard cat had brought her kittens in there. I sat down, right at the back under the hayloft, and the next thing I knew, you and Gray started talking in the loft right above my head.'

'You should have said something, called out.'

'I would have done, but by the time I realised that it was a conversation that should not have been overheard…the things you were saying—

I was too… And then I realised who you were talking about, who you had debauched.'

'Damn it, neither of us had debauched anyone, Laurel!' The gardener lifted his head and glanced across at them and Giles lowered his voice back to normal conversational tones. 'It was fantasy, pure fantasy.'

'Fantasy? What sort of experience did the pair of you have, that you could fantasise like that? It was positively obscene.'

'None. No experience. We were virgins, for goodness' sake, Laurel.' Giles's colour was up, probably more out of embarrassment at having to admit that, rather than shame at speaking of such a thing to a lady. But then this was a totally inappropriate conversation in any case. When she simply stared at him he shifted on the bench, took off his tall hat and raked his fingers through his hair, reducing a fashionable crop to something that recalled the hot, angry and dishevelled youth he had been that day.

'Hell, how can I make you understand? Look, Laurel—young men think about sex a lot. All the time. Constantly. It is part of growing up, becoming a man. Youths will boast and brag and invent and lie like farmyard roosters flaunting their tail feathers to outdo every other juvenile rooster in the neighbourhood.'

'*All* the time? All of you?'

'Young men think almost exclusively about sex and food and drink. Or drink and food and sex, with regular diversions into horses, guns and joining the army and slaughtering the French while mounted on a fabulous black stallion. And then celebrating with food, wine and women. A lot of willing women.'

The picture should have been amusing. She found she was not amused. Laurel closed her mouth, swallowed and ventured, 'And men grow out of this…obsession?'

'On the whole, yes. We get some experience with both women and wine, we grow up, we learn about life and its realities. We get our appetites under control.'

'But you were…*fantasising* about my cousin, about Portia.'

'She was very beautiful,' Giles said, as though that explained, and excused, everything. 'I imagine that every red-blooded male she came into contact with had those kind of thoughts, those kind of dreams about her. Neither of us would ever have behaved with the slightest disrespect to her, in word or action.'

'Except in your heads.'

'Except there,' he admitted. 'That is the nature of fantasy.' He stood up and began to pace back and forth on the gravel path in front of her, one hand thrust deep into his coat pocket.

Men could do that, use physical activity to calm themselves, to work off emotions. Ladies were stuck on seats, pretending to be calm and collected and looking graceful, Laurel thought, clasping her hands in her lap as she made herself think about what Giles had said.

She herself would have been quite safe from being the subject of such fantasies, she knew that. She had not been beautiful, she had not even been attractive, just an awkward, gangly girl. Giles's description of Portia just now had stung. Had she been jealous then, even though she was utterly unaware of ever wanting a man to desire her in that way? She must have been.

'I didn't realise. I thought that you had…that it had all been real. I tiptoed out, too shocked to say anything. When I ran back to the house there was your father and mine and Godpapa Gordon, Portia's father, talking in the study with the window open, all about how they were drawing up a marriage contract for us for when I was eighteen and how Godpapa would witness it. So I rushed in and said I could not bear to be married to you because you were wicked and immoral and had a lover.'

She took a deep breath and made herself go

on. 'And they demanded to know who, so I told them what I had heard and Portia must have been listening because she came in shrieking and then you and Gray arrived and Godpapa Gordon was demanding that you marry her and she was hysterical and you were refusing to marry either of us and Papa was shouting that you had to marry me and I said I would rather die. And he and Godpapa almost came to blows. But you know all that. You were there, after all. I do not know why you have to ask me now. Why you think this is all my fault.'

'Because I could not understand then, and I do not understand now, why, if you were so upset, so shocked, why you did not come and accuse me to my face? We had talked about just about everything, hadn't we? Whenever we had a disagreement we fought it out, argued ourselves into a truce, at the very least. I thought we were friends, Laurel. I trusted you. I thought you trusted me. And yet you were prepared to believe the worst of me and to accuse me of it in front of our fathers.'

'Because I heard it from your own lips.'

Because I was shocked. Because I was jealous, I can see that now. Most of all because I was jealous. Oh, Lord, what have I done?

'We had never talked about that. About sex and men and women.'

'Of course we had not.' Giles looked scandalised. 'You were just a girl still, an innocent. Even when you were older, it was not the sort of thing I could *ever* talk to you about.'

'I was the same age as Portia and you could think about her like that.'

But I was plain and immature, and unaware of anything except that you were my friend. I was just a young girl to you, your little friend who you were kind to and indulged. The friend who was sexless in your eyes.

'I knew the facts of life, I was brought up in the country, after all. I just had never thought about it like that. Not…not people I knew.'

'So you were trying to protect Portia?' Giles stopped pacing and faced her. 'It was not that you wanted to attack me, or were looking for an excuse not to marry me?'

'Of course not! Why would I ever do anything to hurt you? I had no idea Papa and your father were planning that match,' Laurel said with complete honesty. She had thought it was all her own idea to marry Giles when she was grown up and it had never occurred to her that their families were plotting just that outcome. 'And when I overheard you and Gray I thought it meant that you were very experienced with women and were corrupting Portia. I was so shocked.'

I was shocked and envious and hurting and betrayed. I hit out because I wanted to make you see that. I had no idea what damage I was doing.

She wanted to say it, but how could she admit that she had been jealous, that she had considered Giles to be hers, even then, when she had simply been a plain and awkward child? He would be appalled, embarrassed—and he would pity her. Or he would not believe she had no idea what she was doing. For a moment she wondered herself. Had it been unconscious spite? There was even less reason for telling him, if that was the case. Confession might be good for the soul, but she did not feel brave enough for that, it would be worse even than this guilt.

Giles watched the play of emotion on Laurel's face. He suspected this was the first time since they had met again as adults that she was not guarding her expression. What could he see, besides a lovely woman dealing with some very unpleasant memories?

She had shown embarrassment and real shock when he had confessed about those erotic fantasies. And perhaps, just a little interest, although that might have been wishful thinking on the part of his masculine pride. There had been chagrin when she had realised that her fears about what she had overheard had been false and shame over the hornets' nest she had stirred up as a result.

But he could understand her reaction, he realised, feeling almost a sense of shock at the crack in the little nugget of anger and resentment he had hugged to himself all those years. If he had been an unformed cub, then she had been younger still, a girl, innocent and idealistic. It was all forgivable and he realised he was already shedding the angry memories. No harm had come of it in the long term.

Or had it? He had been estranged from his father for years, years during which the Marquess had gambled away their fortunes on those poor investments. Portia had been distressed to the point where she had spent months shut away recovering her spirits and had then married Gray when she was just eighteen. He must have somehow made his peace with her on his third leave in England after he joined the army. Being Gray, he had said nothing about his courtship, nothing about his brief marriage, although Giles was certain it had not been a close and happy one. Would they have made a match of it if it hadn't been for that awful summer afternoon and Gray's sense of duty and honour, driving him to do what Giles had refused to contemplate? And he had let his own sense of betrayal and hurt fester inside him, damaging his memories of home and childhood.

But the past was the past and he was clear that Laurel had not intended harm. He could surely begin to court her without a qualm now they had cleared the air about this? She now understood what she had overheard, even though it had been outrageous of him to discuss it so frankly with her. He could forgive her for what, after all, had not been spite as he had thought, but instead shocked innocence and loyalty to her cousin. He could forgive himself, given time and thought. They could put it behind them now, but not before he made amends for his reaction on first knowing her again.

'I was insulting yesterday morning. I apologise. I had never understood before why you did what you did. I had not realised I was holding on to so much anger still.'

Laurel tipped her head, the gesture that had first stirred recognition in him when they had met on the Downs, reminding him now that somewhere behind that lovely face and graceful figure lurked the strange, gawky, fiercely loyal child who had always haunted his footsteps growing up. He had kissed her on the hilltop in the sunlight amidst the lark's song. His body stirred, remembering the cool scent of her, the warmth of her mouth, the flutter of her eyelashes, dark against a pale cheek.

'You were shocked at seeing me again without warning,' she said, apparently offering him the comfort of an excuse. A first, tentative flag of truce, perhaps. There was no smile. He supposed he was still not completely forgiven for any of it. 'And perhaps you had never come to terms with leaving your home and the country like that, even if you enjoyed yourself in Portugal.'

She tipped her head the other way, regarding him. Her eyes narrowed in thought and she touched the tip of her tongue to her lower lip. He felt his body tense, harden, and then he stopped worrying about inconvenient arousal as she added, 'I assume you lost your virginity there soon enough?'

And I was worried about shocking her with the facts of life just now!

But then, they had always been able to talk directly about whatever was on their minds, except that once. 'Yes. Soon enough.'

It had not been in Portugal. Both he and Gray had fled to London the morning after the confrontation, as far as they could go in that first instinctive dash to get away from Hampshire and the dire scenes they had left behind them. Both of them had been too young to cope with all those churning adult emotions, he could see that now. Gray had gone to his father and asked to join the army as an ensign, much to the Earl of Wickham's delight, for the Graystones had always been a military family.

Giles had taken refuge with Cousin Theobald and found him preparing to go out to Portugal. Theo had never had much time for Giles's father and it had been easy enough to persuade his cousin to take him along as an unofficial part of his entourage.

During that terrifying, exhilarating week of freedom in London he and Gray visited an exclusive and expensive brothel, escorted by Lord Wickham, who had no intention of allowing his heir go off to war without first learning something about the perils that awaited him away from the battlefield.

Giles hauled his mind back from that first enlightening experience and studied the woman who would be ensuring his future faithfulness if she would only consent to do the sensible thing and marry him.

'Why have you never married? Surely you did not allow that overheard conversation to give you a fear of marital relations?' he asked without considering, allowing his thoughts to continue to their logical conclusion. He had been puzzling about Lady Cary's remark all morning. Why should Laurel not want to marry? Then he realised what he had spoken out loud.

Laurel surged to her feet in a flurry of skirts and parasol and outrage, all their fragile harmony destroyed. 'Give me a fear? You arrogant man— as though I would allow two adolescent youths to influence my adult life. I certainly developed a distaste for having my father arrange my future. But Mama died and Papa remarried and Jamie was not happy, so I looked after him and then we lost Papa, so he needed me even more. It was very satisfying, seeing him grow up to be such a fine boy.'

'It must have been,' Giles agreed diplomatically, privately appalled. What had her family been about, allowing her to become, effectively, a governess? And it was no life for a lad either, tied to her apron strings. 'What has happened to him now?'

'Jamie has gone to be a midshipman,' Laurel said with a smile that held both pride and heartbreak. 'So I am now free to do what I want— not that I was not free before, of course—and I choose to come and live with my aunt. Stepmama and I are not particularly compatible.'

'So this is not just a long visit? You are now Lady Cary's companion?'

Lord, but she does need rescuing. A few weeks of Bath tedium and she will overcome any aversion to marriage.

But he did not have weeks, not if he was to be certain of her within the time limit.

'Certainly not a paid companion. We will be living together on equal terms, as two independent ladies.' Her chin was up, she met his enquiring gaze straight on.

'But you had your London Season, of course?' She certainly had the poise and finish of a lady, not a companion.

'No.' Laurel smoothed down her skirts, furled up her parasol. This time her evasion was obvious.

'Why ever not?'

'I saw no point. I was not looking for a husband.'

'I fail to understand why you would not wish to marry.'

'I am two years younger than you and you are not married,' she retorted. 'I would like to go home now, it is becoming a trifle chilly.'

It was no such thing, but one did not contradict a lady. One could patronise her though, which was tempting if the lady in question was Laurel, and he could goad her into losing her temper and saying something revealing.

Giles offered his arm and said, with deliberate provocation, 'But men may marry later and most do. We have other things in our lives beside family and we may father heirs into our sixties if we have to. For women that opportunity for a family is far shorter.'

As he expected, Laurel bristled at this. She was too good at hiding behind a façade when she was in control, he realised, but when her temper was roused the mask slipped. 'Are you saying that a woman's only purpose is to be a wife and mother and that anything else is a waste of time, whereas for men marriage is entirely secondary because you have a full and satisfying life anyway?'

'Yes, that is it exactly,' Giles said, heaping on the coals. He was not entirely sure he believed it himself, but seeing Laurel angry, flags of colour flying in her cheeks and her dark eyes glaring at him, was arousing and surprisingly tempting. He thought fleetingly of Beatriz, schooled in court etiquette, who was always perfectly poised and refined, until that evening when he had held her weeping, breaking her heart on his shoulder.

'All I can say, Lord Revesby, is that you are a very good reason for not marrying—one would have to live with a man with attitudes like yours and that would be intolerable. I would be obliged if you would escort me home this minute.'

On impulse Giles took one of the side paths. If he remembered correctly from the map he had seen at the hotel, this led to the labyrinth.

'I thought you were taking me home,' she said, still bristling.

'This is simply an alternative route,' Giles said to soothe her suspicions. That was true enough. In the enclosed space of the garden all paths would, eventually, lead back to the entrance.

Her quick, irritated steps carried her along with him until he slowed and she looked around and saw they were on a narrow path bounded by tall close-clipped hedges.

'No, it is not an alternative. This is the labyrinth. Now how do we get out of it?'

'Do not be alarmed, Laurel, I will rescue you.' Giles, tongue in cheek, somehow managed to keep his voice serious. This was working out very well and he realised he was beginning to enjoy himself.

'Rescue, you beast?' she demanded with a rapid descent into childhood abuse. He bit the inside of his lip to keep the smile off his face. 'I have absolutely no need of rescue, I can get myself out.' She shook off his hand, turned around and swept off back along the path, passing, he was pleased to see, the opening they had turned in on. If she had gone that way it would have taken alternating left and right turns and she would have been out.

Giles turned and carried on, alternating the turnings until he arrived in the centre. From the distance came the sound of a raised female voice uttering curses that became, to his ear, more and more unladylike as Laurel drew closer.

'Over here,' he called. 'This way.'

Five minutes later Laurel arrived, bonnet askew, her hem trailing twigs, her face pink with what was probably a mixture of exercise and frustration.

'I told you I would rescue you. And you are not chilly any more either.'

'Oh, you—' She marched up and delivered a thump with a clenched fist in the middle of his chest. 'I could hit you!'

'You just have,' he pointed out. And kissed her.

She gave a little gasp of surprise against his lips, which was curiously arousing, and stepped back sharply. Giles told himself to let her go, that this had been a mistake and he should apologise.

And then she moved back, put her arms around his neck, knocking off his hat in the process, and kissed him.

Chapter Eight

It was a more accomplished kiss than Giles had been expecting and he adjusted his expectations rapidly, even as he gathered her in against his body with one hand and untied her bonnet ribbons with the other. Laurel was not experienced, but she was a grown woman, not some adolescent innocent, and her body knew what it wanted, even if she had presumably always been too ladylike to act on those urgings.

She started in surprise when he slid his tongue between her lips, but she did not move away, or even, as he was braced for, bite him. Her own tongue moved cautiously to meet his, a touch that spoke of trust and curiosity and the promise of future sensuality.

Giles pushed her bonnet clean off her head and speared his hand through her hair at her nape, releasing the scent of rosemary rinse and warm woman. Warm woman who wanted him at that moment as much as he wanted her. That knowledge was almost more powerfully erotic than the feel of her curves against him or the taste of her on his tongue. And he must stop. This was too much, too soon.

It seemed that Laurel had come to the same conclusion and that her will was less fogged with desire than his was, because she uncoiled her arms from around his neck and blinked up at him, bemused and indignant. 'Giles, I had absolutely no intention of... I cannot imagine why I— Oh, for goodness' sake! Why on *earth* are we kissing each other?'

'Because whatever our minds are telling us, our bodies want something different,' he suggested, shaken. He was going to marry Laurel because he had to, not because he loved her or thought they would have an easy or happy marriage. Finding himself aroused and aching over sharp-tongued Laurel Knighton was as baffling as it was surprising.

But she is very lovely now, he told himself. *Those deep brown eyes, the rich brown hair, the elegant line of neck and shoulder. Very desirable.*

The thought of mellowing that sharp edge with kisses and more was...tempting.

'I have no wish to discuss my body—and

certainly not yours. And you have only just explained to me what goes on in the swamp that is your mind, Giles Redmond!' She stepped back, her hands up as though to ward him off although he made no move to touch her. 'I— What was that?'

That, he saw when he looked down, was the soft sound of a foot crushing an expensive straw bonnet, pressing silk ribbons into yielding turf.

'My bonnet,' Laurel wailed as she twisted to extricate her foot in its half-boot from the wreckage of her hat. 'You dropped my bonnet on the ground!'

'I did not intend you to step on it,' Giles protested. 'I will buy you a new one.'

'That *was* a new one. I only bought it yesterday.'

'After your encounter with me in the Pump Room?' Even as he said it Giles realised that it was probably not the most tactful thing in the world to suggest that a lady might have been so affected by meeting him that she had rushed out and bought a hat to look beautiful in for his benefit.

'Yes, immediately afterwards, as it happens. And do not flatter yourself that I wanted you to admire it, you arrogant man. I was so put out by that exchange that only a new bonnet would do to soothe my nerves. You are expensive as well as exasperating.' She dangled the bonnet from one bedraggled ribbon. 'Now I have to walk back through the streets of Bath without a hat, like some doxy.'

'We will go back to the hotel and I will order you a chair to take you home,' Giles suggested as he stooped to pick up his own hat and brushed a daisy flower from the brim, using the opportunity to get his breathing under control. Strategically holding the hat in such a way as to conceal his reluctantly subsiding arousal was probably also tactful. It should be a huge relief to discover that he could make love to Laurel with conviction, although the visible evidence was inconvenient. It seemed his body was just as undisciplined as any adolescent youth's, responding more for the physical sex than the emotional tangle of his thoughts.

'And how do I explain how this happened? I will not be able to show my face in the Sydney Hotel again after this,' she mourned. 'And Phoebe had promised such interesting entertainments there.'

'Give it to me.' Giles took the battered hat and impaled the brim on a small branch that was sticking out. 'There.' He jerked it free and handed it to her. 'We were in the maze and the branch caught it, tore it off, it fell to the ground, you recoiled in shock, stood on the hat and so on. In fact, the management will probably feel so guilty about their faulty pruning that they will offer to buy you a new bonnet.'

'You always were the best person for inventing excuses,' Laurel remembered. Strange how thinking of the distant past and Giles as a boy reduced her anger with him as a man. In some ways he had not changed at all. 'Expecting them to buy me a new bonnet would be dishonest. But the story would serve to save my blushes.' She cast him a sidelong glance, wondering if he felt anywhere near as confused as she did. It didn't show. 'Giles, what happened just now?'

'We kissed. I rather thought you had noticed.'

'Of course I noticed, stop playing with words.' She turned and walked down the path out of the central space. That was cowardly, but it meant she did not have to look at him. 'I mean, why should we do such a thing?' she asked over her shoulder. 'We do not even like each other any more.'

'Do we not?' He fell into step beside her, still holding his hat. 'We had a misunderstanding and we explained ourselves to each other. I rather thought that we could cry friends again.'

Once she would have been very happy with that, with being friends. What did she want now? And what did Giles want, swinging from anger and exasperation with her to teasing and kisses? 'I do not make a habit of kissing men.'

'No, I could tell that.'

'Oh! You—'

'That was a compliment, Laurel, not a suggestion that your embraces are not enjoyable. You are very properly inexperienced with lovemaking.'

'A situation you are intending to remedy? Really, Giles, I do not know what your experience might have been in Portugal, but unmarried ladies in this country do not take lovers, not and remain respectable. I honestly do not know what came over me just now.' He was silent as they came out into the open again, his expression as closed as if he had slammed a book shut. 'Giles?'

'I will tell you what came over us,' he said, his voice harsh. 'Simple desire. There is nothing wrong with that, nothing to be ashamed of. And naturally you would not kiss any man whom you did not trust.'

'I can trust you?'

'Of course,' he said.

What was there in that to make him frown so? 'You kissed me on the Downs before you knew who I was, what I was,' she pointed out. 'We were total strangers, so we thought.'

'We were, but sometimes, surely, we can give way to instinct, to snatch pleasure where we may, provided we do no harm. It was the merest touch of the lips.'

It had been magical. An enchantment. And one that she was not sure had worn off yet, because otherwise, what was she doing allowing him to kiss her again? 'But that might have caused harm. I might have fallen in love with you, gone into a decline pining for the handsome stranger who kissed me in the sunlight on top of the world.'

He seemed to take her tone and her false laugh at face value, thank goodness. 'I suspect that two old friends, long parted, recognised each other without realising it, don't you?' There was a pause and that shuttered look came over his face again. 'I would never want to hurt you, Laurel.'

But I hurt you with my lack of trust. Can you ever truly forgive that?

The hotel concierge was appalled that Lady Laurel's charming bonnet had fallen foul of the undergrowth and a sedan chair was produced within minutes to whisk her the short distance home. Outdated they might seem, but sedan chairs continued to flourish in the spa town, snuggly conveying old ladies from hot baths to lodging houses, or ferrying gouty gentlemen up the hills, safe with the strong arms of the Irish chairmen.

Giles paced alongside and, as the chair swayed, she watched him through the glass, trying to read his expression, grateful to be spared the need to talk, to touch him by taking his arm. Inexperienced though she might be, she was certain that kiss had been one of genuine desire, but it had also felt strangely safe. Was that because of their old friendship, or because Giles was a true gentleman? Or perhaps it was the difference between men and women. He could kiss without commitment, without necessarily wanting the person—only the caress.

So what do I want?

She understood now what she had overheard, all those years ago in the barn. She could accept it for what it was, although it felt deeply uncomfortable to realise that young men's heads were so full of such shocking and uncontrolled fantasies. She could forgive Giles, she supposed she already had, but she wondered if she could forgive herself.

But how could I be expected to know about these things?

If Giles had told his father that it was all fantasy, surely the older man would have understood?

We are all to blame, she concluded gloomily. *Giles should have reined in his temper and explained to our fathers. His father should have thought back to when he was his son's age. My father and Godpapa Gordon should have stopped working themselves up into a rage over their daughters' virtue and honour and allowed everyone to calm down...*

It took only moments to reach Laura Place. Giles swept her inside, hatless, to be met in the hallway by Phoebe, who had obviously seen their arrival through the window and was considerably agitated.

'Where is your bonnet, Laurel? What have you been doing to her, Lord Revesby?'

'Lady Laurel had an encounter with unruly foliage in the labyrinth,' Giles said, straight-faced. 'The hat came off and was, unfortunately, trodden upon.'

'Unruly foliage.' Phoebe looked from one to the other and then, to Laurel's amazement, giggled. 'How very original. I have never heard it called that before, Lord Revesby. Good day and thank you so much for returning Laurel before she encountered any shrubbery in a state of actual riot.'

Giles's mouth twitched appreciatively. 'Good day, Lady Cary. Good day, Lady Laurel, and thank you for your company this morning.'

The two of them stood in the hallway as the door closed behind Giles. 'Oh, dear, I should not have been so frivolous about that,' Phoebe said, pink in the cheeks. 'The man is just so charming and so good looking and when he says outrageous things with such a look in his eye… Did he, I mean, was he, er, forward in any way?'

'Absolutely not,' Laurel said as she crossed her fingers behind her back. 'We have discussed what happened nine years ago, we understand each other very well and I think you might say that a peace treaty has been signed.'

Although not between me and my conscience.

'I rather think that everyone involved should have taken a deep breath and counted to five hundred.'

She knew she was going to lose sleep over this, not least because she could see all too clearly that she had managed to make a martyr out of herself, ending up unmarried and miserable. She had done what she had thought was the right thing when she should have trusted Giles enough to ask for his side of the story first.

'What will happen now?' Phoebe asked, cutting into her self-flagellating thoughts.

'I imagine Giles will go to the family's country house. It does not seem that his father's condition is as perilous as he was given to believe and I am sure that the Marquess would much rather that Giles was looking after the estate than kicking his heels waiting on him in Bath. He will probably go to London as well, re-establish his social life.' Despite the kiss and his apparent forgiveness, he certainly would not want to see much more of her now. As far as Giles was concerned the past had been explained, forgiven and could now be put behind them.

'I see.' Phoebe seemed as downcast as Laurel felt. 'Things will be less lively in Bath without Lord Revesby here. I am sure all my friends are agog with envy over us having the acquaintance of such a handsome and eligible gentleman. Oh, well.' She gave herself a little shake. 'We must not repine over the loss of one gentleman, I suppose. Come into the drawing room, Laurel, the post has arrived and there seem to be any number of invitations. We can sort through them before luncheon. I do hope nobody is expecting an introduction to Lord Revesby if he is leaving Bath.'

They sat and sifted through the correspondence. Laurel had, by some miracle, a letter from Jamie, sent from the Solent where he boasted of a lack of seasickness, told her a number of unintelligible things about navigation and the use of a sextant, whatever that was, and complained of a shortage of woollen stockings. She had sent him off with a dozen pairs, so goodness knew what he had done with those.

There were a number of invitations for them both, passed across by Phoebe, and Laurel began sorting them out by date. 'This one looks most impressive.' She held up a heavy gilt-edged card. '*"The Duchess of Wilborough requests the pleasure of the company of Lady Laurel Knighton at a reception..."* It is tomorrow night and the address is the Royal Crescent. Do you know the Duchess, Aunt Phoebe? And why am I invited and not you? It seems very short notice.'

'I already have my invitation. Then it occurred to me to let her know you had arrived and so she has invited you. We were at school together when she was only obscure Miss Barrington with no important connections and some of the girls were top-lofty about it and looked down on her. But I liked her and we were friends and she has not forgotten that. I always receive invitations whenever she is in Bath.'

Phoebe's smile held just a touch of smug self-satisfaction at the thought of her influential friend and Laurel thought she could hardly blame her. She felt quite excited herself at the thought of attending such a fashionable event. Her new life was here in Bath and amongst its society and thinking of that, living it, was what she should do in order to put her muddle of feelings over Giles into perspective. At least the misunderstanding was over, she had been forgiven, he seemed to understand. It was the best she could hope for.

'What progress, eh? What does the chit have to say for herself?'

Giles closed the door behind him and took the seat opposite his father. 'Good morning, sir. How is your foot today?'

'Better, better. Never mind my confounded foot—what about Laurel Knighton? Still as plain and scrawny as she was as a child, poor girl? Still, can't be helped if she is, you'll have to make the best of it. All cats are grey once the bedchamber candles are snuffed out.'

Giles managed not to rise to the bait. 'She has developed into a very handsome young lady, although she still has a sharp tongue and a temper. I danced with her at the Assembly Rooms the night before last and we managed not to come to blows in the middle of a set, although she made no bones about not being pleased to see me. The aunt, Lady Cary, seems to be offering me encouragement.'

'You think so? Interesting.' His father nodded. 'Very interesting. The woman appeared to have the brain of a peahen on the occasions I met her, but I suspect she is sharp enough when it comes to marrying off young ladies. So what else have you done? One dance won't fix her interest.'

'I took her walking in Sydney Gardens yesterday. I explained my part in that fiasco nine years ago, she gave me the benefit of her thoughts on our past history—I may have bruises somewhere, although no actual bleeding wounds—and we parted on moderately good terms.' If his father thought he was going to receive a blow-by-blow, or even a kiss-by-kiss account of this courtship he was much mistaken.

'Have you kissed the chit yet?' *Yes, that is what he expects.*

'I am hardly likely to discuss a young lady in those terms with anyone, Father, even you.' Giles found it was easy to keep a perfectly expressionless face. That kiss had been both memorable and disturbing.

The Marquess grunted. 'So you have kissed her and it was not a great success.'

His father could obviously read him more accurately than he had hoped, although he would have described the experience as confusing rather than unsatisfactory. Giles checked his pockets, found his worry piece and began to turn it between his fingers.

'Confound it, Giles—enough of these namby-pamby attitudes. Get on and seduce the girl if that's what it takes.'

'I will do no such thing,' he snapped back. 'Do you think I want to begin married life having entrapped my bride into wedlock?'

The Marquess erupted from his seat, fetched his bandaged foot a sharp blow on the edge of the toppling gout stool, swore violently and subsided back into the chair. 'Get down off your high horse. I am not suggesting you ravish the girl. Damn it, in my young day we managed our courtship with rather more verve and considerably more finesse.'

Giles resisted the urge to enquire if, by verve, his father recommended throwing a lady over his saddle bow and riding off with her. He picked up the gout stool, set his father's bandaged foot on it with sufficient emphasis to provoke a muffled curse and sat back. 'I am courting Laurel and moving as fast as honour will allow,' he said, contriving to sound infuriatingly starchy, even to his own ears.

'So why are you still here, damn it?'

'Dancing attendance on you, sir, as ordered,' Giles said. Provoking his father seemed to do the older man the world of good. It certainly stopped him brooding about his investment losses.

His father narrowed his eyes dangerously, then barked, 'In!', when there was a tap on the door.

'The post, my lord.' It was the landlord, silver salver in hand.

'I'll be off then, Father.'

'No, wait. There should be something about the Home Farm—yes, here it is.' The Marquess thrust a thick document at him. 'See what you think. It's about time you involved yourself with estate matters.'

'Sir.' Giles took the papers to the table and began to read a complicated tale of leases, under-leases, collapsing field drains and uncooperative tenants.

On the other side of the room his father rustled papers, muttered, swore and occasionally gave a snort of laughter as he scanned the rest of his correspondence. Then he said, 'Aha!'

Giles looked up. 'Everything all right, sir?'

'Hermione Wilborough's back in Bath and she is throwing one of her receptions tonight. Do you no harm to attend, get back into the swing of things. She's up in Royal Crescent. Make a call as soon as you've finished with those documents and she is certain to invite you.'

'She has written to you?'

'No, a mutual acquaintance mentioned it.' He folded up the letter. 'Now, what do you think to that under-lease? Renew or not?'

Chapter Nine

Phoebe bent to check her appearance in the mirror of the ladies' retiring room set aside for the reception. She patted a curl into place with an expression of some complacency. 'We both look very fine, do you not think, Laurel? What a marvellous evening this will be.'

'I agree that you have worked a miracle in two days, Aunt.' Laurel squeezed in next to her to study her own reflection. 'Your dressmaker has rescued my gowns from complete countrified dowdiness—and to be able to produce this one at such short notice is incredible—and your hairdresser has certainly given me a new touch, but I cannot be quite as relaxed as you about a reception at a duchess's mansion.'

Laurel viewed her new gown with approval and her new hairstyle with some wariness. It did seem exceedingly short in places but that, she had been assured, was all the crack. Prodding at it was not going to make her any more comfortable with the effect. She moved to the window and looked out over the spectacular view across Bath, not quite believing that Phoebe had managed to secure her an invitation to such a select gathering.

'Nonsense. Dear Hermione keeps the most welcoming of establishments. It will merely be a friendly soirée, you will see.'

An hour later Laurel had to agree with her. The reception was lavish but the tone light-hearted and she found that she could cope perfectly well on simple good manners and common sense. No one had laughed at her for being a country mouse who had never had a Season, or even travelled to London, and she had managed not to make any dreadful *faux pas* when introduced to a dowager duchess, a bishop and a general in rapid succession.

It was all very elegant and novel and she had eaten several delicious lobster patties and drunk at least one too many glasses of champagne, but Laurel could not help but feel remarkably flat despite the glamour of the occasion. Perhaps she had overtired herself and had not yet recovered from the journey. Or perhaps it was a night of broken sleep and uneasy dreams.

Or perhaps I am missing someone, she admitted to herself.

Giles was confusing and infuriating, but, having found him again, now she missed him. She wanted to talk to him as she had once done every day. Not about anything of huge significance, just to exchange ideas and jokes and confidences.

Everything seemed extraordinarily flat. She had failed Giles with her lack of trust and she had let her judgement be clouded by jealousy.

What if he had been killed in the Peninsula? Stop it. He could have stayed at home and equally easily have been killed in a riding accident or crossing the road...

And then a small group near the entrance moved aside, laughing. The sound caught her attention and she looked across and there, framed between two gorgeously liveried footmen, was Giles. She should not be happy to see him, but she was. Laurel told herself that it would give her the opportunity to put him firmly in his place if he took any more liberties after that kiss in the labyrinth, for one thing, which might also serve to calm her own rather overheated imagination. And there was the undoubted satisfaction of having both a smart hair style and a gorgeous gown of silver net over a pale aquamarine underskirt and no longer looking like a country cousin. That was all it was, perfectly justified feminine pride.

She watched Giles talking to a group near the entrance. The men were laughing, the ladies smiling and flirting their fans, quite at ease. She had no experience in dealing with men, not handsome men who seemed to find her attractive. Giles should be feeling as wary of her as she was of him with their truce and understanding so new between them, yet he had kissed her, paid attention to her, in a way that confused and excited her even as she told herself that she should not want his admiration or his kisses. And perhaps he would not want to offer either if he knew just how she had felt, that long-ago summer's afternoon.

But I still want him. The thought was like bubbles of champagne rising through her blood. *I do not know this adult man, I do not know if I should risk my heart by getting any closer, but...*

Common sense went straight out the door as though a footman was holding it wide for that very purpose. Laurel stepped forward, knowing that it was not at all the done thing for a lady to walk towards a gentleman across a crowded room. She should wait patiently, pretending not to notice his presence until he sought her out, but knowing that perfectly well did nothing to fix her disobedient feet to the spot. They took her diagonally across the floor towards Giles as he walked towards her. They met in the middle, already laughing at each other, and he caught her outstretched hand in his.

'My dear Lady Laurel—what *have* you done to your hair?'

With the laughter in his voice all the years apart vanished like smoke. She was still the girl who had wanted him for ever, he was still the young man who had teased her, been kind to her, been her friend. Only now they were adults. Laurel had no idea what Giles felt about her, but she knew that she wanted him in a way that girl had been too young to understand. She could not have him, of course. He might flirt, he might forgive, but he would be seeking a bride from the new crop of girls making their come-out next Season.

But that was in the future and this was now and she was just light-headed enough to disregard the consequences to her own heart when the evening was over. 'Do you not like my new style, Lord Revesby? It is all the crack.'

'It is ravishing, my lady. Simply ravishing.' He came close and lowered his voice to little more than a murmur so that she had to lean towards him to hear. 'I especially like the way it is cut short at the side of your neck. It exposes so much soft white skin. I want to bite it,' he whispered, so close now that his breath burned trails of sensation across her skin, as intimate as his fingertips would have been.

Against the fine lawn of her chemise her nipples tightened and fretted, the sensation so insistent that she glanced down, certain that they must be visible through chemise and bodice lining and silk. When she looked up, blushing, Giles was watching her face, and she knew he had let his gaze drop to her bosom as he imagined the effect his words were having. She might not be able to read his mind, but she could read his desires very plainly indeed.

'Is there a terrace here?' he asked.

'I… Yes, there must be, don't you think? The French doors are open all along that back wall. Why?' She knew perfectly well why—this was Giles up to mischief, but very grown-up mischief.

'Because I want to make love to you out there,' he murmured. 'Because I want to find a shadowed corner, lit only by the reflected glitter of the lanterns on a pool of water. I want to strip off your gown and take your breasts in the palm of my hand and lick your nipples until you— Good evening, your Grace. I was just saying to Lady Laurel what an exquisite room this is.'

'Wicked man.' The Duchess fetched Giles a sharp rap on the knuckles with her fan. 'You were telling Lady Laurel how her beauty enhances my room. At least, I hope that is what you were saying to account for that blush.'

'Your Grace is, of course, correct.'

The Duchess raised one perfectly shaped eyebrow. 'Flim-flam, you are humouring me, don't think I do not know it. Just like your father—and I am sorry to hear that he is laid low. It must be bad if the poor devil is reduced to drinking spa waters.' She looked Giles up and down. 'You've changed, Revesby. Still, as you were a scrubby boy when I last saw you, that is no surprise. Has your time in the Portuguese Court taught you more than how to do the pretty with duchesses? I seem to have heard rumours that you were a very dangerous young man. Lady Laurel, I caution you to beware.'

'As Lady Laurel is English, not French, she is in no danger, I assure you, your Grace.'

'Not from your weapons made of steel, that is true.' The look that the Duchess gave Giles was unmistakably flirtatious. She gave him another tap with her fan and moved on, chuckling a little.

'Was she referring to—?' Laurel searched

for an acceptable phrase and failed to find one.
'Parts of your anatomy?'

'I believe so. Please rest assured that I am
completely disarmed tonight.'

'Even on the terrace?' Why was Giles flirting
with her when there were so many other younger,
prettier women in the room, or when older, very
attractive ladies such as the Duchess seemed so
very willing to trifle with him?

'You are in no danger from me, Laurel.'

'No?' she murmured, suddenly chilled. She
realised that she had been too overwhelmed by
finding him again to wonder too deeply about
his kisses. He'd had her explanation of what had
happened that long-ago day and he had been concerned about his father and, perhaps, disorientated by being back in England after so long.
All those things could explain why he had forgiven her so easily for the misunderstanding, had
wanted her company, her kisses.

But now he had no anxieties about the Marquess, he was clearly at home and comfortable
in society, so why was he apparently so pleased
to see her and so passionate in his whispered
flirtation? Had Giles come back from Portugal
the libertine she had so falsely accused him of
being, or was it possible that he had other motives for paying attention to the woman who had

sent him into exile in the first place? Revenge, for example. She could hardly blame him.

'Laurel? Is anything wrong?'

'No. No, of course not.' She was being foolish. This was Giles, for goodness' sake, her old friend restored to her. He could not have changed that much—and she owed him her trust above all else. 'I am simply not used to all of this.' She waved a hand around the crowded reception room, with its beautiful, chattering, laughing, confident people in their silks and superfine and their jewels. 'I am a country mouse, used to little local assemblies and domestic entertainments. And I am not used to flirting.'

'I am going too fast,' he said, almost to himself.

'Giles? Too fast for what?'

'For you, of course.' His smile was rueful. 'I should have remembered that society events might be a trifle overwhelming at first. You are older, more mature than the girls making their come-outs and I am treating you as I would a married lady, out for several years.'

'You kiss the breasts of married women on terraces, do you?' She felt the need of the Duchess's technique with her fan.

'Laurel, I cannot pretend that I have been a good boy for nine years. I have not. But here

I am, as I am, and I would very much like to get to know you again, as you are now, a grown woman. And while I am doing that I can promise you that married women, in fact any women, will be out of bounds to me.'

What did he mean? Once she would have asked him directly, but now something held her back. Did he mean that he wanted to enjoy a flirtation with her for as long as it suited them both? That he wanted to be her lover? Or that he was courting her? That possibility almost brought her train of thought to a shuddering halt. No, it was simply her foolish fantasies. Why her, the country spinster, virtually on the shelf, when there would be so many fresh young beauties to choose from? She realised why she dare not ask him outright. He would probably laugh, assuming that she was in jest.

I cannot trust him to tell me the truth about something so personal any more. I misjudged the youth and I know this man even less well. I cannot trust myself either.

On the other hand, keeping him at a suspicious distance was not going to teach her anything about Giles, or about herself. 'I wonder if there are any lobster patties left? And champagne.'

'I would be amazed if the Duchess would tolerate a shortage of either.'

'Then I have a fancy to eat a patty and sip champagne on the terrace.'

'That was not quite what I had in mind, but, of course, what a lady requests, a lady must have.' From his smile she could tell he was not put out by her apparent refusal of his lovemaking.

He was teasing me by being outrageous, she realised.

'And while I am sipping and nibbling we can look to see if there are any pools of water for the lamplight to be reflected in. Simply to admire the effect, of course.' Two could tease.

'We might indeed.' The smile became wicked. Giles gestured to a footman. 'A plate of savouries—especially the lobster patties—and two glasses of champagne on the terrace, if you please.'

The man bowed and hurried off and Laurel slipped her hand under the crook of Giles's elbow. She felt a little self-conscious, people were looking at them and she wondered if she would be considered fast if she went outside with him. Or perhaps they were simply looking at him and wondering who the handsome stranger was.

'You see, there was no need to clutch my arm quite so fiercely,' he murmured as they stepped outside to find several tables had been placed on the well-lit terrace and a number of couples and a few small groups were strolling up and down, chatting in the cool evening air. 'No one is going to be pointing a finger at the fast Lady Laurel Knighton going outside with that wicked rake Revesby.'

'And I do not believe for a moment that you would have done any of those wicked things you were whispering about,' Laurel said tartly, wondering if she was overreacting to the discovery that Giles did not intend to make an attempt on her virtue in the shrubbery.

Would I have allowed him to?

'Would you have let me?' he asked, in an uncanny echo of her thought.

'I do not think you would have risked my reputation like that,' Laurel said, suddenly certain. 'I realised that once I had stopped being flustered and thought about it, or if you had begun to… to take liberties, then I am sure you would have done nothing I was unhappy about.'

Perhaps that was just a little too frank.

'That is very trusting.' Giles pushed a glass of champagne closer to her. 'To assume I would stop if told to, I mean.' When she looked at him, eyebrows raised, he shook his head. 'I would have done, of course.'

'Here is to trust, then.' Laurel raised the wine

glass in a toast. It felt like a momentous declaration. 'We have lost too many years of our friendship to a lack of it.'

'To trust.' Was there something uncomfortable in the expression in those blue eyes that were not quite meeting hers?

'Do you think that perhaps we have forgiven each other too quickly for there to be real trust between us yet?' she probed.

'No.' Giles offered her the platter of savouries. 'You see, I even trust you to leave me at least one lobster patty.'

'Be serious.' She thought about it, studying him. 'If we had met the next day we would have straightened things out, talked it through, however upset we both were, wouldn't we?'

'We would,' he agreed, arrested with a sliver of chicken halfway to his lips. 'I had not thought about it like that, but you are quite right. Somehow, if only we had been able to talk to each other, we would have made it up. Do you realise that if we had, then we would be married by now?'

Laurel dropped the patty she had absentmindedly picked up. Flakes of pastry scattered over the plate.

My instinct had been right all along. He knew we were meant for each other.

Then another reason for Giles's acceptance presented itself—logical, likely, disappointing. 'Did you know about those plans of our fathers' all along? I did not, I had no idea. Would you have agreed to it?'

'I knew they had some such idea in their heads, and I had accepted it, I suppose—it seemed very logical with the land marching together and so on. But it would have been several years in the future and you were too young to talk about such things.'

'Yes, I was, I suppose.' Far too young and very innocent. And romantic without realising it. 'But all that time, you never gave me any idea that you knew.' And all the time that she had felt, in her bones, that Giles was meant for her, it had never occurred to her that he did not feel the same way about a match, that he saw it as simply a logical, practical thing to do.

The land marches together.

But if all he had been doing was dutifully falling in with his father's dynastic plans, then that blew away the rosy glow of her long-cherished picture of them as meant for each other at some deep, primal way, far more fundamental, far purer than agreements over joining bloodlines and estates. It had a sweet pain to it, speaking of what might have been.

'You are not too young now,' Giles said, almost conversationally.

'I— Whatever can you mean?'

He doesn't mean that we should... Surely? Does he? No, of course not.

'What is to stop us getting married now?' Giles was watching her over the rim of his glass.

He does mean marriage, not a dalliance, not friendship.

For a moment the rosy glow flooded back and then she focused on what he had said, how he had said it.

It hardly seems the most passionate of proposals, she thought with a sudden shiver. *Where is the man who kissed me in the labyrinth, the man who suggested doing wicked things out here in the shadows?*

Laurel took a deep breath and found her smile, striving to look amused and sophisticated. 'Why would you want to marry me?' she responded, just as coolly as he had put the question. 'Surely there are any number of younger women you could take to wife? It was you, after all, who reminded me how short a time a woman has to make a good match and bear a family.'

'We know each other, we are old friends. You know Thorne Hall and its people and the neighbourhood. It is all familiar to you, whereas I have been away for years. It seems to me that you would be the perfect wife for me.'

'We have been apart for nine years and are just beginning to repair the breach in our friendship. We knew each other as children, youngsters, not as…as lovers. The idea of asking me has just occurred to you and you cannot have thought it through. You certainly cannot pretend that you wish to marry me because you feel an emotional attachment to me.'

She was not going to use the word *love*, she knew what that did to men—threw them into a panic, and in a male emotional panic they were prone to utter the kind of home truths she had no desire to hear. It was bad enough being told she was perfect because she knew the neighbours.

'Can I not? You think I do not feel fond of you, Laurel? I was so angry over that misunderstanding because it was you, my friend, who overheard and misjudged me, you who thought me a libertine. And did you not enjoy the kisses we shared in Sydney Gardens?'

Only then did Giles reach across the table, take her hand in his.

He should have been holding it, warm and secure in his grasp, all the time he was propos- ing, she thought, resisting the temptation to pull away, to flounce off, all offended pride and hurt feelings.

'Laurel, we could make a good marriage, my father would welcome you with open arms, you would be home again.' His fingers curled into her palm, an insistent pressure through the taut silk of her glove. 'I came to Bath without the slightest notion I would see you here, without any intention of marrying you. But now I find that it is essential to me that we wed.'

Essential? What a very peculiar choice of word.

Yet strangely she could believe it, despite the absence of any protestations of love, or even of affection beyond old friendship. It did have the ring of truth, Giles really did want to marry her. She had always been able to sense, not so much when he lied, but when he was being absolutely sincere, and that sincerity was in his voice now, in his expression, in the grip of his fingers on hers.

Essential.

'I have no idea what my dowry is,' she protested, then realised just how far that comment took her past surprise, edging into acceptance.

Giles shrugged. She supposed that for the heir to a marquessate money was hardly important. But the land would be. She realised that she had no idea how her father had left the unentailed land that had once been her dowry. Presumably it had all gone to Cousin Anthony now.

'We will find out about a dowry and all those tiresome questions later,' Giles said, carrying on calmly while she was lost in a haze of confused emotions. 'I will have to speak to the new Earl, I imagine—is he your trustee?'

If he is prepared to take me with no idea of my dowry that augurs well for his motives, Laurel supposed.

'The old agreement between our fathers—'

'My father wrote to me that the two of them burned it the next day—presumably in the absence of my sorry carcase to put on the bonfire. Father began to correspond with me, you know, after a few months when he realised I was not coming home. And I climbed down off my high horse and wrote back. I cannot say we are exactly close yet, but it is not as though there is a great breach between us. Our marriage would make him very happy, you need have no fear that you would be unwelcome because of our difficult past.' He took her other hand and leaned towards her across the little table, the blue intensity of his gaze in the lantern light almost mesmerising. 'Say yes, Laurel. Say you will marry me.'

Chapter Ten

'And you refused him? But, Laurel, why?' Phoebe stared at Laurel in dismay. She was sitting up in bed, her hair in curl papers that escaped from under her nightcap, the cup of hot chocolate in her hands tilting dangerously. 'I am appalled.'

Laurel had tapped on her aunt's door in her nightgown and robe to catch her at an hour when they could be sure of being alone, before the start of the household's morning routine.

Phoebe sounded both horrified and dismayed, as well as appalled. Laurel had expected astonishment that she had turned down such an eligible suitor, had been braced for a lecture on the foolishness of such a decision, but she had not expected quite such a strong reaction and it threw her off balance. After an almost sleepless night spent tossing and turning until her bedclothes were as tangled as her thoughts, she was not ready to explain herself clearly.

'I did not exactly refuse him, it is more that I did not accept him,' she said, gabbling a little in the face of Phoebe's shock. 'It took me by surprise, you see. I had never imagined that he would propose to me. I said I had to have time to consider.' And one night was not enough, it seemed.

'But, Laurel, how could you hesitate?' Her aunt put down her chocolate cup, held up one hand dramatically and began to count off on her fingers. 'Giles is an earl and will, one day, be a marquess. You have known him all your life and you would be living in, as near as makes no difference, your old home. He is an exceedingly handsome, intelligent young man, in good health, and he brings back a most excellent reputation from the Peninsula. Those are six very good points in his favour.' She threw up her hands. 'Do you want to wait until we can enumerate ten?' She narrowed her eyes and studied Laurel's face. 'Has he done anything to his discredit since you became reacquainted?'

'No.'

'He has not tried to take liberties with you?'

'No.' Laurel considered the truth of that statement. 'Well, none that I did not welcome.'

Phoebe's cheeks turned pink. 'Oh, dear. What have you done, Laurel?'

'Nothing too naughty, Aunt, I promise you. Just that I know that we can add that he is very good at kissing to our list of positive attributes.'

Phoebe went even pinker, but then she smiled. 'I make that seven then.'

Laurel found she was smiling back.

'So why do you hesitate, dearest? I am sure we can find another three good points to convince you.' Phoebe wriggled up against the pillows, the smile vanishing.

'I do not say you should marry him if you do not want to, or have taken him in dislike, but you reached an understanding the other day, you made up your quarrel. I do not understand why you would not wish to accept Lord Revesby. Why any woman not in love with someone else would not wish to, come to that,' she added.

Perhaps I am in love with someone else, with the image of the young man I thought would be mine, the young man I told myself I hated for all those years. Can I love the real man?

'Because I do not know why he wants to marry me,' she said, producing the practical, sensible answer. 'I am twenty-five, nearly twenty-six, and there are many much prettier, much younger, ladies in the Marriage Mart for him to choose from. We have spent nine years apart after a ghastly quarrel and neither of us knows the other as an adult. So, why me?'

'He is in love with you?' Phoebe looked hopeful.

'He has not said so.' Her aunt's face dropped. 'And you would think that if he does then he would say so when he was proposing, wouldn't you?'

'Most certainly. Why would he not? Any young lady would be delighted with a declaration like that from such a man. Not that love is essential for a good marriage, of course,' she added, apparently remembering her duty to see her niece well married. 'And it is no excuse for a bad one. Do you love Lord Revesby, Laurel?'

She almost denied it, but surely she could be honest with her aunt? 'I... I did, long ago, before he left. Not as an adult, of course, but I was sure we were meant for each other. I suppose that was why it hurt so much when I thought that he and Portia were...involved. But that is different from what an adult woman should feel for a man.' She found that her hands were tangled and knotted in the skirts of her robe and made herself relax her grip. 'I really thought I would be happier unmarried, happier forgetting him.'

'You were making the best of things bravely,'

Phoebe pronounced. 'And now you are not sure how you feel.'

Laurel did not like the idea that she had somehow talked herself into pretending opposition to marriage, just to make the best of things. 'I am not at all certain. If I am honest with myself—and I suppose that if I am not there is really no hope for me—if Giles had said he loved me, then I would have accepted him.'

'Men are not good at understanding their own feelings, which does make everything more complicated, of course,' Phoebe said sagely. 'My dear Cary would have sooner shot himself in the foot than admit that he loved me, but he showed it every day, bless him.' Phoebe reached out and tugged the bell pull. 'We need more chocolate.' When her maid came in she sent her for another cup and a fresh jug and they talked of the reception until it came and they were alone again.

'You think Giles might love me?' The chocolate was soothing and invigorating at the same time.

'It might be that he does and feels awkward about saying so, although I doubt that young man has a bashful bone in his body.' Phoebe looked approving at the thought.

She likes a rake, Laurel realised and bit her lip to hide the smile.

'Or he loves you but simply does not recognise it,' her aunt continued. 'Or he is not in love, but feels the two of you would rub along very well together and he would rather that than take a risk on an unknown, probably immature, young lady.'

'If it is the first, that he feels awkward, then he would soon get over his reticence if I encouraged him,' Laurel pondered. 'If the second, then surely that would emerge once we are married. And the third, I suppose, would not be the end of the world if it were not for the fact that I hate the idea of just rubbing along, as you put it.' Giles had produced all those sensible, practical reasons for their match and they had felt as though something joyous in her soul was being smothered. 'I might—'

'Love him as a grown woman should?' Phoebe had turned pink again.

'Yes. I just wish I knew what it is he is not telling me.' Laurel slid off the end of the bed and began to pace around the room, the skirts of her robe swishing around her ankles, the cup clasped in her hands. 'I believe Giles sincerely wants to marry me, but he is hiding something, I am sure of it.'

'If he had acquired a disastrous gambling habit in Portugal, or drinks too much, I am sure we would have heard rumours of such things.'

'More likely a mistress and a brood of handsome dark-eyed Portuguese children,' Laurel said darkly. 'I will ask him.'

'Laurel!'

'If I cannot talk to Giles frankly, then how can I marry him?'

'All men have their secrets, dear. It does not do to insist on total frankness—one might hear things one does not wish to. Men are different from ladies and we have to learn to turn a blind eye sometimes. We must get up and get dressed.' Phoebe threw back the covers and reached for the bell pull again. 'Is Lord Revesby calling today to hear your decision?'

'He is coming this afternoon and taking me to walk in Sydney Gardens where he says we may be assured of some privacy.' Phoebe's expression made her laugh, despite her worries. 'To talk, Phoebe, not to do whatever it is that is making you frown so. I do not think that I can accept him, you know. I have this strong conviction that there is something I do not understand, something behind this proposal. It is so sudden. And yet he does seem quite genuine in his desire to marry me.'

'Oh, dear.' Phoebe hesitated, one foot out from between the covers. 'Ah, well, we must get on with the day. I have just recalled some letters I must write this morning.'

'Yes, I must admit to appalling tactics,' Giles said, not at all happy about having to discuss his failed attempt at a proposal with his father. 'In fact, no tactics at all, but impulse. I had not thought through what I intended to say to Laurel, I simply took the opportunity of finding her at the Duchess's affair last night and put the question because she seemed quite receptive. I could have sworn she was glad to see me, but I made a mull of it.'

The Marquess opened his mouth to speak, but Giles pressed on. 'She obviously considers me a most unsatisfactory suitor and I cannot blame her. You have no need to share your opinion of my cow-handedness, Father, and there is no need to lecture me with advice on courtship either. I am taking her out walking this afternoon and I hope I will make a better fist of it this time.'

'The chit is being coy, I have no doubt. She means to accept you—she would be all about in the head to turn you down, Giles, and she might have been a sad romp as a girl, but she was not lacking in wits.'

'That is all very flattering, sir, but—'

'What time are you going to the gardens?'

'About four, I thought. It is rather cloudy now, but it seems set to improve later.'

'Hmm. Well, good fortune, Giles—and send in my man on your way out, will you?'

Later, as he sat in his room, working out just how he was going to word that afternoon's proposal, Giles realised he still had no idea what he could say to convince Laurel to accept. He had laid out all the practical reasons for her, but the problem was that he feared he knew exactly why she had hesitated—she had expected him to say he loved her.

It was a perfectly reasonable expectation, because otherwise why propose to her and not to anyone else—she had been quite clear that there must be any number of other suitable ladies out there if all he wanted was an eligible bride. But how could he make declarations of a love he did not feel to Laurel? He refused to lie to her—it was bad enough that he was having to deceive her about his motives—but he did not want to hurt her either. Or give her cause to refuse.

Making love to Laurel was another matter. He could do that with pleasure—it was a delight and she was an attractive woman—but he could imagine what she would say, and feel, if she realised that he was quite capable of making love to her while not feeling any deeper emotion than liking combined with sexual attraction.

How much did she understand about men, about sex and desire? Not a great deal, he imagined, not if the sum total of her social life was neighbourhood society and an occasional local assembly. Not that a sophisticated understanding about the capacity of men to separate desire and love would make it any less painful if she realised how he felt.

What if he told her the truth about the financial position, about the debt and her dowry? What if he put it to her almost as a business proposition rather than a romantic one? Giles rocked back in his chair and chewed the end of his quill as he tried to shape such a proposal into something that might be acceptable. Could he present it as an opportunity for Laurel? She would gain the title, a fine estate, security, the chance to have a family. Many women would leap at the offer.

The front legs of his chair hit the carpet with a thud. But not Laurel. She appeared to have the independence she was seeking now and he sensed that the strange, romantic, free-spirited girl he had known would want more of marriage. Much more. Laurel, he very much feared, would want love, an emotional partnership. If he laid out the facts, then she would ask him directly if he would have even thought of marrying her if it had not been for the land and the debt, and the honest answer to that question was *no*. And he could not lie to her, not about that.

'I told Phoebe that I am going to discuss this very frankly with you.' Laurel sidestepped an enthusiastic small boy chasing a hoop along the path. The garden was rather more crowded this afternoon and there were several couples and groups taking advantage of the brightening weather.

'Excellent.'

She looked up at Giles, walking by her side, and was unable to resist a wry smile. 'You said that with almost adequate enthusiasm.'

'I am out of practice for frank discussions with ladies.'

'I am glad to hear it.'

'At least you could tell I am not in the habit of making proposals. I made a sorry fist of it, did I not?'

'In what way?' she asked. It would not do to let him off the hook so easily. And, of course, he might be the veteran of goodness knew how many botched proposals, although that did seem rather unlikely.

'I began with shocking suggestions about

making love to you and then followed that up with an exceedingly prosaic proposal.' Giles sounded gloomy enough to have been thinking carefully about the matter.

'True. Both shocking and prosaic, a most peculiar mixture.'

'May I try again?'

'To make love or to propose?'

'I suspect that reversing the order might be advisable this time.' When she turned her head to look at him she found he was watching her and that the gloomy tone was lightened by the hint of a smile.

'You are trying to make me laugh, Giles. You are a rogue and I suppose you know that perfectly well. Yes, you may try again, but I warn you now, I am expecting to refuse again.' She rather thought he was offering her dream, her heart's desire that she did not deserve and, without love, she did not think she could bear it. She should have trusted him, talked to him and, surely, it was too late now?

'Shall we sit on that bench? It is shielded by roses on either side, we will not be overheard, but it is not compromisingly secluded.' Giles took her nod as approval and turned to cross the grass to the seat.

It was a very good choice, Laurel decided.

The roses smelt delightful and certainly added some much-needed romance. 'Very well, Lord Revesby, you have my full attention.' She folded her hands together neatly in her lap, tucked her feet under her skirts and regarded him with all the prim solemnity she could conjure up. Giles had always known how to make her laugh and she should not be yielding to the temptation to tease him back now, but, oh, he did so lift her spirits.

'*I* am a rogue? You are deliberately trying to put me out of countenance with your Puritan Miss impersonation.'

'I am waiting, my lord.'

Giles rolled his eyes, took a large handkerchief from his pocket, laid it out on the grass and went down on one knee.

'Lord Revesby! We are in public.' She reached out and tugged at his shoulder. Of course the wretched man did not stir.

'Lady Laurel, I am attempting to perform an adequately romantic proposal in the correct style.'

'Well, stop it this moment before someone who knows me sees us. Look—that group of ladies is walking this way! Get up, do, Giles, pretend you have dropped something. I despair of you—why should I marry a man who is as provoking now as he was as a boy?'

'Because I make you laugh?' Giles stood up, retrieved his handkerchief and sat down beside her again, just in time before the ladies passed by.

'Making me laugh is better than making me cry, but it is hardly the basis of a sound marriage. But you did give me all the sensible reasons yesterday evening so I suppose the more…emotional ones are still to be discussed.'

'Laurel, I can give you liking and respect and friendship. Years of shared memories and dreams.' He did not try to take her hands, or move closer and, somehow, that made her believe more in his sincerity.

'But not love.'

'Damnation, here comes another flock of chaperons. I could swear it is the local branch of the Society for the Suppression of Vice, on patrol.'

This time the ladies, a trio, sat down on the next bench, close enough for the murmur of their voices to be heard, if not their words. Laurel managed, somehow, not to give way to giggles.

'I refuse to discuss this in a whisper,' Giles said.

'Quite. Oh, no, here are the first group coming back and I recognise at least one of them.

Mrs Atkinson, good afternoon.' Laurel bowed slightly. Mrs Atkinson, one of Phoebe's bosom bows, returned the gesture, glanced at Giles and walked on with her friends. They stopped a few yards away to admire a sundial.

'And I have just realised that one of the group on the bench is Lady Druitt, who came to visit my father the other morning as I was leaving. We are going to have to move, this place is like Almack's on a Wednesday night.' Giles was beginning to look hunted.

'There's the labyrinth, but at least three parties have gone in while we have been in the garden and no one has come out,' Laurel said. 'The children and nursemaids are all over on the other side of the lawns—are there any other areas?'

Giles dug in his pockets and took out the little map of the grounds that they had been given with their tickets. 'There's a Wilderness, over by the sham castle.' He pointed. 'I can't recall seeing anyone go that way. Shall we stroll over there now before anyone else appears?'

Arm in arm, Laurel demurely twirling her parasol, they strolled towards the shady side of the grounds where the faux ruins could be glimpsed above small tress and artfully wild shrubbery.

'I asked about love,' she prompted.

She saw Giles look down at her hand on his arm. She was very conscious of his masculinity, the strength under her fingers, the muscles in the long thighs hinted at beneath the tight buckskin of his breeches. 'I can promise you truthfulness and trust,' he said before the silence became awkward.

'And you do not look for love in marriage?'

'No.'

'Or out of it?' she asked before her courage failed her.

'No.' They were into the Wilderness now and he stopped and met her questioning gaze, his own eyes blue and clear and sincere. And bleak. 'I do not. And I swear I would be faithful to you, Laurel. Always.'

Chapter Eleven

It was not a game any more, not an almost-unreal situation. Giles was serious about this and she had to make a decision. 'I do not know what to say.' Laurel slid her hand free and walked on. 'I had intended to say no. I had expected that you would either flirt with me and try to seduce me into agreeing or that you would have changed your mind and realised that you had just spoken on a whim last night. Or perhaps that you would produce the same sensible reasons as you did before. But you have promised me something very different—honesty and trust. We could be friends again, couldn't we? We could make something of this on that basis.' She gestured as she spoke, sending parasol and reticule tumbling to the grass.

Giles dropped to his knees, picking up her scattered belongings. He stayed where he was, looking up at her, and it was hard not to reach out and touch his face, tug at his shoulder, pull him up to kiss her. But they needed to talk this through, not be lost in some physical attraction.

'Yes. We could. Laurel, earlier, before I proposed at all, you said you had decided not to marry—that was not because of any distaste for the intimate side of it, was it? Your kisses say not, but kisses are not all there is to it.'

'I know that.' She did reach out then and urge him to his feet. 'When I had recovered from the shock of what I had overheard that day in the barn I did some investigating. It is remarkable what one can find on the bookshelves of even the most respectable houses when the libraries are old and large and things are forgotten and overlooked.'

'You shock me now.'

'You think women should be ignorant of the physical facts of marriage? My reading certainly made me aware of why girls are so strictly chaperoned.'

'No. I do not think women should be ignorant, but I would like to think there are things that you and I could discover together. Will you say *yes*, Laurel? It would make me very happy if you did.'

'What was that?' A twig snapped, somewhere behind them.

Giles looked round. 'A bird, perhaps. It cannot be people—they would not be so quiet.'

'No, of course not. Oh, I do not know what to do for the best. Let us walk a little further, I really do not want to be interrupted.' She should not even be considering marrying a man who did not love her, one with whom she had such a past history. She expected to feel a sharp reaction to her own foolhardiness, goosebumps or qualms or dizziness, but all she could feel was a warm glow of happiness. Perhaps... Giles did not love her, but together they could build a strong marriage, she was certain of it.

'This is very confusing, you know. I have been an elder sister, almost a governess for so long. Then I decided that I would be an independent single lady and now you are trying to turn my life upside down.'

'And back to where it was nine years ago.' Giles bent down and took both her hands, raised them to his lips. 'Shall I try seduction again? It seemed to make a very favourable impression last time.'

She tugged her hands free. 'Giles, I cannot think when you do that.' Half-a-dozen steps took her around another bend in the path and into a damp and overgrown glade. 'Oh!'

The three men who had been crouched down

around a sack on the ground stood up, slowly, moving apart as they did so. There were objects on the sack, she saw, purses and something like a cudgel, a knife—no, three knives. She glanced at the men as she backed away. They were dressed in coarse homespun, boots, slouch hats. There was no chance they were gardeners taking a break from their labours. Laurel had never knowingly encountered a footpad before, but she had a very good idea that she was seeing some now.

'Come back to me, Laurel.' Giles's voice behind her was low, confident. He raised it, pitched to reach the three men who were closing in on them, walking slowly, spread out as if they were edging game towards catch-nets. 'Sorry to disturb you, gentlemen. We are just leaving.'

'Not so fast, cully.' The voice came from behind them. 'Not until you've turned out your pockets and we've had a look in the lady's purse.'

Giles caught Laurel's arm and spun her round behind him, her back to the wall of shrubs. Now they had one man barring the way out and the three in the glade who were stooping to pick up their weapons.

'Laurel.' Giles's voice was a mere breath. 'I'll take the one on the path. Get by us when I do and run like the devil is after you.'

And leave you to face four armed men? I think not.

'Yes,' Laurel whispered back, edging round behind him as Giles took off his hat and flicked it at the man, the sharp brim hitting him in the mouth. He gave a roar of rage, batted away the hat and charged at Giles, past Laurel.

She ran to get behind him, then pulled the hatpin from her bonnet, took a firm hold on the strings of her reticule which held her guinea purse and slapped him in the back of the neck with it. He stumbled, swore, half-turned and she stabbed him in the shoulder with the hatpin, then hit him again as he tripped over a fallen branch and crashed to the ground.

'Help!' Laurel shrieked as she pulled the branch from under his legs and began to belabour him with it. 'Help! Murder!' It wasn't a very heavy branch, but it still had a mass of tiny whippy twigs on it and she thrashed it, keeping him down as she kept shouting. The man wrapped his arms around his head and rolled away sharply. There was an unpleasant dull thud as his temple hit a stump half-buried in the leaves and he went still.

Laurel dropped to her knees, ripped off the narrow ribbon around the waist of her pelisse and tied his hands.

In the glade Giles was facing two of the footpads. The other one was down, clutching his shoulder and groaning, the hilt of a knife sticking out between his fingers. His companions were edging cautiously closer to Giles, one with a long-bladed knife held out in front of him, the other swinging a club. Giles bent and pulled a flat-bladed knife from his boot.

To call out would be to distract him and she could see nothing she could do to help. Distantly she could hear shouts. Assistance was coming, but here, now, Giles was facing two large armed men who had very little to lose by maiming him.

And then he moved straight at the man with the cudgel who lifted it and lunged forward to meet him. Giles spun round, kicked, high and hard, and the knife went spinning from the other man's hand. He slashed with his own, sending the footpad reeling back clutching his chest and Giles closed with his snarling companion, who brought the club down on Giles's shoulder.

Laurel slapped her hand over her mouth to cut off the cry as Giles buckled at the knees, then turned the fall into a roll, crashing into the attacker, knocking him off his feet. After that, it was quick. As the thud of running feet grew louder behind her Giles had the man face down, his arms behind him in a lock that was not allowing him to as much as twitch.

The glade filled with men, it seemed to Laurel, dazedly taking in the fact that Giles was not only unhurt, but had fought with a focused, skilled ferocity. She pulled herself together and pointed out her struggling captive to one of the two gardeners who had arrived, armed with sickle and hoe. He hauled the man to his feet while the other went to help Giles secure the other two, producing enough garden twine to truss half-a-dozen footpads. Two gentlemen were also there, one who looked like a visitor, the other she recognised as the manager. They both ignored Giles, the gardeners and the footpads, hurrying to her side instead.

'No, no, I am perfectly unharmed. Do assist Lord Revesby.' She batted away the smelling salts held under her nose, declined the offer to be carried to the hotel and caught the manager by the arm. 'Send for the constables and a magistrate at once!'

'Of course, of course.' The man ran off, leaving the other gentleman, who seemed more sensible now he was not attempting to revive her, and the gardeners to haul the offenders off.

'Tell the constables I will call and give them my account as soon as I can,' Giles called after them, then, the moment they were alone, he turned on Laurel. 'You told them you were un-harmed. Is that true? Yes? Thank God. And what the devil were you thinking of? I told you to run and get help, you could have been killed.' He tow-ered over her, dishevelled, bleeding from a cut on his cheek, exuding anger.

'Run and leave you?' she demanded, as fu-rious as he, suddenly. 'I never did that and you know it. You taught me to fight after the time Jerry Hopkins, the miller's son, and his cousin were drowning those kittens and I tried to stop them and they pushed me into the mill pond. You pulled me out and you beat them both and then you taught me what to do if anyone attacked me. And I did, too, although I didn't get the chance to kick him where it hurts like you said to do. I stabbed him with a hat pin though.'

'Kick him where... I told you to do that?' Giles took her by the shoulders and stared down at her. 'Hatpin. I have never been so scared in my life as when I saw you were still there. Lau-rel, there were four of them.'

'I know. You were wonderful, Giles.' She reached up and touched the skin close to the cut on his face—it was already bruising.

'No lady should see such—'

'Idiot,' she scolded. 'I am Laurel, not some

lady with the vapours.' Then she was in his arms,
her body tight against his, his mouth hot on hers
and her hands were burrowing into his hair, her
fingers feeling the elegant curves of his ears, the
brush of that strand of hair that had always fallen
into his eyes, even when he was a boy, even now
with his expensive, modish crop.

It felt right to be kissing Giles and the taste
of him was familiar now after just that one kiss,
here in the heart of the Wilderness. She wanted
him, she realised as the blood sang in her ears
and her heart thudded against his. His skin smelt
of sweat and anger and crushed grass and she
wanted him more than she ever had.

She would say *yes*, because surely she could
not feel like this, he could not be kissing her like
this, if there was not something very special between them.

'Lady Laurel!'

Giles spun her round, pushed her behind him
as he turned to face whoever it was who had spoken. Dizzy, disorientated, Laurel clutched at his
shoulders as she leaned against him, panting a
little. Her bonnet had fallen off at some point in
the battle, she realised, and her bodice was half-
undone, her breasts straining against the flimsy
covering of her chemise. She had not been aware
of Giles unfastening anything, but he must have

done or the hooks had ripped free when she had wielded that branch…

'Ladies, you will excuse us, but this is a private conversation.' He sounded furious, even as he kept his voice at a polite conversational level.

'Conversation?' It was Lady Druitt. 'We saw you coming into the Wilderness—most unwise, Lady Laurel, I must say—and then there was screaming and we saw those men being dragged out. Naturally we hastened in here. Lady Laurel, kindly remove yourself from behind Lord Revesby. This is all shocking, quite shocking.'

'Lady Druitt, Mrs Atkinson.' Laurel somehow got her bodice fastened and stepped out from the shelter of Giles's broad shoulders. Both of the ladies had their friends clustered behind them. The ladies stared avidly, creating an agitated chorus of shocked gasps and tutting. 'There is nothing shocking whatsoever, unless it is that the management of the Gardens had a nest of footpads skulking in here. They should have broken glass on top of the wall—a child could climb it. Thank you, but I have no need of your…assistance. Lord Revesby acted with courage and despatch.'

'Of course you have need, young lady! Have you no shame? What have you to say for yourself, Revesby, luring Lady Laurel in here and then exposing her to such violence?'

'That you have just interrupted a proposal of marriage.'

Laurel put her hand on Giles's arm. Through the fine woollen cloth she could feel him vibrating with anger. He was still primed with aggression after the fight and then there had been that passionate kiss and she suspected that if there had been a man with this flock of clucking hens he would have hit him. As he could not lash out physically at women Giles was keeping hold of his temper with ferocious will.

'Which one can only hope has been answered in the affirmative,' said Lady Druitt. 'Your poor father's health when he hears of this—'

'My father the Marquess,' Giles said, subtlety reminding them that they were all comprehensively outranked, 'will be delighted to hear that Lady Laurel is to be his future daughter-in-law.'

Laurel opened her mouth to protest that she had not yet agreed, then closed it again. They were completely cornered. She could refuse Giles only at the expense of a scandal that would ricochet around Bath like an exploding shell. Phoebe's position as her hostess would become impossible. She would have to go back to Malden Grange in disgrace, back to being the dependent spinster stepdaughter. There really was no choice. And besides, now her hand was forced she felt a surge of relief. This was what she wanted. Giles, whether or not he loved her.

'Naturally I answered in the affirmative,' she said coolly. Inside she was shaking, but she was going to back Giles up to the hilt. The way he had moved to shield her, instantly, without hesitation, the way he had fought for her was worth a thousand words. 'Lord Revesby is a gentleman of honour who would never presume to kiss a lady to whom he was not affianced. If you would excuse us, ladies? My aunt, Lady Cary, is waiting in expectation of our good news and I would not have her hear about the incident with the footpads from any other source.'

What was Mrs Atkinson smirking about? It was not a very pleasant smile, not the expression of someone whose dear friend was about to hear welcome news, more the smug, knowing look of a conspirator. Surely the ladies had not all followed their progress around the Gardens in the hope of snooping on a scandal? Perhaps Mrs Atkinson was not such a good friend as Phoebe thought.

Laurel swept out of the Wilderness with Giles at her side, a gracious smile plastered on her face. As they passed the ladies he stooped and picked up her bonnet.

They stayed silent until they were outside, then

Giles walked swiftly around to the side, out of sight of the main lawns. 'Hell and damnation,' he muttered. 'We both look as though we have been in a riot. Associating with me is hard on your hats.' When she laughed, perhaps a little shakily, and tied her bonnet ribbons, he said, 'Laurel, you are quite unhurt, aren't you? You wouldn't lie to me?'

'I would never lie to you, Giles. I am shaken, I will admit, but I have not as much as a scratch.'

He was pale under the tan—from anger, she had thought, but perhaps worry for her—and some colour came back at her words. 'Were you going to say yes?' he asked. 'Would you have agreed to marry me if they had not come upon us?'

'Yes,' she said, trying to be honest. 'Seeing you fighting for me made me realise how much I…how much I admire you. And then when you kissed me, I was certain.'

'Thank heavens for that, because I do not think we have any choice now, short of igniting a scandal.'

'You sound relieved,' Laurel said, warmed by the ring of sincerity in his voice. Why she should doubt him when it was he who had been pressing for this engagement all along, she did not know, but there was no mistaking the fact that he welcomed it.

* * *

'I *am* relieved.' Giles looked down, but was frustrated in his attempt to see Laurel's expression by the brim of her bonnet. 'That is the usual emotion of a man who has been pressing his suit when he is accepted, I imagine.'

As he said it he experienced a qualm. Possibly *relieved*, although accurate in his case, was not the most tactful choice of words. *Delighted*, *happy*, even *ecstatic* might be expected. His brain was still fogged with fighting fury and the effects of that kiss. Laurel was not the only one it had affected.

'And delighted and happy,' he added, smiling as he said it, despite the pain as the bruises made themselves felt. It was something he had learned early with the diplomatic corps—if he smiled it put warmth and sincerity into his voice.

But this was not a matter of deceiving a possible enemy for an hour or so, a day or two, or ingratiating himself with someone whose influence would be beneficial for Britain. This was Laurel, the woman with whom he would spend the rest of his life.

She might have been hurt, even killed.

He thought of those knives again, of the rank smell of the gang, of the brute anger and greed in their eyes. And he thought of her courage, her un-flinching reaction, and felt a thrill of pride in her.

'I am relieved,' she confessed. 'Relieved that we got out of there without it becoming any worse than it was—both with those men and with Lady Druitt and her cronies. Thank you for the way you dealt with the ladies.'

'For what? I should not have been kissing you like that somewhere we might have been inter-rupted at any moment. As we were.'

By that coven of old crows, he thought bitterly, mixing his metaphors with a certain relish. He knew why he had kissed her perfectly well: he had slain the dragons for her and that kiss had been a claiming on the field of battle.

'For keeping your temper and for snubbing them in the politest manner. *"My father the Mar-quess"* was masterly.'

She sounded quite cheerful. 'You are certain, aren't you, Laurel?' What had come over him? He should be running to get a special licence, not giving her every opportunity to turn him down.

'Yes. Of course I am. What is the matter, Giles? Have you changed your mind?'

Chapter Twelve

'Changed my mind? No, certainly not. But you have just had a shock and I do not want you to feel trapped by what has just happened.'

'Of course not. Will you come in with me to tell Aunt Phoebe?'

'I had better, before the news of the fight or the old crows squawking reaches her. Should I be approaching your stepmother for her blessing, do you think?'

'Definitely not,' Laurel said with a vigorous shake of her head. 'I am of age—we do not need anyone's permission, or blessing.'

'Who are your trustees? Your cousin the Earl, I assume?' He knew perfectly well it was and remembered in time to make it a question.

'He is the only one, although Mr Truscott, Papa's solicitor, would be involved if Cousin Anthony met with an accident or could not act for me.' She stopped suddenly, halfway along Great Pulteney Street. 'This does feel very strange. I never imagined that I would marry. Now I can hardly think of all the things I should be doing.' Her hand on his arm was not quite steady. Shock was beginning to make itself felt, but he knew better than to fuss over her in the street.

'We will tell Lady Cary first.' Giles began walking again and she fell into step beside him. 'Then I will go and tell my father, who will be delighted, but I think I had best break the good news by myself, in case he is feeling unwell.'

In case he leaps out of his chair with a whoop of joy and says something damning in front of you, more like.

'You can write to your cousin to prepare him. I will write, too, we will need to meet together with our lawyers to sort out the settlements.'

What else? *Ah, yes.*

'Where would you like to marry? Malden Court, Palgrave Castle, the Abbey here? I will need to know to sort out the licence.'

'I suppose Malden. That would be easiest for you, would it not?'

'My convenience is a minor matter.'

'I would not want to impose upon Cousin Anthony and his wife by inflicting an entire wedding on them. And I suppose it would seem

like a snub to Stepmama if I am not married at
Malden.'

'You do not sound very happy at the thought.
Is it the house or your stepmother that makes
you hesitate?' Of course, she had no idea that
the house would be hers on her marriage to him.
Now he had a stepmother-in-law problem to
solve. Hopefully the Dower House was in good
order and Lady Palgrave willing to retire to it
with good grace.

'Stepmama,' Laurel admitted.

'I will sweet-talk her,' Giles promised. 'So,
Malden Grange in a month?'

'A month…'

'Is there any reason to delay?'

'No, I do not suppose there is.' Laurel tightened her hold on his arm. 'We will be married
in a month, I can hardly believe it.'

Lady Cary, it seemed, had no problem believing their news. The butler had the front door
open before they set foot on the steps and she
was waiting in the drawing room almost quivering with anticipation. One look at them and
she gave a shriek and tottered back into a chair.
'Lord Revesby, your face! And, Laurel, whatever
has happened?'

Giles made sure Laurel was sitting down and

sent Nicol for hot sweet tea and then let her tell the tale. She seemed to need to talk and he was concerned for her.

'Oh, thank goodness you accepted Lord Revesby, dearest! So brave, such a hero!'

At least, that was what he thought Lady Cary was repeating over and over, but as she was hugging Laurel in an all-enveloping grip her voice was a trifle muffled. 'She took so long to make up her mind,' she said to him, rather more intelligibly when she finally let go. 'I am so relieved, dear Giles. I shall call you Giles, for you are to be my nephew and, after all, I knew you as a child.'

Giles, emerging from another of her enthusiastic embraces, straightened his crumpled neck-cloth and assured her that he would be honoured.

'I would have done anything to see you so well established, my dear.' She turned back to Laurel. 'I believe you two are made for each other.'

'I should tell you, Lady Cary, that we had an unfortunate encounter in the Gardens with a number of ladies, some of whom I believe are known to you. They encountered us in the Wilderness, embracing in the aftermath of the attack, and created quite a scene, despite being assured that we are engaged to be married.'

'Mrs Atkinson, for one,' Laurel said. 'She was positively smirking. Anyone would think she was delighted to have discovered us behaving indiscreetly, not shocked.'

'I am sure they meant well, dear.' Lady Cary looked exceedingly flustered to Giles's eye. Presumably she would have the coven descending on her at any minute twittering about poor chaperonage and making her life a misery.

He was certainly not going to be around to add fuel to the flames. 'I must leave you and go and report to the constables, then break the good news to my father. I hope you will both dine with us this evening, but I must see how his health is first. I will send a note.' He held out his hand to Laurel and, when she took it, raised it to kiss her fingers. 'You have made me very happy.'

Giles dealt with the constables and the resident magistrate easily enough and was assured that he would be informed in ample time of the date of the trial at the next Quarter Sessions. A visit to his room at the Christopher set his clothing to rights and Dryden cleaned the cut cheek and applied an infallible lotion of his own devising which stung like the devil.

Now he should go directly to break the good news to his father and take the dead weight of worry and guilt off his shoulders. Giles strode into the High Street and then up Bond Street, intending to cut through Quiet Street into Wood Street and from there into Queen Square.

Instead he found his feet had taken him into George Street, heading away from his father's lodgings. With a shrug he turned into Gay Street, went around the Circus and out on to Crescent Fields with the view out to the south across the city and the River Avon.

Giles sat down on the dry grass and stared at the sheep grazing in the pasture below him, incongruous with the elegance of the Royal Crescent at his back. They reminded him of the sheep dotted across the Downs when he had stood with the woman whose name he had not known and had been seized with the impulse he still did not understand to kiss her.

He flexed his grazed knuckles and let the last of the fight ebb out of muscle and nerve, but he could not relax. It did not take much thought to tell him what was so disturbing him—his conscience was giving him hell. His first duty was to his father and to his inheritance. He knew that, with an understanding that went bone-deep, back to the very first things he had learned as a child. It meant he must marry well and appropriately and he was prepared to do that, even though he had now lost any element of choice in the matter.

None of this was new, a suitable marriage was what was expected of aristocrats.

Laurel was most certainly suitable—and, it turned out, she was the only choice compatible with his duty. So far, so…satisfactory. Giles grimaced at the choice of word. What of Laurel? Why had she accepted him? He did not deceive himself that she had been swept off her feet by the sight of him fighting. He thought he had been very clear about not being able to offer her love, so it was not that which was making his conscience so uneasy. He had not lied to her, he was certain, racking his memory in an effort to reassure himself that he had not uttered any actual falsehoods.

Except by omission. He knew about her inheritance and he stood to gain by that, far more than she was aware. And if it was not for that inheritance he would have avoided her after that fraught encounter in the Pump Room and taken his bitter memories of her away with him.

So, some good had come of this. Giles leaned back on his elbows and stretched out his legs, eyes narrowed against the sunshine. He and Laurel were friends again, each understood what had happened all those years ago, each forgave the other. The sun was warm. Giles put his hands behind his head, tipped his hat over his eyes, shut out the sight of Bath and surrendered to the wave of sleep that washed over him.

Friends do not deceive each other.

The thought swam up through the buzz of bees, the faint cries of children playing further along the Crescent Fields and the hum of the city below him. He was deceiving Laurel by omission by not telling her about the provisions of her father's will.

On the other hand, an inner voice of practicality said, *it is for her own good. You are giving her back the life she should have had, the title that should have been hers, the future—the children—that she would have had if it had not been for that misunderstanding. You are saving her from the life of a spinster.*

He opened his eyes, all desire to sleep banished, and sat up.

And besides, the ruthless voice said, *you cannot back out now—think of the scandal.*

He wished he had a friend to talk to, but they were all in Portugal. Nine years out of the country had left him with only the acquaintances of childhood and youth in England. There was Gray, of course. But he was back on the Yorkshire estates he had inherited just before peace had come and he had sold out. He could hardly write to him—this was not the sort of thing one committed to paper.

Giles got to his feet, dusted hay stalks off his coat and put on his hat. It was done now and there was no going back. He wondered, as he walked down the hill to the back of Queen's Parade, his feet skidding on the dry grass, what the secret service was that his ancestor had performed for the king. That had resulted in the prize of a marquessate. Had it left him feeling any more queasy about his honour than this did?

'You must allow me to give you any assistance in my power to make your move to the Dower House as smooth as possible.' Cousin Anthony, now Earl of Palgrave, directed his gentle, rather aloof smile at his predecessor's widow. He had arrived the evening before in response to the news that Laurel had returned to Malden Grange from Bath with a fiancé and there was a need for settlements to be discussed. 'At your own convenience, naturally.'

'You do not mind me being married from here, Cousin? I would very much appreciate it if Stepmama was to be here with me until then,' Laurel said hastily, seeing her stepmother's lips tighten. It did not seem that the passage of time was reconciling her to the need to move from her marital home. Laurel could hardly blame her. 'Unless you are wanting to move in yourself before the wedding? I am sorry, I should have thought of that.'

Laurel cast her stepmother a harried glance. She was not finding her any easier to live with—in fact, a break of a few weeks had only made it worse. But it would be the depth of ingratitude not to include her fully in the wedding preparations or to make her feel at all unwanted.

'Forgive me, Laurel. I had forgotten that perhaps you are not fully aware of the provisions of your father's will,' Cousin Anthony said.

'I was there when it was read,' she said, puzzled.

'Yes, of course, but you would have still been shocked and distressed by your father's passing. There is a section of which you may not have realised the importance at the time—the Malden Grange house and estates are held by me in trust. The terms of that trust are set out in separate documents which your father did not see fit to make public. Did he not discuss them with you?' He looked away as he spoke, his attention apparently fully on the papers he was shuffling on the table in front of him.

Perhaps, Laurel thought, he was embarrassed at having to deal with a frosty widow and a young

woman he hardly knew but whose marriage settlements he must negotiate. 'I recall something
about a trust being mentioned when the will was
read, but I assumed it was to do with the entail—
if I thought of it at all.' Now she was completely
puzzled as to why he was mentioning these provisions now. 'Papa had said nothing to me of it,
but he did die suddenly—his heart attack was
not expected.'

'That must have been it. You see, Cousin Laurel, the Malden estate and various monies are left
to you on your marriage.'

'To me? But why did no one tell me that?'

Papa must have forgiven me after all.

The thought made her want to smile, but that,
naturally, would be most inappropriate.

'I assumed you knew. You made no comment
on my decision to use Palgrave Castle as my seat
and not to request that you and Lady Palgrave
move to the Dower House.'

'I…we thought you were being very kind in
not disturbing us in our old home while we were
in mourning and that you preferred the Castle for
the present. Stepmama—did you know of this?'

'I did not.'

She seemed even more displeased, Laurel
thought. Was it resentment that her stepdaughter would take her place as lady of this house? If

it was, there was nothing to be done about it other than to be as tactful as possible. But… Once she married it would no longer *be* her house. In fact, it never would be. It was not hers until she married and, the moment she was married, everything passed to her husband. To Giles.

That was an unsettling notion. It had never concerned her until now, because she had believed she had only the money settled on her to provide the income for her allowance and living expenses. Now she was an heiress.

'Does Lord Revesby know of this?' she asked, sharply enough to bring the attention of the other two snapping back to her.

'It would have been most inappropriate for me to discuss the terms of the trust with anyone it did not affect,' Cousin Anthony said stiffly, his attention still apparently riveted on ordering the papers. 'Now that you are betrothed I will, naturally, include these matters in my discussions with Lord Revesby in the course of the settlement discussions.'

'So Papa has left the entire Malden estate to me.' Stepmama raised her head and looked across at them. She was seated at the other end of the Chinese salon, writing wedding invitations, but frequently breaking off to look at them as though, Laurel thought resentfully, she and Giles would start ripping each other's clothes off if left alone for one moment. She moderated her voice. 'Had you any idea?'

'My father wrote to me while I was in Portugal as you know.' Giles crossed one leg over the other and tugged a seam straight. 'Quite early on he told me that your father had torn up the agreement they had made in anticipation of our marriage. That, you will recall, passed Malden to you on his death—to us, in effect. My father, in an equal rage, picked the scraps up and threw them on the fire and then the two of them got drunk on brandy. Papa blamed his subsequent headache on me. Your father obviously thought better of that decision as time healed his anger and disappointment and so he added those instructions.'

'Is your father surprised at mine changing his mind?' she persisted.

'They had once been very close.' Giles shrugged as though to say, *Who knows? Perhaps...* He took a snuff box out of his pocket, looked at it as though he had no idea where it had come from, then put it back. He kept his hand in his pocket, toying with something.

Stepmama is embarrassing him, playing the chaperon so obviously.

It was not like Giles to fidget like that. He had always seemed to her to have an extraordinary capacity for stillness and concentration, even as a boy.

'So what do you want to do with the estate?' he asked, taking her by surprise.

'Me?'

'It is yours.'

'Until the wedding,' Laurel pointed out, unable to suppress the sharpness in her tone. 'And then it becomes yours.'

'Ours,' he said, with a smile that had an extraordinary effect on her toes, making them curl up in her slippers. 'Shall we live here?'

'Do you not want to be with your father?'

To live here with Giles. How very strange that would feel. And yet, she was hardly unused to seeing him in this setting—he had run tame here as a boy, accepted as one of the family.

'My father and I would probably brain each other with the decanters after a few weeks. Talking of relatives…' He raised his voice a little and took his hand from his pocket as he stood up, holding it out to her. 'Shall we take a stroll on the terrace, Laurel?' He spoke softly again. 'I have something to tell you that will probably have you uttering a most improper word.'

'Yes, the fresh air would be pleasant,' she said

demurely, her thumb rubbing over an odd callous on his forefinger. Perhaps it was from fencing, or using a gun, it was not in the right place to be caused by reins. She forgot it, even as the question flitted through her mind, and they made their way out, ostentatiously leaving the doors from the salon wide behind them. There were no comfortable seats on the terrace, only stone benches, and there was a slight breeze off the lake, so provided they stayed in view for most of the time they were safe from Stepmama following them out.

Chapter Thirteen

'What is it that will have me swearing?' Laurel
asked.

'The ladies who so accidentally encountered
us in the Gardens—I do not think that it was
coincidence they were there at all. I suspect that
your aunt put Mrs Atkinson on our track and, it
occurs to me now, Lady Druitt is an old friend
of my father.'

'You mean that Phoebe and your father con-
spired to have us caught in a compromising situation?' He nodded. 'That is outrageous!' Laurel
took a few agitated steps along the terrace, then
came back. 'On the other hand…'

'On the other hand that, hard on the heels of
the attack, did help you make up your mind. I
thought I should mention it in case it made a
difference.' His mouth was set in a hard line. 'I
would not have you entrapped into this marriage.'

'Oh, Giles, that is very sweet of you. And very scrupulous and honourable.' Oddly, his expression did not lighten at the praise. 'I could give them both a piece of my mind for interfering, but they meant well and I am happy that your father is so strongly in my favour.'

'Thank you, it is a relief that you feel like that. And while we are on the subject of relatives—do you wish for Lady Palgrave to live with us when we are married?' Giles asked bluntly, surprising an equally frank reply out of her.

'No! Most definitely not. I am not certain that we would hit each other with the decanters like you and your father, but I fear embroidery hoops at ten paces is quite likely. Besides, it would be difficult for her to surrender control of a house where she has been mistress for years and yet continue to live there. I am sure she will be very comfortable in the Dower House where she can create her own home as she likes.'

'At a safe distance from us.'

'Precisely,' Laurel agreed, straight-faced.

'We have not discussed a honeymoon,' Giles said, with another of his rapid changes of subject.

'Do we need one? It seems like a great deal of work to organise something at such short notice, as well as all the wedding preparations.' Giles made a sound suspiciously like a snort.

'What have I said now? Oh, am I supposed to want a honeymoon? I never really understood what they are for.'

This time it was definitely a gasp of laughter. 'I believe—not that I have any experience, of course—that a bridal tour enables the newlyweds to meet one another's relatives.'

'We know them. All the ones we would want to, that is. I realise that it is a long time since we encountered any of them together, but they will hardly be strangers to us.'

'Or the happy couple might wish to be romantically alone amidst the splendours of nature— the Lake District, Italy…'

'We have agreed that this is not a love match,' Laurel pointed out, perhaps a little tartly. She tucked her hand under his arm in a conciliatory manner, much as she might have done if they'd had a childhood falling out.

'True,' Giles agreed equably. Reminders about that did not appear to discompose him. 'Or the real reason, I always suspect, is so that the blushing bride does not have to face familiar staff and servants in the mornings for a while.'

'Oh.'

'Now I have made *you* blush.' Giles stopped at the end of the terrace, out of sight of the salon windows, and turned, bringing Laurel round to stand in front of him. 'I would apologise, but it is a very fetching effect. I had not realised you could colour up so charmingly.'

He sounds almost as though he desires me. I suppose he does. Men are able to separate physical desire and love and, as he explained all too plainly the other day, men think about desire a great deal.

'Am I offending you?' He was watching her, probably reading her mind, betrayed by the blood ebbing and flowing under her skin. 'Shocking you?'

Laurel shook her head.

'Only you kiss me without restraint and I had hoped that part of our marriage would not be a…difficulty for you. Would not be distasteful.'

'I think that is a question, is it not? No, I do not think it will be a difficulty or distasteful. It will involve a great deal of blushing because, whatever you think of my kisses, they are not the product of much practice, I can assure you.'

'Do you think we should remedy that?' Giles's eyes were focused on her face, heavy-lidded, their deep clear blue smoky with an emotion she did not have to be experienced to interpret.

'Are you suggesting that we anticipate our wedding night?' How very strange that she could talk to him so frankly when she ought to be scurrying back to her chaperon's side, shocked and flustered. It was not as though she really knew Giles as a grown man, however close they had been nine years ago.

Not that I had known all his secrets, as it turned out.

'No, I am not, much as I am looking forward to it. But I thought perhaps a little familiarity with each other might make things easier.'

'That is another question, disguised as a statement,' Laurel said, crossly. 'You always used to do that, I recall. Or you would make statements in the form of a question. Very maddening.' When Giles grinned at her she added, 'And of course there was that utterly infuriating male habit of answering questions absolutely literally—you were a complete master of that.'

Was it her imagination or did his gaze shift away from her face for a split second, almost as if he felt guilty about something? It must have been a trick of the light, because his attention was certainly on her again now.

'You haven't answered my first question at all,' he retorted. 'I seem to recall a little summer house on the island in the lake, completely out of sight from the house and, once one has taken the rowing boat to get there, quite safe from interruption.'

'But what are you suggesting?' Laurel realised that they were walking again, diagonally away from the house, down the lawn towards the lake edge. She really must stop letting Giles distract her so. Her feet seemed to have the habit of following him, whatever her mind thought of the matter. 'We have kissed already and you said you do not wish to anticipate things...'

'There are things and things,' Giles said mysteriously. 'Things between kisses and wedding nights, certainly. Things that I hope you will enjoy.'

'That you would enjoy also?'

'My pleasure just now is in what gives you pleasure.'

The sensual growl in his voice sent shivers racing deliciously down her spine. She knew the facts, of course, she was country-bred and reared after all, and had sought out what information she could find, as she had explained to him, but the details, and putting them into practice—now that was something else altogether.

Stepmama had attempted an awkward pre-nuptial lecture on the subject when she had heard about the betrothal. She had emphasised the importance of submission to one's husband's will and how children were a recompense for this distasteful, but necessary duty, but Laurel was suspicious of the implication that physical relations were something to be endured, or at best, tolerated. If sex was so unpleasant for wives that it required a conscious act of submission, then why did some women so obviously enjoy it, to the extent of committing adultery or gaining the reputation for being fast and immoral?

'Have I shocked you? You have gone very quiet, which is not at all like you.'

Laurel looked around and found they had reached the little boathouse, no more than an open-sided structure with a pitched roof to keep the rain off the punt and the two rowing boats that had been pulled out of the lake.

'I was thinking that there seems to be a conspiracy amongst married women to keep unmarried girls ignorant of the realities of marriage. If—'

Oh, for goodness' sake, this is Giles and I am about to be married to him! If I cannot say the words to him, how can we ever discuss things?

'If sexual intercourse is not enjoyable for women, as they try to pretend, why do women commit adultery?'

Giles had bent to pull a rowing boat clear of the shelter, but at that he looked up and laughed. 'Perhaps those women are in search of a man whose bedroom skills are better than their husbands'.'

That was interesting. 'So having…sex is a skill?' If she kept on saying the word perhaps she would learn to stop blushing.

'Making love is.' Giles had the little boat bobbing at the waterside now. 'Anything male can have sex, provided all the parts are in working order. Making love now—' his smile was warm and intimate and just for her '—that is an art.'

And one you have no doubt practised to perfection, Laurel thought, catching the sting in the tail of that explanation.

After all, one does not learn to play the piano or paint a picture well just by wishing to do so. Giles had told her he had been a virgin when he had left home, but he had lived nine adult years of his life in Portugal in the company of soldiers, diplomats, men of the world. And he was handsome and charming and probably most of the women of Lisbon were still patching their broken hearts back together after his departure.

'Was there anyone special in Portugal?' she asked, taking his hand and stepping into the rowing boat. It was quite a while since she had tried that, especially wearing pretty slippers and a respectable morning dress that she needed to keep clean and dry, and she made a mull of it, causing the boat to rock. That seemed to take Giles by surprise, too, and he had to step into the water to steady both it, and her, before she could sit down.

'Portuguese ladies are very striking in looks,' Giles said eventually when he had got on board himself, sat down and sorted out the oars. 'I spent the first week trying to keep my mouth shut and managing not to stare. Their colouring is much like yours—dark hair, large brown eyes—but their skin is more olive, not your English roses and cream. Their taste in dress is more flamboyant, too, with touches of traditional costume even in highly fashionable gowns. And of course the national character in Portugal and Spain is more demonstrative than in polite circles here—'

He broke off as the boat bumped into the landing stage on the tiny island. 'Here we are already. A few strokes of the oars and the dragon is left behind. Quick, Lady Palgrave has come out on to the terrace to look for us.'

Giles jumped ashore and held out his hand to her. It was like their childhood escapades playing hide and seek, Laurel thought, laughing out loud as they scurried round the shrubs and reached the other side of the islet. 'Do you remember hiding here from Fawcett, the old gamekeeper, that time we let all the terriers out by mistake?'

'Lord, do I! And there was hell to pay because

his prize bitch encountered some mongrel from the village and was ravished before he could separate them.'

'They were sweet puppies though, and you did find good homes for all of them.'

'So I did.' He held back some arching rose briars to let her through the tangle of shrubbery. 'And here is the summer house, looking a great deal smaller than I recall from my youth.'

'Things do look smaller. Childhood exaggerates everything.' Laurel pushed open the door. 'It is still in good condition and clean though. I used to let Jamie row over here quite often when it was hot. He would fish and swim and I would read novels and we would pretend to Stepmama that we had been studying natural history or something serious.'

Memory did not exaggerate you though, she thought as she turned to see Giles following her into the summer house.

He stood in the doorway of the miniature Greek temple, silhouetted against the bright sunlight outside, and she caught her breath. Memory had given her the image of the youth—gangling, quiet, not yet grown into his body and showing no signs of the man he would become. *My man*. Now he was solid, confident in his body, relaxed and yet with an edge of alertness.

'For a schoolroom this has the two essentials as a boudoir for seduction.' He came in, leaving the door open behind him. 'There is a comfortable couch and, as far as I can see, no spiders. Spiders are the death of passion.'

'Indeed? You speak from experience, no doubt?' She was jealous, she could hear it in her voice.

'Of spiders in such circumstances? No, I am glad to say. They would be a serious impediment—I am terrified of the things.' Giles made a show of lifting the skirts of the chintz cover on the couch and peering warily beneath. 'And as for mice…'

'Wretch.' Laurel lobbed a cushion at him and found herself caught up in his arms and tumbled on to the couch. 'You used to keep pet mice in the schoolroom and I recall you putting spiders in the soup tureen when Lady—' The rest of what she was about to say was lost as Giles kissed her.

She had thought she was beginning to understand kissing, but it seemed she had been wrong. This was different, this slow, languid open-mouthed caress. It was deep and personal and intimate. She could taste Giles. The flavour of tea and the sweetness from the tiny macarons they had nibbled at politely a short while ago, that she had expected. But there was something that she recognised from their previous kisses, something that must be simply him, his unique taste, his essence.

It was disturbing and arousing, almost as arousing as the slow slide of his tongue across hers, the tiny nips and licks at her lips, the movement of his hands on her body.

Laurel wriggled, wanting to get closer, wanting to feel him, skin to skin, even as the wary, self-conscious part of her brain protested that she was shy, that he did not love her, that really this would be so much easier the first time in the darkness of the bedchamber...

'What is it, Laurel?' Giles broke the kiss and propped himself on one elbow to look down at her. 'Am I going too fast?'

'No. It isn't that. Giles—will you take your clothes off? All of them?'

'Me? I was rather hoping to remove yours.'

'Please.'

He thought about it for a moment, his lids heavy over the deep blue of his eyes, his lips a little swollen from their kisses. 'You will feel more in control of things. I see.'

'Yes, yes, I would. I had not expected you to understand that.'

'I used to understand you very well, Laurel. I could read your expressions, the way you held yourself, the gestures you made with your hands. You have grown so confoundedly pretty that I must have been distracted up to now—but I am learning to see the old Laurel again.' As he spoke he swung his legs down from the couch and pulled off his boots and stockings, then unwound his neckcloth.

Laurel curled up against the head of the seat, watching as Giles stood and shrugged out of coat and waistcoat. 'You have changed, too.'

'I should hope so.' His grin faded as he looked down at her. 'You have your curious robin look— head on one side. Laurel, the male body might come as a bit of a shock to you.'

'I doubt that,' she said, more confidently than she felt. 'I have seen Jamie growing up, don't forget—and you were not exactly shy about diving into the lake when we were young. Oh, and I have seen statues.'

'Boys, youths in cold lakes and statues are not exactly good guides to what an aroused adult male looks like,' he said, his voice muffled as he pulled his shirt over his head. 'And I think you might say that I am aroused.' He emerged tousled, tossed the crumpled linen aside and paused, hands at the fastenings of his breeches.

There was a significant ridge just there. To distract herself from it Laurel reached out and touched the hair that dusted across his chest. 'Is that soft?' It was darker than the sun-bleached hair on his head and felt both springy and soft as he leaned down to let her brush tentative fingertips across it. When her forefinger caught his right nipple she heard his quick intake of breath.

'It changed when I touched it.' She brushed her finger over it again, and then the other one. 'How interesting.' Startlingly, her own nipples stiffened as well.

'That is not quite how I would describe it,' Giles said, his voice on the cusp between laughter and something else altogether. Under her hand his skin was smoother than she expected, the well-defined muscles beneath it harder.

'How do you get muscles like this?' She ran the flat of her hand down the arm that was bracing him against the wall as he bent over her. 'You moved so beautifully when you were fighting those men.'

'Riding, swordplay, boxing. And in the Peninsula it is often not possible to ride. It is tough terrain to walk in—one gets fit quickly.'

'Behind enemy lines, you mean?' She could not see his face clearly, but she felt the tension in his arm. 'You do not want to talk about it?' she stated when he did not reply.

'No. No, I do not.' He straightened and she

saw he was trying to soften the snub with a smile. And then he unfastened his breeches and let them fall, taking his drawers with them, and she stopped wondering about the war.

'Oh. Oh, yes, I see—' She broke off, fascinated by the heavy length half-rising from the dark curls at his groin, and reached out her hand. Giles stepped back and that part of him visibly thickened and lifted of its own accord.

'If we are not to anticipate our wedding night then, I beg you, Laurel—do not touch.' There was the laughter again and, this time, a husky hint of breathlessness that gave her the most extraordinary sensation of power.

If I reach out and stroke... And that would not be fair, he is trying to keep this within the bounds that we agreed.

She trusted him and it was not right that she should make it difficult for him to keep his word. 'Very well, I will behave. Shall I take all my clothes off, too? It seems only just.'

'I really do not think that would be a good idea.'

That was definitely a faint moan. How very intriguing.

'In fact, I am going to put some of mine back on, if you don't mind.' He reached for his breeches without waiting for her reply, fastened them and pulled on his shirt, leaving it untucked.

'How do we make love with our clothes on?' Laurel had a horrible suspicion that she was pouting and got her expression under control.

'Like this.' For a big man he could move fast, she discovered. One moment she had been sitting up, the next they were both lying on the couch and Giles's hand was sliding up under her skirts, up over the silk of her stockings, the fine fabric snagging slightly on the callouses on his fingers.

Then the bare skin of his palms was on the bare skin above her garters and heat quite apart from the warmth of his flesh on hers flooded through her, deeply, intimately. Laurel muffled the little sob of surprise against his shoulder and clung on as his hand moved upwards, smoothing over the curve of her thigh, gently, insistently, parting her legs. She felt herself tense, then, as though her body knew far better than she did what she wanted, needed, she relaxed, opening for him, letting the questing fingers stroke upwards, parting her intimately.

'Laurel?' Giles breathed in her ear and she nodded, made some sort of inarticulate sound—agreement, trust, assent—she was not sure what it was.

She was aware of one finger sliding deeper,

entering her. It felt thick and her body resisted. She was suddenly not at all certain about agreeing to this—and then Giles touched something at the same time and the pleasure took her breath as she arched into his hand and lost the power to analyse just what was happening.

'Yes, sweet, yes, *querida. Perfeito*…let go for me.'

How could she let go when whatever it was he was doing was ravelling her so tight, so impossibly tight, that she would surely break?

'Yes, like that, Laurel, just like that…'

And then she did break and let go and cry out and…

Chapter Fourteen

'I saw stars.' Laurel stirred as she lay in his arms, then opened pleasure-drugged dark brown eyes.

'Is that a good thing?' Giles managed to ask. He was shaking, he found. Shaking because he was racked with desire to take this to its conclusion, cursing himself for using Portuguese endearments, of all the clumsy mistakes to make. Laurel did not need it rubbing in that he had had lovers before, although she obviously knew.

He made himself relax, enjoying the feel of her as she snuggled closer, trusting him, secure in his arms.

She believes in me, he thought bleakly. *Trusts me. How much would that hurt her if she knew why I offered for her? I should never have asked her to marry me. I should have thought of something, some way to make the money, some way to get the land back without this marriage.*

And yet—how? His duty was to his father and to his name. The match he had offered Laurel was perfectly acceptable in the eyes of society, especially for a lady virtually on the shelf. Most reasonable people would say it was highly advantageous to her.

You are justifying yourself, his conscience nagged.

He had lied to her by omission by not telling her about the land sale and the debts. Giles pulled himself together with an effort. This was Laurel, his friend, the girl he had been estranged from for far too long, and now she was happy that they were together. She had accepted that this was not a love match, he was not deceiving her about that.

'Giles?' The sleepy contentment in her eyes had turned to puzzlement. He needed to keep alert because she could read him too well, even in a sensual haze. Laurel sat up, her hands on his chest, and frowned. 'What is wrong?'

'Guilty conscience,' he admitted. Might as well tell the truth about something. 'I should never have made love to you.'

And there I go with another half-truth.

'Your stepmother is going to be furious that we sneaked off together and she will make your life miserable by nagging you about it, I have no doubt.'

'I thought you were not happy because I had all the pleasure and you have had none.' Laurel pushed away from him, her hands firm on his chest for a second. Giles looked down, remembering them scratched from blackberry picking, bruised from tree-climbing, muddy from fishing. Now they were the pampered hands of a lady, the lady he had tied himself to for life.

And she is tied to me, my ring will be on that finger soon enough.

'I had my pleasure in seeing your pleasure, feeling it,' he told her as he got to his feet and put his clothing in order.

And that at least is the truth.

It had been arousing watching Laurel come apart under his touch. There had been something more than that, although he could not put a name to the emotion.

'Hmmm.' She looked at him doubtfully, then smiled, a wicked twist of her lips. 'I will have to make it up to you when we are married. But we had better get back, or at least be seen rowing about on the lake. Stepmama will not nag me, merely sigh heavily and tell me I will have to behave with decorum when I am a countess. You, of course, may receive a lecture, so be prepared to look suitably repentant.'

She does not suspect that anything is wrong.

Giles pulled on his boots and checked his neckcloth by touch. Hopefully any disorder would be put down to the exertions of rowing, not to disgracefully stripping off to gratify the curiosity of his betrothed.

He led the way down from the summer house to the boat and helped Laurel in, a certain masculine smugness counteracting the guilt. Her expression when she had looked at his naked body, the interest and the frank admiration, the curiosity that hinted at so much delightful sensual exploration, those all promised that their marriage would be satisfactory in the bedchamber at least. But there must be no more lies, no more deceit. Or, given that was probably impossible, no more than absolutely necessary.

Something was wrong with Giles. Laurel pretended not to notice as she smiled and pointed out dabchicks and water lilies and did her best to ignore the tingling along muscles she had not realised she possessed and the fizzing in her veins that was like too much champagne, only better.

There had been something in his manner that had not been quite right from the beginning. He was hiding something from her, she sensed. Once she would have teased it out of him, or demanded outright to know what it was. But this was no longer the young Giles, this was a man, and presumably his secrets were not the kind to be revealed to avoid persistent teasing or to be tricked out of him by catching him unawares. For all she knew they might be state secrets, military intelligence, or he had seen something in the course of the fighting that had made a profound impression, something he was not yet ready to speak about.

Whatever his secrets were, she had to respect them and certainly not jump to conclusions about them—she had learned her lesson about doing that all too well. But there was something else, something that had happened when he was making love to her. He was regretting having done it, she could tell. For a moment she had wondered if it was her, if he had found her not attractive enough, but the hard evidence of his arousal against her body had not changed—he had wanted her at the beginning and he still wanted her now.

Laurel hid a sudden smile: how very inconvenient for men that their desires were so evident in the fashions of the time. No doubt some vigorous rowing would allow him to have everything under control by the time they got back to the house.

Thinking was not easy with her brain befuddled by the onslaught of unfamiliar sensual pleasures. Perhaps she was analysing too much, worrying that their new-found reconciliation would be wrecked by the perils of marriage where the possibilities for misunderstandings, for hurting each other, were so great. Even so, it nagged at her. What was it that he wanted her to be to him? Would she be able to satisfy that need?

Stepmama was cool when they returned, but she seemed to accept the explanation that they had gone rowing to take advantage of the breezes on the lake. Even so, Laurel felt herself rebelling at the implied grudging approval. She was not eighteen, nor was she the spinster daughter any longer. She was old enough to know her own mind and, whatever doubts lurked in the shadowy recesses, she wanted to marry Giles. Now.

'We have not actually posted any of the invitations, have we, Stepmama?'

'No. I had intended doing that tomorrow when we have checked over the list one final time with Lord Revesby. I would not like to omit anyone.' Lady Palgrave ticked off another name on the paper by her side.

'How long would it take to obtain a special licence?' Laurel asked Giles.

'Three days, provided I can find the Archbishop at Lambeth Palace. I believe he is in residence. If I have to go down to Canterbury, then two more days, perhaps.' He kept his expression perfectly neutral, but there was laughter in his eyes and she guessed he knew exactly how she felt. 'Or we could elope to the Border, although that is a long journey and would cause talk. A special licence would be tidier and more conventional, shall we say?'

'A special licence?' Lady Palgrave dropped her pen, making a large blot in the middle of the invitation list. 'Laurel! Is there something you should be telling me?'

'Something…? Oh, my goodness, no. It is just that I suddenly realised that I do not want to *get* married, I want to *be* married.'

'I see. So, I am to pack my bags and take myself off to the Dower House in three days' time, am I?'

'Of course I would not ask something so distressing of you, Stepmama.' Laurel sat down with a bump on the nearest chair. 'I have only realised now how I feel. Giles, would you mind? Did you want a large wedding? Only, I fear that it means that we must take that honeymoon after all—I would not inconvenience Stepmama for the world.'

'We will elope to London.' Giles sat down, too. 'Scandalously run away to the town house.

I will obtain the licence and we may be married at whichever church you wish. We will lure in two witnesses off the street if you want to do without guests entirely. Think of the saving in champagne,' he added in a whisper.

'What will people say?' Lady Palgrave demanded.

'I have no doubt that those with unpleasant imaginations will be counting the weeks until our first child is born,' Laurel said coolly, ignoring her stepmother's outraged expression. 'I see no reason why we have to make a great parade of our wedding for the curious. Provided the Marquess does not require the town house, of course.' Honeymooning with her new father-in-law would be nearly as embarrassing as sharing the house with Stepmama.

'No danger of that. Parliament is not sitting, of course, so my father will stay at Thorne Hall for the summer. Our engagement has improved his health wonderfully—I expect he will be out riding the estate and making life hideous for his steward before much longer. I am certain that he will be delighted to assist you in any way with your move to the Dower House, Lady Palgrave.'

'When shall we go?' Suddenly the prospect of marriage to Giles was a reality, whereas before it had seemed dreamlike. He had made love to her, he had agreed to elope with her, he understood her. All those doubts, all the little niggling suspicions that he was holding something back, that he was not being completely open with her, seemed to have evaporated.

'Tomorrow?' he asked. He was laughing at her, she realised. Not mocking her, but amused by her excitement, just as he had laughed with her when they were children. So often she had been the one to have the madcap ideas, but it had been Giles—quiet, studious, apparently undashing Giles—who had put them into operation and had made them work, just as he was doing now. *Although where that quiet, studious boy has gone...*

'Yes,' she agreed. 'Tomorrow. I can be ready if you can.' She threw it out almost as a challenge.

'But your clothes!' Her stepmother seemed to be wringing her hands.

'London has no shortage of excellent shops and is full of modistes who would be delighted with the prospect of creating Lady Revesby's new wardrobe just at a time when the city is quiet,' Giles pointed out. He leaned closer and whispered, 'Besides, you will not need clothes on honeymoon.'

'I wash my hands of both of you,' Lady Palgrave said, as she virtually tossed her pen into the tray. 'You will at least keep me informed of your plans to return here?'

'Of course, ma'am. If London becomes too hot as the summer progresses we may go to the coast—but rest assured, you will have at least three months to remove to your new home.'

The next morning Laurel felt a certain longing to have at least three *days* to relocate to her own new home. Binham had enlisted every maid in the house to assist with packing and the footmen had been staggering up and down stairs until well into the evening, but the big travelling coach was finally loaded with trunks and bandboxes. Binham herself, rigidly disapproving of both this informality and haste and the company of Dryden, Giles's manservant, was sitting amidst the luggage clutching Laurel's dressing case as though that might protect her from whatever the valet had in mind to pass the journey.

Bridge followed on, driving Giles's curricle with another groom on one riding horse and leading Arthur, and the cavalcade was led by an elegant travelling chaise borrowed from the Thorne Hall stables.

'This must be the least discreet elopement in history,' Laurel commented as Giles handed her into the chaise. 'So much for slipping away to be married with no fuss.'

'A procession like this would certainly be somewhat incongruous on the road to Scotland,' he agreed, settling beside her on the blue-plush upholstery. They waved to Lady Palgrave and the staff lined up on the steps to see them off and then sank back with perfectly co-ordinated sighs of relief. 'Alone at last,' Giles said as the carriage turned on to the road that led towards the turnpike.

'Mmm.' Laurel stifled a yawn. 'Goodness, I hardly got a wink of sleep last night. We were packing until eleven and then I kept waking up thinking of things that I had forgotten.'

'Sleep now.' Giles put his arm around her shoulder and pulled her close to his side. 'We've a long way to go…' His voice faded as she closed her eyes. Safe and secure… Giles was there, the old Giles, the friend she had always relied on, the new Giles who was her lover…

'An excellent journey, thank you, Downing, but I confess I am glad to have stopped moving and I suspect that Lady Laurel is, too.'

The butler bowed to Laurel, who was smiling gamely as she looked around her with an air of bright attentiveness which must surely be feigned. She had slept most of the morning, then dozed again after luncheon and for the last two hours had been clearly biting her tongue so as not to demand when they were going to arrive. Not the most patient of travellers, his bride-to-be, he recalled from their encounter at Beckhampton.

The St James's Square house was kept in constant readiness for the family and a swift glance round told Giles that their unannounced arrival had not found Downing and his staff wanting. Only the merest hesitation on the butler's part revealed his surprise at seeing the young master arrive with an unmarried lady on his arm and a mountain of luggage in train.

'Laurel, this is Downing, our butler. Downing, Lady Laurel Knighton and I are eloping.'

'Indeed, my lord? My felicitations, my lord, my lady,' Downing said with a fair attempt at his usual unruffled dignity. 'Which suites would your lordship wish me to prepare?'

'I will have my usual rooms and Lady Laurel will be most comfortable in the Rose bedchamber, I believe. Here is her woman now. You really do not want my late mama's suite, Laurel, trust me. Gloomy rooms, they need redecorating and besides, they are on the floor below. Yes, Downing?'

'Might I enquire if your lordship's presence in London is widely known? Will you be receiving visitors, for example, my lord?' Downing gazed at a spot about a foot above Giles's head. 'The Marquess is…'

'The Marquess knows all about it, so does Lady Laurel's stepmother. We are not so much eloping as avoiding a large wedding. Let me see—if I can get the licence tomorrow, then we can be married the day after and I'll send out the announcements. Until then I suppose we had best not be at home to callers. And please ensure that the staff are officially unaware of Lady Laurel's presence in this house until after the wedding. I want to avoid gossip.'

'All the neighbours must have noticed your arrival.' Laurel gestured towards the vehicles at the kerb and the grooms with the horses. They were effectively blocking the street and already people had stopped to stare.

'I will be out tomorrow sweet-talking the Archbishop's chaplain and you will be out and about shopping, I have no doubt. We will not be at home to be called upon. Can the kitchen produce some supper in half an hour, do you think, Downing?'

'Certainly, my lord. Peter, show Lady Laurel and her woman to the Rose Suite and see to the luggage. Michael, assist his lordship's man. Hot water will be sent up directly, my lord.'

Laurel followed the footman with a pleasant smile for the staff that she passed. Her back was straight, her manner perfect. Giles let out a sigh of relief he had not realised he had been holding. She had grown up in a fine house, was used to servants and to formality, but she had been living quietly for years and this was the first time he had seen her faced with a difficult situation where her poise and confidence would be tested.

She had every quality he would have been looking for in a wife, he told himself—he could thank the Fates that the loss of the land and the debt had not forced him into a marriage with an unsuitable woman. What if he had been driven to marry the daughter of some wealthy merchant or industrialist looking to buy his family into the aristocracy? Worthy men, he had no doubt, but their daughters would not have been raised to be mistress of large estates.

He could offer Laurel a setting in which all her natural talents, and her character, could shine. This was a good match for her, too, but his conscience would not allow him to be easy. There was too much he was hiding from Laurel, too much he could hardly bring himself to face.

'…a diplomatic gentleman. Or should I say, nobleman.' Downing had apparently been speaking for some time.

Giles pulled himself back into the present. 'I am sorry, Downing, my attention strayed. You were saying?'

'Lord Trencham's house next door but three has been let to a foreign nobleman, I understand, my lord.' Downing was efficiently directing the flow of footmen and luggage around Giles as he stood in the middle of the hall like a boulder in a stream.

With a murmur of apology he stepped aside to let the staff do their work. 'Do we know who he is?'

'A diplomatic gentleman is all that I have been able to ascertain, my lord. A most convenient address for his purposes, no doubt.'

'No doubt.' They were so close to St James's Palace that it could be reached on foot in a few minutes, not that anyone attending Court would ever be so casual about their status. A carriage would be used, even if the wheels hardly turned two-dozen times from door to door. Which reminded him, he would need a town vehicle for Laurel and a riding horse for her. Arthur, his own grey, had come with the curricle. The practicalities of marriage would be a welcome distraction from the less tangible elements. Emotions, for one thing.

Chapter Fifteen

'Our minds are in tune, it seems,' Laurel said as she came into the small dining room where supper had been laid out. 'I was going to apologise for my dreadful informality, but I see you have decided on comfort, too.' She had changed into a simple morning dress in amber lawn with a darker ribbon trim and had caught up her hair in a more elaborate arrangement. Giles thought how well the gown suited her and how much better the less ornate style that she favoured suited her, in contrast with the frills and ornament that the Portuguese ladies of rank inevitably wore. Laurel's beauty could speak for itself, whereas Beatriz's loveliness had to compete with ringlets and jewellery and fringed trimmings.

Stop thinking about Beatriz.

That had been an appallingly close shave. If Dom Frederico had not been so understanding—

or perhaps had not been so determined to see the arranged match go through and therefore desperate to avoid talk about his daughter—Giles could have ended up facing either an enraged father or outraged fiancé on the duelling field or causing a diplomatic incident. He wasn't sure which would have been worse.

'Thank you, Downing. We will serve ourselves. I will ring if we need anything.' As the door closed behind the last of the footmen he pulled out a chair for Laurel and took the one opposite at the oval table. 'Soup?'

'It smells divine.' She lifted the lid of the tureen in front of her. 'Potage Crécy. May I serve you some?'

They ate slowly, too tired for more than a little soup and a breast of chicken with lightly cooked greens. Laurel shook her head when Giles offered her a confection of whipped cream and glacé fruits. 'Will I mortally offend your cook if I do not? I must send my apologies for my poor appetite.'

'You are tired. Mrs Pomfret will not expect us to demolish this feast—but she feels she would lose face if she does not serve enough for a regiment. Her nose is always vastly out of joint when Papa is in residence and he brings Anton, his French chef, with him. Laurel—'

How do I put this? Best to be quite frank.

'The Rose Suite is opposite mine. I do not want you to feel uneasy about that. I will not be disturbing you tonight, or tomorrow night.'

'You will not?' Laurel looked disappointed, which was flattering, he supposed. 'Why not?'

Why not?

'You are tired tonight.' That was the truth. 'And I feel we should wait until our wedding night.' Perhaps she would be tired then as well. It would be an emotional day. He was trying to find excuses not to sleep with her, he realised. He wanted her, wanted her in his bed, wanted her lips on his, wanted to be inside her, to be one with her. But once he had done that then she was his wife, irretrievably his wife.

And who are you attempting to fool? You are going to marry Laurel whatever your conscience is telling you. You are not going to confess to knowing about her inheritance. You are not going to tell her that it was the reason you courted her. You will marry her and you are not going to entertain some fantasy about not consummating the marriage because that would give her a way out of it. That is not an easy way to reduce your sense of guilt.

'I do declare that you are a romantic, Giles Redmond.' Laurel's smile heaped more coals on his conscience. Now she was finding something likeable in his prevarications.

'I must be. You have found me out,' he said with an attempt at lightness.

'I will enjoy finding out all the things about the adult Giles that are different from the youth. What other secrets are you hiding from me?' Laurel smiled back with such warmth that he felt insensibly soothed.

'Let me see… My three other wives, my career as a pirate captain, the fact that I snore…'

'No! We must call it off at once. I am quite prepared to tolerate the other wives, if they are amiable, and the piracy sounds exciting, and doubtless profitable, but I cannot marry a man who snores.'

He had forgotten her sense of the ridiculous. It had always amused him and it did now. 'I suspect that all men snore.'

'That *is* a blow.' She wrinkled her nose in thought. 'I know the answer—separate bedrooms for us, my lord.'

'We will see about that, my lady,' Giles said with an exaggerated leer that made her laugh out loud.

Hell, but I want her.

Even as he thought it he saw the dark smudges under her eyes, the way she had leaned back into the support of the chair, the way the laugh faded away to a smile. Laurel was bone weary with travelling and with the emotional impact of what they had agreed to do. What he felt and what he wanted did not matter, Giles realised, only what was best for Laurel.

'And you are going to your chaste and lonely, but very comfortable, bed just as soon as you have finished that tartlet.'

'As my lord commands.' There it was again, that flash of mischief, the way she had always teased him, never allowing him to take himself too seriously.

'Are you going to be a disobedient wife, Laurel?' He got to his feet and rang the bell.

'I believe I will be. I have had nine years of being so very good, you see. I think I am long overdue my rebellion,' she said as he pulled out her chair for her to rise. As the door opened to admit Michael, the footman, her wicked smile vanished to be replaced with one that was perfectly demure. 'Goodnight, my lord.'

'Michael, escort Lady Laurel to her suite. Is her woman there? If not, send her up.'

'Yes, my lord. I believe that all is in readiness for her ladyship.'

'Goodnight, my dear.' He permitted himself a chaste kiss on her cheek, tried not to notice the fleeting caress of her hand on his shoulder, the scent of lily of the valley, the way her eyelashes curled on her cheek when she closed her eyes for a second. When had his skinny little friend become this beautiful, disconcerting woman?

'It is exceedingly difficult not having any acquaintances to make recommendations for shops,' Laurel observed as the carriage made its way through Mayfair side streets. They were in search of one of the modistes whose name she and Binham had gleaned from scouring through the pile of fashion magazines that Peter, the footman, had produced that morning. 'I assume that if a particular dressmaker has a design featured in *La Belle Assemblée* or the *Repository* then she must be fashionable, but for all one knows she could have paid the publishers to be included.'

'These gowns do seem to be in the first stare, my lady.' Binham passed her a print of a ball gown worn by a willowy brunette with improbably tiny feet, who was posed against a broken pillar in the Tuscan style, one hand dramatically raised to her brow.

'Tomorrow for the wedding I shall wear my new rose-pink morning dress with the dark green pelisse and kid shoes,' Laurel said, looking askance at the pose in the print. If ladies were supposed to throw themselves into attitudes she was going to feel very self-conscious. 'There is no hope of getting anything ready to wear and I do not want to reveal the fact that I need a gown to be married in. Have you the list? I think this must be Madame Ranier's shop.'

The double-fronted shop was painted a tasteful mint green with touches of gilt and the windows displayed single gowns, draped over velvet stands and accessorised with a few well-chosen items. 'This looks acceptable, my lady.'

'I agree.' Laurel gathered up her reticule and descended on to the pavement. Fashionable dressmakers could be as snobbish as the grandest dowager, she had heard. She fixed a faint, aloof smile on her lips and swept into the shop.

'Madame?' The smart assistant was certainly promising. At the rear of the shop a curtain moved. Laurel assumed she was being assessed.

'I am Lady Laurel Knighton. I require an extensive new wardrobe and as I am unfamiliar with London I am hoping to find a modiste to suit me.'

The curtains parted and a middle-aged woman with dyed black hair and a figure that suggested the most rigorous corseting emerged. 'My lady. I am Madame Ranier. I would be most happy to show your ladyship some of our work.'

Sharp black eyes flickered over Laurel's face and figure.

She could almost read the thoughts. *Not in the first blush of youth, no ingénue. Well-made outfit, superior maid. Private carriage with a team of four.*

'Hortense, a chair for Lady Laurel.'

'Thank you. I trust I may count upon your discretion, *madame*?' She lowered her voice and the modiste came closer. 'I am to be married very shortly. My future husband and I wish to avoid the vulgar display of a public wedding, you understand. In his position…' She let her voice trial off suggestively. 'My wedding gown is, naturally, already made, but I require morning dresses, walking dresses, a riding habit and, perhaps, at this stage, two evening gowns. And I need them as soon as possible.'

'A ball gown, my lady?' Laurel could almost hear the clink of guineas being added up in the dressmaker's head.

'Later, perhaps. And I would be most obliged for your recommendations for milliners, cordwainers and haberdashers.'

It was nearly two when Laurel arrived back at St James's Square, hungry and weary, but very pleased with her morning's work. Most of the items she had bought would be delivered that afternoon, but Binham was guarding one magnificent striped hatbox containing the bonnet to be worn at the wedding.

As they were getting out of the carriage a young lady came down the steps of a house three doors down. She turned north towards them, her maid on her heels, and seemed to be scrutinising the numbers on the doors. It took only a moment to bring her level with Laurel and she came to a stop, her way blocked by the open carriage door, Binham disputing the carrying of the hatbox with the footman and Laurel herself.

'I do beg your pardon, ma'am.' Laurel sidestepped and, inevitably, the other woman did, too, so they were still face to face.

But surely I know you?

The words were almost out of her mouth before she realised that the reason the stranger seemed familiar was because she looked like Laurel, although several years younger. Dark hair, dark brown eyes, decided eyebrows, a full mouth, close to the same height. But this was not a mirror. The other woman was far more of a classical beauty than Laurel—her nose was just the right length, her brows arched more elegantly, her mouth was not quite so wide.

'We are neighbours,' she ventured, then hesitated when instead of the expected polite smile or greeting she received a stare of unmistakable suspicion. 'Good day to you.' Laurel turned on her heel and marched up the steps, smarting at the snub.

There was no sign of Giles in the front hall, but he had apparently only just come in, for Downing was holding his hat and cane.

'Well, really! The rudest woman has just come out of a house next door but two, Downing. Did you see her? We were blocking her path, so I apologised and smiled and said something about us being neighbours and she looked at me as though I had insulted her and cut me dead. And the ridiculous thing is, she looks just like me— it gave me quite a start. Mind you,' she added, 'I would not be seen in that poisonous shade of pistachio green with so many flounces. Who lives in that house, do you know?'

'That must be a lady from the newly arrived foreign gentleman's household, my lady. I believe they are Spanish. It was a most regrettable encounter, my lady. I do not like to think of anyone treating you rudely, let alone a neighbour. It does not bode well for the tone of the Square if new residents are not courteous.'

Laurel shrugged. 'It cannot be because she disapproves of me, because she cannot know anything about us. Probably she was piqued because my walking dress is so much more flattering to our colouring than hers is.'

Downing made a sound that was possibly agreement. 'His lordship is in the drawing room, my lady.'

She opened the door and glanced inside. Giles was engrossed in a letter, sitting with one hip hitched on to the table, the rest of the post scattered beside him. She watched him for a moment, enjoying the way the sunlight from the undraped window showed off his profile and picked up the sun-bleached highlights in his hair.

That hair, the golden colour of the southern sun that his skin still held, set off a train of thought that she did not quite understand. She was uneasy, she realised.

Laurel stepped back into the hall, pulling the door gently closed behind her. 'Downing, do you think you can find out exactly who is living in that house? Their nationality and, if possible, their name?'

'Certainly, my lady. I have in fact just despatched Peter on just that errand.'

'With what excuse? He can hardly march up to the front door and demand to know who lives there.'

'He will go down the area steps and knock

at the tradesman's entrance. He is a bright lad with, if you will excuse me mentioning it, my lady, rather a way with the girls. He will find an excuse for calling and then, shall we say, charm his way inside, have no fear.'

'Good. It is not that I mind that woman's hostility, exactly, but it is disturbing. And Lord Revesby was in the Peninsula and not all the inhabitants would be exactly friendly… Many of the Spanish sided with the French, for one thing.'

'And with his nuptials imminent we do not want his lordship disturbed. I quite agree, my lady.' Downing permitted himself a faint smile.

Laurel went back to the drawing room, making enough noise as she entered to make Giles look up from his letter. He tossed it on to the table and stood up.

'Did you succeed with the licence, Giles?'

'Yes, there was no problem with it, thankfully. There was something of an interrogation and I had to take an oath, but it seems I look respectable enough to convince a clerk in holy orders that I am who I say I am and that you are of age and willing to marry and so on and so forth. I will send one of the footmen to collect it later today—apparently the actual document is a parchment the size of a small tablecloth and

encumbered with a seal and ribbons and goodness knows what else, so they do not hand them
out there and then. I called on the vicar of St
James's, close by on Piccadilly, and he is willing to marry us tomorrow morning at ten, if that
is not too early for you? He says we should have
the church to ourselves and can provide a verger
and his clerk as witnesses.'

With a special licence they could have married
at the house but, much as she wanted to avoid
fuss, that seemed rather hole-and-corner to Laurel and she was glad Giles had not suggested it.

'It never occurred to me that there might be
a difficulty, but I suppose you have been out of
the country for so long that you are not generally
recognised. It is very trusting of them to hand out
licences so easily with only the man there. After
all, for all they know, you might be an unscrupu-
lous fortune hunter tricking me into marriage.'

There was a deadly little silence, then Giles
said, 'I believe my family is sufficiently well
known for there to be no question of that in their
minds.'

'Yes, of course. An ill-chosen jest on my part,'
she said hastily. What was wrong with Giles? She
had never known him to get on his dignity like
that—he had positively snapped at her. Was he

regretting their match, or their decision to virtually elope? Or perhaps it was simply the apprehension that anyone might feel before making such a drastic change to their lives.

It occurred to Laurel that she, too, was making a drastic change, one even greater than Giles's. After all, she was not used to high society and town life. Perhaps he was concerned that she would struggle to become a fitting countess, let alone, eventually, a marchioness. Strangely she felt no apprehension about it. She was well educated, reasonably intelligent, raised to be a lady—she would learn the details of her new life soon enough.

Perhaps soothing an irritable husband was a necessary skill. And he would soon see that she could rise to whatever occasion she was confronted with, even if she had spent nine years as a rustic wallflower. That conjured up a picture of the straggling wallflowers that seeded themselves into any nook and cranny of brickwork around the garden.

'What is amusing you?' Giles had recovered himself again. He was tired and anxious that she was all right and the wedding would go well, that was all, she told herself.

'Just a foolish image as I followed a train of thought. Now, let me wipe that smile from your lips by recounting the tale of my shopping expedition. As you have not told me what my allowance is to be, I have spent as I pleased, have opened accounts all over the place and have told them to send all the bills to you.'

'I will inform my banker to brace himself,' he said with a grin. 'Now, a late luncheon is ready, I believe.'

Laurel remembered that she was hungry and found that the cook was as capable of producing a delicious cold collation as she was of presenting a reviving supper or a hearty breakfast. As Giles had dismissed the footmen again and they were alone she asked, 'Should I ask to see Cook and the rest of the staff? I am not quite sure what my position is—this is your father's house and I would not like to give offence by seeming to assume responsibilities that are not mine.' Giles's mother had given birth to a daughter who had died within a few days, Lady Thorncote with her. It had been many years ago, when Giles had been about five, she supposed, and Thorne Hall had its housekeeper, of course, the supremely competent Mrs Finlay. Here things had obviously run very smoothly with the cook and butler in command.

'I would be glad if you would.' Giles passed a plate of boiled ham. 'I certainly do not want to be approving menus and as for the contents of the linen cupboard—I surrender them entirely to your capable hands. Wait until a day or two after the wedding and then talk to Cook and Downing and arrange things between you.'

That all sounded reassuringly unfussy. Everything seemed to be going so smoothly and yet Laurel felt uneasy, on edge. It could be pre-marriage nerves, she supposed. Stepmama had delivered another awkward and confusing little lecture about One's Marital Duties, which had nearly reduced Laurel to unseemly giggles. If she had been completely innocent she would have been both alarmed and perplexed by the murmured phrases and rather alarming imagery, but as it was she was looking forward to the experience with only a few qualms, so it could not be that affecting her mood.

'Giles.' She spoke so abruptly that he put down the forkful of ham that had been halfway to his mouth.

'Laurel?'

'You are quite, quite certain that you want to marry me, aren't you? Because it is not too late to change your mind. No one except Stepmama and your father and the servants know I am here.'

'Of course I want to marry you. I want nothing more than to marry you.' He spoke without hesitation. 'Is something wrong? Are you chang-ing *your* mind?'

'No. Not at all. It is simply that I cannot quite understand why you want to marry *me*.'

Chapter Sixteen

Giles looked at her directly, his eyes very blue, that blazing blue she had learned to associate with extremes of emotion when he was young. 'Believe me, Laurel, it is the sum total of my ambition to marry you and only you. I will do my utmost to make you a good husband, I swear it.'

It shook her, the intensity of that declaration. There was almost something desperate about it. Was his conscience troubling him because of their long-ago misunderstanding? Was he afraid that she had recoiled from marriage as a result and he was now on a mission to save her from spinsterhood?

'I believe you,' Laurel said, as serious as he. 'I will try to stop fretting—I suppose it is having my life turned so comprehensively upside down that is making me unsettled.'

* * *

After luncheon Giles retired into the study, pleading a mountain of paperwork and correspondence and no secretary to assist him. Laurel set her foot on the bottom step to climb the stairs to her room and see how Binham was getting on with the newly delivered purchases and her outfit for the wedding.

'My lady?' Downing appeared from the baize door at the back of the hallway. 'Peter has returned from our neighbours' house.'

'Has he discovered who they are?'

'A noble Portuguese family apparently. The English maid Peter was talking to was a little confused by their foreignness and certainly has taken against their own servants, which I suppose is inevitable. The head of the household is supporting the Portuguese Minister Plenipotentiary in some matters of trade negotiations, it seems.'

'The duty on port, I suppose,' Laurel mused. It was a coincidence that no sooner had Giles returned to London from Portugal than natives of the country had set up home virtually next door, but with the war over at last it must be inevitable that matters of trade would need discussing and Portugal was, she recalled, England's oldest ally. 'Thank you, Downing. The young lady must simply be very short-tempered and resented us blocking her path.'

She must remember to tell Giles about this. He might enjoy having someone to reminisce with about life in Lisbon.

'The sun is shining. Shall we walk to our wedding?' Giles, who had breakfasted in his rooms, met Laurel in the hallway at half past nine. 'It is only a short distance to the church and I must say I would enjoy showing off my lady looking so beautiful. That is a delicious bonnet, but the face beneath it is even more so.'

'You are a flatterer, sir.' But she allowed him to kiss her hand and then her cheek. 'And you are looking very fine yourself.' Dryden had trimmed Giles's hair and he was turned out in biscuit-coloured pantaloons, glossy Hessian boots, immaculate white linen, a dark claret waistcoat subtly embroidered with gold and all set off with a swallowtail coat in midnight-blue superfine. His buttonhole sported a rosebud the exact colour of her own gown, doubtless the result of consultations between Binham and Dryden. 'I would like to walk very much.'

Giles clapped a tall hat on his head, pulled on his gloves and took a leather portfolio from Downing. 'The licence itself. Shall we go?'

St James's Square was still quiet as they crossed Charles Street, turned along the northern edge and then turned right up York Street. The church was immediately before them at the top of the short slope, sitting at the junction with Jermyn Street. Beyond its grey stone walls would be the bustle of Piccadilly, but all was tranquil here, except for deliveries and shop staff sweeping front steps.

A flower seller was setting up her stall just before the entrance to the church, a small boy at her side struggling to fit bunches of foliage into buckets of water. 'I knew I had forgotten something.' Giles stopped and consulted the woman.

They waited while she made up a neat nosegay of pink roses, ferns and a frothy white flower that was new to Laurel. She tied it with trailing white ribbons, obviously used to making up bouquets for brides, and handed it to Laurel with a beaming smile. 'Blessings on you, ma'am, and your handsome gentleman!'

Giles paid and Laurel took his arm again as they mounted the few steps into the wide stone corridor that ran along the west end of the church, linking the Jermyn Street and Piccadilly entrances. The cool and quiet of the interior, the familiar church smell of damp and snuffed candles and dust that she had always thought of as the odour of sanctity, transported her from the outside world and into the reality of what she was about to do.

I am marrying Giles. After all these years, after so much pain. I will make this work, we will be happy and he will never regret marrying me, she vowed as Giles pushed open the doors into the nave and they walked side by side down the aisle to the waiting vicar.

The service ran its course, the words so familiar from the many weddings she had attended and her study of her prayer book the night before. Then the vicar asked, 'Who gives this woman to be married to this man?'

Silence. Neither of them had thought of that, she realised. 'I do,' Laurel said. 'I give myself.' Beside her she heard Giles expel a long breath—relief, or shock at her presumption? Then she saw he was smiling and that so was the vicar. It was a good omen, she thought fleetingly before her attention was drawn back into the exchange of vows.

'For better or worse…'

I am not going to regret this marriage and neither will he.

'For richer for poorer…'

Beside her she felt Giles stiffen and wondered for a fleeting, uneasy moment if the settlements had been very unequal, then forgot in a wave of emotion as the ring slid on to her finger.

Laurel had not been certain who would witness the ceremony. A dour verger, perhaps, or the sexton—who would also be, ominously, the gravedigger. But no sooner had the words 'I now pronounce you man and wife' been uttered than several figures came forward, eager, it seemed, to sign the register.

There was the verger, cheerful, bald and skinny in his dusty black cassock and there was the flower seller, who must have left the boy in charge of the stand while she came in to watch the wedding.

Goodness knows what a pickle he is making of bouquets, Laurel thought.

Hard on her heels were a pair of respectable elderly ladies who must have come into the church to say their morning prayers and who were telling the verger how very excited they were to have been present at such a romantic wedding and finally there was the sexton, his cassock apparently hastily donned, for his old boots were showing beneath it and it was hitched up at the side to reveal his working breeches.

'Only two witnesses are required,' the vicar began.

'Oh, I think we must have all of them, don't

you, my dear?' Giles took her hand and squeezed it. 'After all, it is not every day that the heir to a marquessate is married to his childhood sweetheart, is it?' he added, giving their audience exactly the thrill he had intended.

At which point the two sentimental ladies began to weep and the flower seller came forward and added a silver ribbon to the rosebud in Giles's buttonhole and the sexton produced a large red-and-white-spotted handkerchief and blew his nose with great vigour.

The verger unscrewed the large brass knob on the end of the long verge he carried as his badge of office, revealing that it was actually a beaker. He tipped up the staff and filled the vessel with a dark brown liquid. 'Best French brandy to drink the health of the happy couple,' he announced.

'Not in church, Brooks!' The vicar shepherded them all into the vestry. 'How many times must I tell you, Willie?' But he took his own sip when the beaker was passed to him and the two ladies mopped their tears and made a confused and rambling toast and the hollow stave produced enough brandy for the happy couple to drink as well, once they had signed the register and the others were jostling to take their turns with the scratchy steel pen.

'I think I am a trifle tipsy,' Laurel whispered,

holding firmly to Giles's arm. 'I am not used to spirits at the best of times and I hardly ate any breakfast.'

'Shocking,' Giles murmured. 'And we are going to have to reel back through the streets because I did not order the carriage to collect us either. I can see that we are going to be a notorious couple, lowering the tone of the neighbourhood.' He shook hands with the vicar, threw the two elderly ladies into confusion by kissing them both on the cheek, tipped the verger and the sexton and assured the flower seller that he would make a point of directing his staff to buy flowers from her on a regular basis.

They all trooped outside where Giles gave the small boy a half-crown which was greeted by whoops of delight. Jermyn Street was busier now and people gathered round to stare at the bridal party. 'This is going to be the talk of Mayfair,' Giles said. He raised his hat politely to a group of giggling housemaids, then bowed to a haughty matron who raised a lorgnette as her barouche drove past.

'Who is that?'

'No idea, don't recognise her, but then I hardly know a soul in London—or in England, come to that. I must join some clubs, look up some of the officers I knew in the Peninsula. We will get calls enough once the announcement is in the paper, and I told Downing to send it off as soon as we left this morning.'

Giles turned to walk along Jermyn Street. Laurel saw that they were still trailing some of the spectators and faces appeared at the windows of shops as they passed. Perhaps brides on foot carrying bouquets were not a common sight in Mayfair. 'We could have sold tickets. I am sure Astley's Amphitheatre would be glad to have such an audience for a performance.'

'Do you mind?' Giles tucked her hand snuggly against his side. 'Perhaps I was wrong and we should have had the wedding privately at the house.'

'No. This was lovely. I feel very much married.'

'Not so *very* much yet. I have not kissed my bride. I hope you will forgive me that, but I feel we were giving enough of a show as it was.'

'Giles, where are we going? This is in quite the opposite direction to the Square—look, we are at St James's Street already.'

'I have a surprise for you.' Giles tossed a coin to the crossing sweeper and guided Laurel in his wake through the busy traffic of Piccadilly and into the street immediately opposite. 'And now we are here. Grillon's Hotel for one night. Possibly the shortest honeymoon on record.'

'An hotel? I have never stayed in one.' But even in the depth of the country she had read about Grillon's on the society pages of the newspapers. All the best people stayed at Grillon's and now she, Lady Laurel Knighton—no, *Lady Revesby*—was joining their ranks. She tried not to stare about her at the polished wood, the wide carpeted sweep of the lobby, the small groups of people passing in and out of the doors, all of them far too well bred and sophisticated to be gazing about as she longed to do.

They were escorted upstairs by a tailcoated man who was apparently the manager. 'We have no luggage,' Laurel whispered.

'All taken care of,' Giles said as they reached a panelled door.

The manager opened it wide to reveal a sitting room. 'My lord, my lady. If there is anything you require, please ring.'

'Thank you,' Giles said, in clear dismissal. The man bowed himself off and Giles bent, put one arm behind her knees and swept her off her feet and up against his chest. 'I realise this is not my own threshold and I will have to repeat the exercise when we go home, but it feels right to do it now.'

Laurel curled her arms around her husband's neck and hugged him tightly as he leaned back to push the door closed behind them. They were married and her childhood certainty that they were meant for each other was vindicated after nine long years. It would take a little getting used to after she had managed to convince herself that she was quite content to be a spinster and an independent woman, but it would be all right because this was meant to be.

They still had to get to know each other again, learn how to make the marriage work, but she wondered, as Giles set her on her feet, how she had ever doubted him in the past. Now there was nothing but trust between them and on that foundation they would build not only a marriage, but a family.

The urgency of Giles's mouth on hers told her that he was contemplating beginning that family at the earliest possible moment, a sentiment with which she was entirely in accordance. Her bonnet was askew and the ribbons were half-strangling her. She had to stand on tiptoe to kiss Giles with the eagerness she felt and the bouquet was scratchily pressed between her bosom and his chest and was prickling her chin. Laurel tossed it back over one shoulder without breaking the kiss, then heard a small shriek of delight.

Giles stopped kissing her and lifted his head just enough to murmur, 'We are not alone.'

'No, it seems not,' Laurel agreed, disentangling herself. She wondered if she was quite as pink in the face as she felt. She pulled her bonnet straight and turned to find Giles's valet Dryden. Beside him, clutching the slightly battered bouquet, was Binham looking happier than Laurel had ever seen her.

'We were just departing, my lord. Everything is in order according to your instructions. Come along,' he added in a mutter and gave Binham's arm a tug.

To Laurel's surprise her maid did not protest at such treatment, merely bobbed a curtsy and hurried after the valet, holding tight to the flowers.

'What is the matter with her?' Giles demanded.

'She is somewhat confused after catching the bridal bouquet—by tradition that should mean she is the next bride.'

'Heavens, I hope she does not have her eye on Dryden. The woman terrifies me.'

'Me, too, at first, I must confess. Stepmama employed her without consulting me and I had every intention of dismissing her with excellent references and finding someone more amenable, but she is actually mellowing.' She looked around. 'Are we alone here now?'

'That was my idea. Binham and Dryden have brought over everything we might need until tomorrow, there should be champagne on ice, and the hotel will send up food and hot water and so forth when we ring for it, at whatever time, day or night. It occurred to me that carrying you over the threshold in the Square and then continuing straight upstairs and vanishing for twenty-four hours might cause you some embarrassment.' He was working on the bow of her bonnet ribbons as he spoke.

'It would be equally awkward to be sitting around for the rest of the day waiting for dinner to be over and pretending that we were not just married and dying to be in bed.'

'Are you? Dying to be in bed with me?' Giles set the bonnet aside, pulled off his gloves with his teeth and began work on the row of buttons down the front of her pelisse.

'I find myself quite resigned to the prospect,' Laurel said demurely. He was remarkably adept with fiddly buttons.

'Minx. You never were very convincing as a demure miss. Whenever we were in trouble as children you would stand there looking far too innocent to be believable.' The pelisse slid off her shoulders and Giles tossed it on to a chair along with his tall hat, then shrugged out of his coat. 'The bedchamber should be that door there.'

They stumbled into the other room, wearing considerably less than they had started with. Giles's waistcoat and neckcloth had gone, apparently while he had followed her across the sitting room, caressing her out of her gown as she retreated before him. His urgency was exciting and the flutter of nerves quite disappeared to be replaced with a sensation that Laurel recognised as arousal, warming and teasing parts of her that no young lady was supposed to be aware of, let alone think about. Since that interlude on the island she had found herself thinking about them more than she should and about Giles's body, naked in the sunlight.

'I had better draw the curtains.' Giles gestured towards the view of the windows on the opposite side of Albemarle Street. 'Ah, there are thin blinds, that is better.' He drew them down, filtering the light into a softness that still allowed them to see each other clearly. 'Now, Lady Revesby...' And then he seemed to lose the desire to talk because while he had turned away to locate the blind pulls she had taken the pins from her hair and stepped out of her petticoats.

Giles's breathing hitched as he ran his hands

into the tumbled curls that she had washed so carefully in rosemary infusion, that Binham had brushed and brushed as it dried so every lock was glossy and slippery over his fingers.

He lifted her with one arm around her waist, the other still in her hair, and laid her on the bed, following her so they were locked together on the high mattress. He went still, unspeaking, looking down into her eyes, then he bent his head and kissed her. It began as a slow, gentle pressure, but as she kissed him back, slid her arms around him and tugged at his shirt, he became more urgent, his fingers tangling with the ribbons and laces of her underthings until Laurel sat up and pulled off her chemise herself.

'You will have to unlace me.' She found she was beyond shyness.

Quite shameless, in fact.

It was unspeakably erotic, to turn her back to give him access, to feel the nip of his teeth on the nape of her neck as he freed her from her corset, his hands coming round to cup her breasts as the laces yielded and the stiff boning released them. His thumbs fretted across her nipples and Laurel looked down to see them stiffen, pushing impudently against his fingers. She was cradled between his spread thighs, against his chest and she could feel clearly that he was erect and hard, his arousal pressing blatantly against her buttocks.

The nerves fluttered back, but in a way that was strangely exciting. Laurel wriggled, pressing against him, her head tipped back on his shoulder. *'Giles.'*

Chapter Seventeen

Giles moved, turning her on to her back on the bed, pulling the loosened corset away. He bent to kiss her breasts, then he dragged his shirt over his head and got off the bed to free himself of the rest of his clothing. When they were both naked he stood there looking at her, then reached out and stroked his hand over the slight swell of her stomach, down into the curls.

'Shall we make this irrevocable?' he asked, his voice husky. His desire was evident in his body, in his face, in his voice, but the strangeness of his words made her frown for a second, confused. Surely there was no question of this not being irrevocable? They were married now in the sight of the church and the law. But perhaps he was as overset as she was, emotions tangling his tongue.

'Oh, yes, Giles.'

I would rather you had asked me if we should make love...but that is only a euphemism, a form of words after all. It need not have anything to do with the emotion of love, I suppose.

It made her feel a little wistful for a moment, but only a moment, because kissing when two naked bodies were pressed together, when two naked people wanted each other, in love or not, there was no room for brooding, Laurel found.

Giles was gentle but sure, not giving her time to fret that she did not know what to do. Her body seemed to understand the fundamentals in any case, she thought hazily as his weight came over her and she instinctively raised her knees to cradle his hips and pressed back when she felt the blunt pressure nudging at her entrance.

She was expecting it to hurt, but his fingers insinuated themselves between their bodies, worked the magic as they had in the summer house and when he pushed into her she was crying out with pleasure, not with pain.

It felt a little strange, then a little sore and then very wonderful, as she came back to herself, to feel Giles within her, joined with her. She opened her eyes and saw the concentration on his face, the hard lines of his tense neck and throat, saw his eyes close for a second, then he opened them, his gaze fierce on her face, his expression almost one of pain before he cried out, something in a language she did not know, and collapsed against her, his face buried in the angle of her neck and shoulder.

The weight of a fully grown, completely relaxed man was more than she had expected and Laurel found herself sinking into the Grillon's luxuriously soft feather mattress.

I am being swallowed by clouds, she thought, then had to stifle a little gasp of laughter against Giles's shoulder at the thought of being squashed into a cloud by an angel, because this was surely heaven.

'Do you find my lovemaking amusing?' a muffled voice enquired, vibrating against the skin just above her right breast.

'It was heaven and now I feel as though I am sinking into a very fluffy cloud under the weight of a rather large angel.'

Giles levered himself up on braced forearms which had the interesting effect of pressing his lower body tight against hers. 'I have no idea what size angels are supposed to be, so I am not sure whether to be insulted because you are saying I am fat.'

He was smiling down at her, that errant lock of hair falling across his forehead. He looked formidable and very male and, at the same time vulnerable because he had surrendered himself, lost himself, with her, just as she had been lost with him. 'Now I come to think of it, aren't angels supposed to be sexless? Yes, I am insulted.'

Laurel gave an experimental wriggle. If she did that... Oh, yes. 'I really do not think you can be an angel after all.'

'What a relief.' Giles slid down her body, his tongue exploring as he went.

'Giles? *Giles!* What are you...? Oh, Giles, *yes.*'

Her husband, wickedly reducing her to a quivering mass of delight, said nothing.

Giles leaned back in his father's great carved chair in the study and surveyed the post neatly stacked on the worn green leather of the desktop. Back to reality. He picked up a pen and jotted *Employ secretary* on a blank piece of paper. If this much had accumulated while they had been gone for only two days at Grillon's, then there would be considerably more when news of his return to London spread more widely.

He picked up the top item, then sat, contemplating the first two days—and nights—of married life. When his eyes finally focused on his reflection in the glass doors of the bookcase opposite he saw he was smiling fatuously. *Moonling*, he mouthed at himself.

That first day and night had been so good that at breakfast the next morning he had suggested staying for another night. The sight of Laurel curled up at the end of the bed, her nightgown slipping off one shoulder as she ate fingers of toast and honey that he was making for her, removed the slightest desire to go back to St James's Square and deal with the real world.

When a drop of honey dripped from the toast and into Laurel's cleavage, making her laugh, he dropped the knife, threw off his robe and devoted himself to licking her clean of honey. That took at least an hour, what with having to spread more on her body and then check there was none behind her ears, or her knees, and having to respond to wriggling and giggling and bold exploration of any parts of his anatomy that came within reach of her fingers or the honey spoon.

'We may as well stay for luncheon,' he'd said and then the afternoon had slipped away with bathing and sleeping and lazily making love and talking of this and that and nothing very much until it was time for dinner and it became much easier to simply stay where they were for the night.

At three that afternoon he had carried Laurel over the threshold once more and she had retired upstairs, primly informing him she had things to attend to in her wardrobe, which he strongly suspected meant that she was taking a nap. Something that he felt in need of himself, if he was honest. He must be getting old, he thought, shaking his head as he broke the seal on the first piece of correspondence. Although perhaps making love, on and off, for forty-eight hours, was some excuse.

Most of the correspondence was business, but there were at least a dozen letters welcoming him back to England and congratulating him on his marriage. Several included invitations and he set all the social correspondence to one side to look through with Laurel later.

So far, Giles had to admit, married life was proving far better than he had hoped. It was surprisingly easy to make love to Laurel without feeling guilty about it. Perhaps he ought to feel guilty about not feeling… He gave himself a brisk mental shake. Not feeling guilty at all would be preferable. But he would have to stop himself speaking Portuguese in the throes of passion.

Laurel had been a delight. Responsive, sensual and brave, she seemed to have overcome whatever qualms a virgin might have about the marriage bed and, Giles suspected, he was going to enjoy himself keeping up with her demands and her imagination.

She also kept her sense of humour in the bedroom. That nonsense about angels and clouds still made him smile. If he could not marry for love—and finding love must be a total gamble—then he could not think of a better bride. He only hoped he could make Laurel happy because she deserved to be, she had brought him so much.

Downing opened the door. 'This has just come by royal messenger, my lord.'

'From the Palace?'

'From Carlton House.' He extended a silver salver with a thick folded envelope in the centre, its heavy red seal exuding importance.

'Is he waiting for a reply?'

'No, my lord.'

Presumably, *Yes, Your Royal Highness* was the only expected response to whatever this was. It had to be from Prinny, of course, coming from Carlton House and not from the Palace. Giles broke the seal and read the contents. 'Damn.' An invitation from the Prince Regent was only to be expected, but this was for tomorrow evening and he had no idea whether Laurel had anything suitable to wear or even how she would feel about being plunged into one of Prinny's 'little' receptions when she had not even got her bearings in London.

He got to his feet. The sooner he found out, the better, because if he had to make their excuses they had better be good ones. The Regent was prone to sulks if thwarted and, while the last thing Giles wanted was to be part of the Carlton House set, he did not want to offend the heir to the throne either.

When he scratched on the door to the Rose Suite Binham opened it immediately, then swung it wide when she saw who it was.

'Your mistress is not resting?'

'I am through here, Giles,' Laurel called. She was in the bedchamber in front of the long pier glass, holding up a gown of yellow silk with an overskirt of pale green net. 'This has just come from Madame Ranier—what do you think? It is very lovely, but I am not at all sure when I would wear something quite this splendid. It is not a ball gown, but it is certainly full evening dress. Perhaps I should wait until we have some suitable invitation before taking it.'

'We have just the occasion.' He held up the embossed card. 'The Prince Regent invites Lord and Lady Revesby to a reception at Carlton House—tomorrow evening.'

Laurel stared at him, mouth slightly open, then

gave herself a little shake. 'The Prince Regent? Um… Very well. Then this will be perfect, I think.' She laid it on the bed and began to count things off on her fingers. 'Unless I have to wear feathers—but that's only for the Queen's Drawing Rooms, isn't it? I do own a tiara… Shoes and stockings and gloves, of course, I will need to find those to match tomorrow, but there should be no problem.'

He had expected her to show more alarm, or apprehension at the very least, but Laurel was clearly not going to allow herself to be over-awed. 'I will send round directly to Rundell, Bridge & Rundell and have the yellow-diamond parure brought out of storage and cleaned, that would be best with that gown. Are you sure you are not nervous about this? Carlton House and Prinny can be somewhat overwhelming.'

'I have read all about both the Regent and his house. It sounds as though it is in the most appalling taste, but I have to confess to be agog to see it. Is he very top-lofty and difficult?'

'Not at all in that sense, provided he receives due deference, of course. Once he sees he is getting it, then he relaxes and becomes positively convivial. But you must not be alone with him, not for a moment. His hands wander alarmingly, so they say.' He hesitated, wondering how much to warn her. 'In fact, one hears that the company may be a trifle *warm* at anything hosted by the Regent. I wouldn't wander off into any quiet corners.'

'I promise I will not allow myself to be lured into compromising situations, or shocked either.' Laurel tilted her head to one side and studied him. 'Are you concerned that I may not be up to this and might let you down?'

'No, never that. But I do not want you feeling that I have tossed you into the deep water of London society and left you to sink or swim. Especially as you have no friends here to advise you.'

'But I will have—not that I have had time to write to any of them yet. I know at least three married ladies who may be in town and I have several distant cousins, now I come to think about it. I haven't seen them for some time, but they do have London addresses. And I will make friends soon enough.'

'But not with the Carlton House set,' Giles warned. He glanced around. Muffled sounds of drawers closing came from the dressing room where Binham was working with the door closed. 'Laurel. Are you happy? Is everything all right?' What was the matter with him? She looked and sounded perfectly content, so why was he feeling so insecure about his new wife's feelings? It was almost as though he… No. It was only his wretched conscience again.

Being Laurel she did not laugh off his question, or become coy. 'Yes. I am happy.' She went a little pink and lowered her voice. 'I very much enjoy…the bedroom with you. I love this house, the staff are very pleasant, I am thrilled to be in London and…' she came close and lifted one hand to touch his cheek '… I am married to quite the most handsome Earl in England.'

I am petrified, Laurel confessed to herself.

But she was not going to admit it to Giles. She had her pride—besides, he was worried enough about her, what with the thought of Prinny's roving eye and the shocking behaviour of his set and the fact that she had no experience of how to go on in London society.

But I look the part.

Her image in the mirror was reassuring. She was a countess with all the right trimmings of fashionable gown, gorgeous jewels and elegant accessories. Now all she needed was the correct attitude and that meant relaxing and being herself. It would be nerves that would betray her lack of experience, not naturalness.

'Thank you, Binham, that will be all.' The folds of the evening cloak swirled around her as

she paused at the bedchamber door. 'There is no
need to wait up for me.'

'But, my lady, that gown is impossible to remove by yourself. And your hair—'

'His lordship will assist me,' Laurel said without thinking. Binham blushed and she was afraid
she had done so herself.

'You look magnificent.' Giles was waiting at
the foot of the stairs as she came down.

'Thank you.' *And so do you*, she wanted to
add, but did not say so. It was becoming increasingly difficult to keep the way she felt about him
out of her tone and she was uncertain that Giles
would welcome the thought that she was becoming too emotionally attached. If he had shown
any signs beyond liking and desiring her then
perhaps she would have plucked up the courage. As it was, she was using all of her courage
up pretending to be sophisticated about meeting royalty.

Carlton House was as close as St James's
Palace, simply a left turn as one left St James's
Square, rather than a right turn. But, of course
they could not be seen to walk, the carriage had
to come out and they must sit in splendour for

half an hour in the slow-moving cavalcade to the gates.

'Will you know anyone?' she asked Giles. 'You have been out of the country for so long it must be difficult to get to know people again.'

'There could well be army men I met in Portugal and possibly diplomats home on leave or between postings. And I might discover the odd childhood friend, although probably I won't recognise anyone at first sight—or them me. My father put me up for both Brooks's and White's clubs, so once I've shown my face there things will be easier. Are any of your acquaintances likely to be there?'

'I have no idea. Amanda Pettigrew married the Earl of Preston last year, so she might be. Maria Foster's husband is a Whig Member of Parliament, a Mr Tompkins, but he is a great critic of the Regent, so they most definitely would not be invited to Carlton House. Look—we are through the gates at last.'

'What are you saying under your breath?' Giles leaned down and asked, low-voiced, as they joined the line snaking up the steps and under the great portico, trying not to tread on trains and flounces.

'I am reminding myself not to look over-awed

and not to giggle at things that are in terrible taste,' she whispered back.

'Like this hallway, for example.' Giles looked round at the oppressive gilt and crimson, studded with mirrors, all as bright as daylight under the mass of candles and lamps. 'I suppose there is *some* marble left, somewhere, in Italy. They cannot have used it all, whatever this looks like.'

The rooms were laid out so that they had to process through front hall, main hall, a series of anterooms, the throne room—which was almost too much for Laurel's equilibrium—and finally the Great Drawing Room and the Regent himself.

She was proud of her curtsy, right down to the ground and then up again without a wobble, and prouder still of Giles. The Regent knew who he was and had obviously heard good things, although Giles was looking exceedingly uncomfortable at the praise.

'Behind enemy lines, what? Damn dashing, I call it. Good show. No wonder we beat Boney hollow with men like you on our side! What do you say, eh, Lady Revesby?'

He creaks when he moves, Laurel was thinking, fascinated by the man in front of her. *It must be corsets. What if he goes pop?*

'I am exceedingly proud of my husband, your Royal Highness. Although he is too modest to

enjoy praise, however well merited, your approbation must be deeply moving and valuable to
him, as it is to me.'

They backed away to make room for the next
arrivals. Giles was quivering with either indignation or laughter. Both, it turned out when he
had her behind a vast potted palm.

'You *baggage*! It was a miracle that I did not
dissolve into whoops there and then. *Moving
and valuable* approbation, indeed. You deserve
spanking.'

'You wouldn't—'

'Only in play.' He lowered his voice to a husky
murmur. 'You would enjoy it.' He straightened up
abruptly. 'General Hastings, good evening, sir.'

Laurel got her expression under control, although not either her pulse rate or the half-
scandalised, half-aroused thoughts that Giles's
words evoked. She was introduced and said all
the right things and then waited patiently while
her husband was drawn into an analysis of some
border issue in the Peninsula that he, apparently,
had viewed on the ground.

They could be involved discussing it for ages,
she thought, becoming bored. She was interested in Giles's life in the Peninsula—not that
he showed any willingness to talk to *her* about
it—but discussions of catchment areas and river

flood levels were not enthralling. She looked around. There were other ladies strolling about without partners and the room was full, with people clearly spilling into adjacent reception rooms, so she would not be conspicuous if she walked around by herself, too. She might see someone she knew and, if nothing else, she could glean a wealth of impressions for some very lively letters to Stepmama and Jamie.

The next room was slightly smaller and rather less crowded, although the reflection of the myriad candles on so many reflective surfaces hurt her eyes and the heat was stifling. She looked up at the chandelier and then down again abruptly as she bumped into someone who gave a sharp squeak of alarm.

'I do apologise—you are not hurt, are you? I was not looking where I was— Oh, we have already met. We are neighbours, I believe.' It was the hostile young lady from the Portuguese household in the Square.

She did not look any more pleased to see Laurel than she had the other day, but at least she appeared to be about to speak. Laurel smiled encouragingly. Perhaps the young lady was shy, or her English was poor. She should make an effort because it did not do to be on poor terms with neighbours.

'Tell me,' the young woman said in heavily accented English, 'is St James's Square a place where noblemen keep their paramours...' She moved her hands as though searching for a word. '*Amantes*...their mistresses?'

Does she mean what I think she means? That she thinks that I am a courtesan? Yes, that question was just as rude and just as direct as it sounded.

'No, it is not,' Laurel said, with a smile that showed her teeth. 'It is where they keep their wives.'

Whatever it was that was agitating the young woman, that response seemed to knock her completely off balance. The delicate olive complexion turned an unhealthy shade of grey, her eyes widened and she stepped back, her hand to her mouth. 'Wives?' she said. '*Esposas?*'

Chapter Eighteen

Heads were turning. Laurel took the young woman firmly by the arm and walked her towards an alcove, partly screened by looped-back curtains. 'Please let us through, the lady feels faint.' It worked, the crowd parted and a footman hastened over with offers of water and smelling salts.

'Water, if you please. Oh, and a glass of champagne.' Laurel had a suspicion she was going to need that herself. 'Now, sit down, fan yourself and tell me what is the matter? Who are you and what have I done to deserve such rudeness?' *Or such hostility.*

'I am Beatriz do Cardosa, daughter of Dom Frederico do Cardosa.' She put up her chin and said it as though she expected Laurel to know the significance of those names and be cowed.

'Your father is with the Portuguese Embassy?'

'*Certamente*, in a position of the most important. And who are you, *senhora*?'

'I am Lady Revesby, wife of the Earl of Revesby.'

At which point Senhorita Beatriz, or whatever her correct title was, slumped down in a faint. It was too ungainly to be anything but genuine. Laurel caught her before she collapsed on the floor, hauled the other woman upright on the sofa against her and fanned her vigorously. She caught a glimpse of their reflection in one of the mirrors lining the alcove. They could be sisters at first sight, if it were not for Beatriz's Mediterranean skin tones.

The waiter arrived with the glasses. Laurel dipped her handkerchief in the water and flicked it on Beatriz's face. When she stirred and moaned Laurel seized the glass of champagne and took a reviving sip. The alcohol seemed to do very little to combat the nausea that was threatening to overset her. This very beautiful, very young Portuguese lady knew Giles and fainted at the news that he was married. What else could a wife deduce other than that they had had an *affaire* in Lisbon?

But this was not some experienced, sophisticated widow, or dashing but bored wife whose husband neglected her. Laurel would have to be an innocent indeed not to realise that Giles must have had liaisons with ladies like that. His skills in bed alone told her that he had not spent nine years in monkish chastity. But this was, if she was not much mistaken, the pampered daughter of a very important family and a virgin. Or at least, she should be. *Giles, what have you done?*

She took another gulp of the wine and returned to reviving Beatriz. Betraying anything other than concern for a fainting stranger in this crowd would be fatal. The gossips would seize avidly on any hint of something amiss and worry at it until everything was revealed. Besides, she had her pride. After some determined dabbing with the soaked handkerchief the other woman finally opened her eyes and recoiled from Laurel as far along the sofa as she could manage.

'Tell me it is not true!'

'That I am Giles's wife? It most certainly is. We were married three days ago, here in London. The notice was in the newspapers.'

'I do not read them, my English is not so good to read. But I do not believe you, you lie to me.' She seemed one breath away from hysteria.

'Why should I do that? I have no idea who you are, even.' Although she was increasingly certain she knew what this woman might be to her husband.

'But I have come to England to marry Giles—

he loves me. We make to be fugitive together, that is the right word?'

'Elope together,' Laurel corrected. 'Unfortunately for you, he and I eloped first.' She kept her tone dry, ironical, because the alternative was to give way to screaming anger. Tears would come later.

'I saw you the other day. I had found out what is his house, the house of his father. I know it is a good *presságio*—omen, you say, I think? A good omen that it is so close to the house my father takes. And then I see you arrive and I think you must be the mistress and I am not happy, but I tell myself that Giles loves me, he has always shown me how much he cares and that he will be lonely and will need a woman. He is a man of the world. Me, I understand this.'

'I can imagine.' Laurel stood up and tossed back the rest of the champagne, wishing she had the bottle. 'Stay there. Do not move.' She could not think of another thing to say and certainly nothing to do that was either acceptable in a royal household, or even vaguely civilised, so she turned on her heel and went to look for Giles.

She found him easily enough, despite the crowds in the rooms, because he had not left the main reception room and because of his height. Laurel wove her way through to the corner where the sun-bleached blond of his hair was visible and found him in conversation with two men in army uniform and a distinguished man who had a foreign air about him.

'Ah, my wife.' He turned, smiling, holding out a hand to draw her into the circle. 'Let me introduce you.' She had a smile fixed in place, but he must have seen something was wrong despite it. 'Laurel? Is anything amiss?'

Yes, you deceiving toad, everything is wrong, she wanted to say, but bit back the words.

'An old friend of yours is here and has been taken ill,' she said. 'I think they would appreciate your assistance, Giles. If you would excuse us, gentlemen?'

'Who is it?' Giles asked as he followed her. 'I did not think you knew any of my acquaintance yet.'

'She introduced herself,' Laurel said tightly. 'There, in that alcove.'

Giles said something under his breath, a sharp sound more shock than anything. Then, *'Beatriz?'*

It had only taken a brief glance at her partly concealed face and figure for him to recognise her, Laurel realised. 'As she was expecting to elope with you she was understandably upset when she discovered she was speaking to your wife.' Somehow she kept her voice low and steady and a bright smile on her lips.

'Elope? But that is *insane*.' Giles seemed to get himself under control with an effort of will and lowered his voice. 'Of course I was not going to elope with her. I did not even know she was in the country. She is just a girl—and besides, she is betrothed.'

It seemed to occur to him that there was a wealth of information in those few words and none of it anything that Laurel wanted to hear. 'That is to say—'

'She appears to believe that she is betrothed to you, or, at least, that the two of you have an understanding,' Laurel said, cutting him off. She did not want to hear excuses. Not now while she was using up all her energy in maintaining a civilised façade. 'I suggest you go and speak to her before she informs anyone else that Lord Revesby was planning to elope with her. She thought I was your mistress, by the way. She seemed quite accepting of that—her understanding of men's *needs* must be rather better than mine is.'

'Hell, Laurel—' Giles turned to face her fully, his face betraying strong emotion, but whether it was anger or guilt or something else, she could not tell.

'Go to her. You cannot leave her in that state, heavens knows what she might say or do.'

As she spoke Beatriz stirred and looked around, saw them. She made as though to rise.

'You are right, I will have to try to contain this.' His voice was tight with what she had no trouble, this time, as interpreting as anger. 'It is not what it seems. Wait for me, please, Laurel.' He took her hand, squeezed it, then strode towards the alcove.

Wait for him, stand around while he soothes his...whatever she is. I will do no such thing.

The moment his back was turned, Laurel made her way as quickly as she could to the entrance. So early in the evening it did not take long to retrieve her cloak, or to send for the carriage.

Laurel was home within half an hour of walking away from Giles.

'A migraine,' she told Binham who, fortunately, was still up. 'My head is splitting. I will go straight to bed if you can just help me out of this gown.'

When the maid had left Laurel locked the bedchamber door and retreated to her bed. She had to think because she did not believe she could manage to speak calmly to Giles, not yet.

Always assuming, she thought miserably, *he*

wants to talk to me, calm or not. Always assuming he comes home. I trusted him.

It felt as though he had received a heavy blow to the back of the skull. He was still conscious, on his feet, moving and hearing words, but even when he put them together into sentences that made sense, the meaning was impossible.

Beatriz in London? Beatriz talking to Laurel, telling her he was intending to elope with her?

And yet there she was, her beautiful face turned to him as he came closer, a desperate, foolish, hope in her eyes.

'Giles! She was lying to me, lying. Was she not? She is your mistress, *sim*?'

'*Não,*' he said forcefully. 'No. She—Laurel— is my wife.' He sat down next to her, picked up a discarded wine glass and tried to keep his expression bland and open, as though this was simply a casual conversation. 'What are you doing here, Beatriz? Why have you been saying those things to my wife? You know perfectly well that there is nothing between us and never was, beyond a little flirtation. Nothing. *Nada,*' he repeated when she just stared at him blankly.

'But in Lisbon you made love to me with your eyes. You were so kind, you help me, you hear how impossible is this marriage that they want to make with me and this…this *sapo*.'

Toad, Giles translated with that part of his brain that was not screaming, *Run!*

'I understood why you must leave, why you cannot speak to me. At home I am too much guarded and besides, Papa has so much influence. You could have been arrested or worse. But I am here now. Papa has a post of the most important with the diplomatic mission. Here in England we can run away—go to this Gretna Green I have read of and there we can be married.'

'But I *am* married.' He found he wanted to shake her. How could she not understand? 'And you are betrothed and your father would never accept our marriage. And besides—I am sorry, Beatriz, but I do not want to marry you. I never did.'

She fixed those lovely eyes on him, her lower lip, sweetly curved, that looked as though it must taste of cherries, trembling. 'But I do not understand. You *love* me.'

'No, I do not. I never said such a thing. I never kissed you or wrote to you or did anything other than flirt with you and let you weep all over me.' It was like wading through deep water trying to make her understand. 'I know you are upset about the man they want you to marry, but this is no answer. Imagine the diplomatic row if you do anything rash—think how angry your father would be. It could harm relations between our countries. Beatriz, you cannot think only of yourself. I am married and you, in a way, are representing your country. You must stop this.' He felt like a brute, but she was not going to accept that her foolish fantasy of escape was not reality unless he forced her to.

'You do not love me.' Her voice was low, shaking, as she turned away. 'You betray me.'

'Damn it, Beatriz. *Grow up.*'

But she had turned her shoulder to him and, in the midst of a royal reception, there was absolutely nothing he could do. He would have to leave her, although it felt like abandoning her. If they attracted notice with her on the brink of tears, the talk would be appalling and her father would be furious with her all over again. And there was Laurel to consider.

Laurel. My wife. He stood up, scanned what he could see of the room. It was crowded now, noisy and hot. He began to quarter the room systematically searching. Laurel would be—what? *Upset* hardly seemed to be adequate, confronted with what appeared to be damning evidence of her new husband's philandering with an innocent young lady. Distressed, angry, deceived.

Betrayed. Hurt. That was what mattered. Laurel would be hurt to discover that she could not trust him and he found that the thought cut like a knife.

Giles made his way to the entrance, discovered that Lady Revesby had collected her cloak and summoned her carriage not twenty minutes before. Was that all it was—a few minutes? It had seemed like an hour in there with Beatriz.

He was within minutes of home so he walked, thin evening pumps painful on the uneven flagstones as he strode along, his evening cloak swirling around him.

A woman stepped out of an alleyway in front of him. 'Looking for a good time, sweetheart?'

She recoiled when he snarled at her, his pulse thudding as he relaxed his hand on the hilt of the thin knife he carried in the lining of his coat. *Not a footpad.* That would have put the crown on the evening, arriving home battered from a fight.

The front door swung open as he ran up the steps. 'Her ladyship has retired, my lord. The decanters are—'

'Thank you. You can lock up now.' He made himself walk calmly up the stairs. If the footman had not noticed anything wrong with Laurel then there was hope that no one else had either, although it was really impossible to keep things from the staff.

There was a thread of light under Laurel's door. He scratched on a panel and tried the handle. Locked. He tapped. 'Laurel, it is Giles.' No answer.

He could fetch a master key. He could pound on the door and demand to be let in. He could even put a shoulder to it. All of those would make him feel better for a moment and would make Laurel feel worse. Giles went to bed.

Laurel got up at five and unlocked the door before there was any chance of Binham coming in. Although when she looked in the mirror at her face and then saw the bed, churned into a tangle of sheets by a sleepless night tossing and turning, the maid would have to be working with her eyes closed not to notice that something was amiss.

Giles had tried the door last night, had knocked, but had gone away without trying to speak to her when she had made no reply. Perhaps he, too, was trying to hide this from the servants. At least he had come home very soon after she had left him. He had not been somewhere with his Beatriz.

Cold water splashed on her face made her feel more alert. Was Giles awake? Had he, like her, lain sleepless all night? Her robe was on the floor, kicked there during the night. Laurel put it on, jammed her feet into her slippers and went across the landing. She was not going to skulk in her bedchamber, waiting for Giles to produce whatever explanation, or ultimatum, he was planning on. Either he was feeling at least as bad as she was, or he was asleep and she would wake him, catch him unawares and get the truth out of him that way.

Then she stopped, went back and sat on the bed and twisted her wedding ring, shiny and new, round and round on her finger. Once she had believed the worst of Giles and had so nearly ruined lives as a result. She had sworn to herself to trust him, so this time she would, she resolved, getting to her feet. She would listen and she would talk and she would understand. And then she would judge, because she loved him and love, surely, did not condemn.

The door was unlocked and she did not knock. Giles was out of bed, sitting slouched in a low armchair by the window, tossing some small object from hand to hand. He was wearing a heavy green-silk robe, his feet bare and she sensed that he had not slept. Perhaps he had been there all night.

She could have sworn she made no sound entering, but he looked round and came to his feet in one rapid, fluid movement, stuffing the thing he had been playing with back into a pocket. 'Laurel.'

'Giles.' She closed the door and went to sit on the window seat, her back to the light. There was no reason why she should let him read her expression, not yet, and she was very interested to see his. As she tucked her feet up on to the cushions and pulled the skirts of the robe around her she wondered a little at her own calm. Shock, perhaps.

'Are you——? No, of course you are not all right.' He stayed on his feet, facing her, the chair between them.

'I would like you to explain, please.'

Giles stared at her, his eyes narrowed as though trying to pierce the veil of shadows hiding her expression. 'You want me to explain? You sit there calmly giving me the opportunity to explain?' He looked not just puzzled by her behaviour, he seemed…hurt?

As though I *have wounded* him, she thought and suddenly understood.

'You think because I am not weeping or shouting that I do not care? That because I seem calm, then this is of no importance to me—that you are of no importance?'

Yes, that is just what he thinks, the idiot man.

He was braced, ready for her reproaches, her anger, his shoulders rigid, like a soldier facing a firing squad. He had slept no more than she had, to judge by the dark smudges under his eyes, the colour of his skin, pale under the fading tan.

'You have every right to be distressed, angry, hurt and to say so. I have never known you to hold back before from telling me your feelings. I can only assume you do not care enough. And I cannot blame you. I rushed you into this marriage, I told you nothing of my past in Portugal.'

'Nine years ago I rushed to a conclusion and caused a catastrophe. I hope I can learn from my mistakes, Giles.' Somehow she was keeping her voice steady, which surprised her. Perhaps because this was simply too important to let anything stand in the way of honesty between them. 'When I promised to marry you I also promised myself that I would trust you. I am trusting you now to tell me the truth and then you can rely on me to tell you how I feel.'

'Hell.' Giles scrubbed both hands up over his face. 'I do not deserve you, Laurel.'

Chapter Nineteen

'No, you do not deserve me,' Laurel agreed readily and surprised a twitch of the lips out of Giles.

'I met Beatriz at the Court in Lisbon. She was very heavily chaperoned, but my credentials were good, I was with the British Mission, I was acceptable as a dance partner. She is a very graceful dancer, she is beautiful, she was fun to flirt with.' He sat down in the chair, facing her, letting her study his face and weigh his words. 'She is very young, of course, and sheltered and, I fear, rather silly.'

Laurel blinked. *'Rather silly'* was hardly a lover's expression.

'She had been betrothed since she was an infant to an aristocrat of the royal blood. Unfortunately they never met, so she was able to tell herself it was not a reality—until the day when she finally encountered him. The poor man is hardly a very prepossessing specimen and much older than she is. She was violently upset, all her romantic ideas and daydreams shattered. I cannot say I blame her, any young woman would find him a disappointment.'

'I do not understand how you come into this.'

'I had flirted with her, talked to her, made a bit of a pet of her, I suppose, unwisely. It never occurred to me that she might be getting…attached. One evening I found her in the conservatory in floods of tears, tried to comfort her, ended up with an armful of sobbing, distraught female. Her mother found us, me doing nothing more lascivious than attempting to mop up her tears with a large square of best Irish linen, but she was seriously worried that there was something else going on.

'I had a most uncomfortable interview with her father, but I did, thankfully, convince him that nothing untoward had occurred. I could always leave the country, but if her reputation was tarnished it would have been appalling. It never crossed my mind that what she felt for me was anything more than a silly fairy story she had told herself as an escape from the reality of who she had to marry, because of course I had to stay right away from her. And, thank heavens, the

French were defeated, part of the Mission was sailing for England and I got permission to go with them.'

'Why didn't you tell me about her?'

'I thought it was all past, a storm in a teacup. I had no idea that Dom Frederico might come to this country, let alone that he would bring his family with him. Certainly not that we would find ourselves living virtually next door to them. I did not believe that it would do any good to rehearse my past.' He shifted, looking uncomfortable. 'Besides, I did not want to talk about the poor girl, however foolish she was and however blind I was to how she might feel about me. It did not feel right to speak of her unhappiness.'

'No. I can understand that.' And she could and admired him for it. Another man, someone less secure in themselves, could have made an amusing story out of the foolish girl's desperation and infatuation, but he had not.

'I would not have wanted to hear about it unless I had to,' Laurel said. 'It was her secret. You are right—you should have been more alert to her feelings, more cautious. But telling me all about it would have been rather like those married men who are unfaithful just once, then feel they have to confess all to their wives which eases their conscience and makes their wives utterly miser-

able. Not that you were being unfaithful to anyone, of course.'

'That is remarkably understanding of you,'
Giles said drily. 'I had expected anger and hurt.'

'I am not exactly *happy*,' Laurel countered,
equally dry. 'But I cannot see what good it will
do either of us for you to be wallowing in guilt
over something that you should not feel guilty
about. Your intentions in Portugal were innocent
and you acted honourably to retrieve the situation and you married me in good faith. The only
thing I do not understand—'

'What is it?'

'Never mind.' It was tactless in the extreme
and it was her fault for falling so easily into a
frank exchange. The relief of finding that Giles
would speak of this with openness had made her
careless.

'No, tell me, Laurel. We are stripping the truth
to the bone this morning, are we not?'

She grimaced at the brutal analogy. 'It is just
that... I expect that Beatriz is finding it difficult
to cope with a strange country and language as
well as the shock of finding you are married and
that is why she is behaving rather...foolishly.'
It was impossible to think of a less pejorative
word, but it was, she supposed, better than *idi-
otic*, which is what came to mind. It did make

things worse, the realisation that the adult Giles had been as enchanted by a lovely face as his adolescent self had been.

He recognised that Beatriz was, as he put it, *rather silly*, but he had still flirted with her because she was beautiful. The fact that she, Laurel, was now accounted good looking was no balm to the remembered hurt of the plain girl that she had been. Beatriz appeared to be a type that attracted Giles—was that why he had proposed to her, because she looked very much the same?

'What do you mean?' he asked, wary now.

Speaking of her own youthful insecurities was both damaging to her pride and pointless. Laurel braced herself for the reaction to her apprehension about Beatriz. 'She could not seem to grasp that as we were married then there was nothing she could do about it. That you had, quite properly, broken off contact with her and that just because she was now in England it did not make things any different. It was like talking to a toddler, trying to reason with them and explain that no amount of crying and screaming was going to make things different from what they are.'

'Hell. You think she will create trouble?' Giles scrubbed his hands over his face again, the rasp of his morning stubble just audible, they were sitting so close.

I love the feel of that roughness on my skin first thing in the morning. Oh, Giles, just when I thought that marriage was going to be straight-forwardly delightful. I am the foolish one.

'I thought it was just me,' he admitted suddenly. 'I thought that I was so shocked that I could not properly take in what she was saying. But she was talking about Gretna Green and refusing to listen when I told her that I was married. You are right, this could stir up one hell of a storm.'

'She is young and she is sheltered and spoilt, no doubt. She must have thought that any man would be bewitched by her because she is so very beautiful. I expect that you are the first thing she has wanted that she could not have.' She imagined Giles flirting with Beatriz, ignoring her foolish chatter because she was so lovely. Her spirits, which had begun to rise as they talked, plummeted again.

'She looks like you,' Giles said.

'She looks like I would if my nose was not a little crooked and my teeth were perfectly even and if my chin was not quite so pointed and my eyebrows arched more and my deportment was perfect. Her eyelashes are much longer,' Laurel said sharply, horrified to see that her fingers were curling into talons. She straightened them out as she tried to keep the bitterness out of her voice. 'Is that is why you kissed me on the Downs? Because I looked like Beatriz? Is that why you wanted to marry me, because you had always known that she was not for you, but I am an acceptable substitute for her?'

Giles's face seemed to tighten as though the skin had contracted over the flesh beneath. She had hit a nerve, it seemed. *'No.'* Giles made a sharp gesture of denial with one hand. 'I swear to you, on everything that I hold sacred, that is not why I asked you to marry me.' He knelt before her, caught her hands in his, held on when she tried to push him away, annoyed as much with herself for her foolish suspicions as she was with him.

'Listen to me, Laurel, please. I flirted with Beatriz and I had *affaires* with ladies at the Court who were looking for the same uncomplicated relationship that I was. I came back to England having ended the current liaison amiably, believing that Beatriz would be marrying her princeling and knowing, too, that I must do the expected thing and marry. And you came back into my life. And I found I must wed you and no one else.'

She looked deep into those blue eyes. The blue took her back so far into the past, almost as early as she could recall, back to Giles looking at her as he was now. Giles making promises, Giles reassuring her, Giles making her laugh. He was telling her the truth now, she sensed.

Or he is telling it as he understands it, a cynical little voice murmured in her head. *He does not consciously believe he married you as a substitute for that lovely girl, but very likely he did. But then, what did you expect of this marriage? A fairy tale?*

'I believe you.'

And I love you, which probably makes me as foolish as Beatriz.

He got to his feet, her hands still in his, and tugged gently until she stood. 'Laurel. You are my wife and I will always be faithful to you, I swear.'

He believes it, so I must also, she told herself, because once trust cracks and wavers it crumbles and falls away entirely.

Laurel's wide brown gaze was steady on his face as though she was reading a document.

Perhaps she is, the evidence in my trial. She seems prepared to find me innocent.

He had not lied to her, but he had not told her the truth about why he married her either. But was that something he felt increasingly compelled to confess to for the sake of his own scruples or because she would want his honesty? That remark about unfaithful husbands easing their own consciences by sacrificing their wives' peace of mind was telling.

'Laurel, I want you. Only you, for ever and here and now. Twenty minutes ago I would have said that I was fit only to sleep, once we had spoken. Now I find that the bed is calling me, but not for sleep.' And it was true. He was quite painfully aroused and her swift downward glance confirmed that she realised it, too.

'We will keep each other awake,' she said, the old wicked smile suddenly there on her lips.

Forgiveness, then.

He was not certain for what. He could not, he thought, blame himself for anything except carelessness in not recognising that Beatriz was developing a *tendre* for him. But he had hurt and distressed Laurel, given her a sleepless night and that was on his head. She was his wife and it was his responsibility to protect her. Although now, as he stood up and drew her into his arms, protection was not exactly what he had in mind.

She was wearing only a thin silk robe over an even more flimsy nightgown and his body hardened and ached as she leaned in to his embrace.

'What are all these things that are so wrong

with your looks?' he asked as he steered her towards the bed, taking a detour on the way to lock
the door. 'Eyelashes that were too long?'

'Too short.'

'Just right for the perfect curl.' He kissed her
eyelids, feeling the lashes tickle his lower lip.
'And your nose?'

'Crooked.'

He bit it lightly. 'Adds interest. Perfection is
so dull.'

'And my teeth are uneven,' she said with a
gasp as the back of her knees hit the edge of the
bed and she fell on to the mattress.

'Now that requires careful investigation.' Giles
climbed on to the bed beside her. 'And the most
thorough kissing.'

Laurel seemed to have no objection. Her arms
went around him and her mouth opened under
his and she sighed as his tongue traced the curve
of her teeth. She was quite right, although he had
never noticed before.

'All the better to whistle with,' Giles said when
he came up for air, dizzy with the scent and taste
and feel of her. He rolled over on to his back and
Laurel settled against him, her chin on his chest.
'Ouch. Your chin is definitely pointed. Still, I
can tolerate one fault, I suppose. Let me inspect
these unsatisfactory eyebrows.'

Laurel obligingly wriggled higher against his chest, causing his body to arch instinctively. She came up on her elbows and looked down at him, eyes wide with sensuality and, beneath that, trouble still lurking in the pansy-brown depths.

'I have no opinion on eyebrows except that yours seem eminently kissable to me.'

She laughed at him, just a little, her eyes narrowing, the skin at the corners crinkling.

It wasn't Beatriz's eyes I saw when I looked at her, as she thinks. It was Laurel's eyes I saw when I looked at Beatriz, that was what drew me to her in the first place, that is what made me smile at her. But that...that is not logical. I never saw Laurel as an adult woman until I came home.

She blinked, the laughter still there, and the trouble, deep and dark, and the affection for him, the affection he did not seem to have killed.

Her eyes have not changed, not since she was a child, not since she was the young woman I left, so angry and confused. I smiled at Beatriz because somehow I recognised deep down that she looked like who Laurel would become. Only I was wrong. Laurel is so much more lovely, every little imperfection that she sees adds up to character and charm.

Then the shock of it took his breath. In his

exile Beatriz had been a substitute for this woman, the one he had always been intended to marry. But that meant—

'Giles, have you gone to sleep with your eyes open?' Laurel sounded understandably put out. 'Because you have been lying there staring at me for a good minute and, delightful as my eyebrows are, I cannot believe they deserve that much scrutiny.'

'But your eyes do,' he said and sat up, shrugging off his robe and reaching for the ties on hers. 'I could drown in your eyes and I intend to.'

She moved under him, supple and warm and demanding, wanting him, it seemed, as much as he wanted her, gasping her encouragement as he explored her body. She used her tongue and lips and hands on him, inciting him, arching up to meet him as he thrust. Laurel closed around him, hot and wet and as smooth as silk velvet, her muscles gripping him, drawing him to the heart of her.

Mine, mine, mine...

Her nails were digging into his shoulders, her legs were tight around his hips, their bodies slithering and slipping with the heat of their lovemaking as Laurel came to pieces in his arms, calling out, sobbing out, his name.

'Giles!'

My name. She forgives me, she wants me. Perhaps as much as I want her.

'Laurel. Laurel.' He said it again and then again like an incantation, a prayer as he lost himself in her.

'Giles?'

Something pointed and warm and wet was tickling his ear. Giles cracked open one eye on to a landscape of cream and pink flesh, of soft skin rising in gentle hills and valleys, of the rose-brown textured surface of one nipple. He blew gently and it tightened and the tickle was replaced by a warm huff of breath. Laurel had been licking the rim of his ear.

'You are squashing me, rather, Giles.'

'I am sorry, love.' He slid off the delicious warmth of her on to the cool, rumpled sheet.

She turned her head away abruptly. 'It doesn't matter, although breathing was a challenge.'

He came up on one elbow facing her as she turned back to him. He must have imagined that momentary reaction. 'My lady, you should have woken me sooner.'

'No. I like being that close to you, it makes me feel…' She shivered. 'I can't explain. Giles—we are all right, aren't we?'

'I hope so.' It was a long time since he had

felt real fear, the sort that gripped the guts and sent the pulse wild and clouded the brain. The last time had been when he had flattened himself inside the hollow trunk of an olive tree with a French patrol leaning against it, sprawled in its shade, settling down for a siesta in the heat of the day. He had been in civilian clothes, quite enough to have him shot out of hand as a spy if they had found him, or tortured to wring every last drop of intelligence from him.

Somehow he had kept still, silent, unmoving except for the constant turning of the worry piece in his pocket, over and over, rubbing against the callouses it had formed, calming him, slowing his breathing, helping him endure. The fear had resolved after two hours when the patrol had ridden off. When he had seen Laurel come into his room that morning he had felt the same sick apprehension, not of torture and death, but of discovering that he had lost her, hurt her.

'Yes,' he said, reaching out to touch her face. 'We are all right, you and I. There might be some repair work to be done.'

'With Beatriz, I am certain of it. We cannot leave things as they are. With us, I do not think so. I never stopped trusting you, Giles. You have never lied to me, I know that now. I will never leap to conclusions about you again, I have learned my lesson. It was a horrible night, last night, I will admit it. I was angry, which was why I locked the door because I could not risk saying something hasty, in temper. I had to calm myself, think it through, but I knew that somehow you would be able to explain.'

I never stopped trusting you.

Hell, if she ever discovered just how little he was to be trusted with her feelings, how he had proposed to her simply for gain, then he would have broken something unique and irreplaceable. It felt like walking on a knife edge over a precipice.

'Where are you off to in that very fetching hat?' Giles asked as Laurel looked round the edge of the study door after luncheon.

'Just along the Square. I am going to pay a call on the ladies of Dom Frederico do Cardosa's household.'

Giles got to his feet, scattering pages of a letter around him. 'After last night?'

'Especially after last night. You cannot possibly go round there until he is reassured that he had not been wrong to believe you innocent of anything beyond some light flirtation. And she needs to realise that no amount of pouting and dramatising herself is going to restore you to her.

After that, then I am hopeful that we can all meet without fireworks going off.'

He looked so dubious that she went right into the room and kissed his cheek. 'It will be all right, you'll see, my—my dear.'

You called me my love *this morning, so casually. I wish I could say the word as easily to you.*

Laurel gave herself a brisk talking-to. There were fences to mend and bridges to build and possibly, to carry her muddled metaphors to the limit, dams to construct. She had asked Downing to send Peter to establish when the Portuguese ladies would be receiving and he had reported that, so far, they had only the smallest social circle and tended to spend the afternoons at home without visitors. That gave her hope that they would receive her, if only to break the monotony of their day.

Her card was received and she was ushered through to a reception room while the English butler established whether the ladies were At Home, but she had hardly seated herself when he reappeared to take her through.

Senhora do Cardosa was seated between two girls who must have been her daughters from their resemblance to Beatriz. She was short and stout within severe corsetry, but her hair was still glossy and black and her eyes had retained their beauty. She rose to shake hands. 'Lady Revesby, you are kind to call. My younger daughters, Cecilia and Daniela.' The girls rose and bobbed curtsies and sat down again without saying anything. From their expressions Laurel guessed that was shyness, and perhaps limited English, rather than any hostility.

'We are neighbours, *senhora*,' Laurel said. 'I felt I should welcome you to London, especially as my husband knew yours in Lisbon.' Now what would happen? She was braced for almost any reaction.

Chapter Twenty

There was no actual hostility flowing from the woman opposite her, just a great deal of reserve, but that might be normal for her. 'He spoke of Dom Frederico's diplomacy and…understanding.'

Ah, yes, there was a reaction, a slight tension, a flickering glance towards an embroidery hoop lying on a chair to Laurel's right, out of reach of the two daughters.

'I had hoped to meet your daughter Beatriz again. We spoke briefly yesterday evening, but she was not well, I think. I do hope she is not indisposed?'

Senhora do Cardosa said something in rapid Portuguese to her daughters who immediately got up, curtsied and left the room. She turned back to Laurel, lips pressed together, and looked at her for a long moment. 'You look very like my daughter, Lady Revesby.'

'Yes, I noticed that. She has far more perfect features than I do though, *senhora*.'

'She is a foolish girl.' Her look now was questioning.

'Very young, perhaps. Time cures that, for all of us. I am entirely in my husband's confidence.'

'Ah.' The older woman looked relieved.

Perhaps, Laurel thought, *she feels reassured that if Giles was prepared to tell his wife about the matter then it must all have been as innocent as he had protested in Lisbon.* 'It would be regrettable if there was any awkwardness…' She let her voice trail away suggestively.

'Most regrettable. I am certain that you and I, Lady Revesby, we can manage matters between us.'

'I am sure of it,' Laurel agreed.

'And so we have a conspiracy, Senhora do Cardosa and I. There will be strict segregation of the sexes whenever our households encounter each other at social gatherings. I will talk to her and her daughters, you may converse with Dom Frederico. We will all be seen to be on the best of terms and Beatriz's blushes will be spared. Once

Beatriz has come to terms with your married state then we will exchange dinner invitations.'

'To say nothing of sparing my blushes, my clever wife. You should be a diplomat.' Giles stood up and gathered Laurel in for a kiss, ducking to negotiate the wide brim of her Villager hat.

'Her mama was anxious about her betraying herself with unseemly behaviour, so it took very little diplomacy, just tact.' She delighted him by immediately untying the bow, casting the new hat on to the sofa without as much as a glance to see where it had landed and linking her hands behind his neck, the better to be thoroughly kissed.

'Would it be very unseemly behaviour to make love to my wife on this desk?' He turned, bringing Laurel round so with one gentle push she was lying over the polished mahogany, a jumble of estate papers squashed beneath her as he went to his knees, threw up her skirts and parted her legs.

Through the muffling of a froth of petticoats he heard, 'Giles—the door is unlocked!'

Giles expressed his opinion of the door, his mouth moving against the moist woman-tasting folds which produced another faint shriek. 'Don't stop!'

As he had no intention of doing so, Giles kept on licking and sucking, his hands clamped either side of the slim hips writhing above him.

He spared a fleeting thought for the state of the three maps, two leases and one field survey on the desk, then smiled and began to nibble.

'Someone is coming.'

'I sincerely hope so,' he mumbled, using his tongue with pinpoint accuracy. As Laurel came to pieces he slid out from under her skirts, stood up, pulled her up to sit on the edge of the desk and leaned over the scattered papers, screening her from the door with his body.

'The afternoon post, my lord.' Downing proffered the salver.

'Thank you.' Giles swivelled, took the post and waited until the butler closed the door behind him before turning to look at Laurel.

She was pink in the face, her hair was coming down, her skirts were crumpled and shards of broken red and blue sealing wax speckled her spencer. She met his gaze and collapsed into giggles. 'Oh, you *wretch*. I heard that board in the hallway creak and I was in terror of someone entering.'

'Admit it, it was exciting,' Giles managed to say through his own gasps of laughter.

'It was outrageous and now it is your turn.' Laurel leaned back, resting her hands on the desk. When he moved to lock the door she shook her head. 'Sauce for the goose,' she said. 'Leave it.'

'You are a very wicked woman.' Giles threw up her skirts again and moved in between her thighs as he unfastened his falls.

'I know.' She held on tightly as he sank into her and held still, shivering slightly with the sheer pleasure of the silky heat. 'I was brought up badly—there was this dreadful boy who led me astray at such a young age.'

'Shocking.' Giles began to move slowly, savouring the slide and suck of their bodies in unison, loving the little sighs and moans Laurel gave. 'What did this frightful lad do?'

'Took me dancing on the green in the moonlight, taught me how to climb a tree, let me go fishing with him, took the blame when I did something dreadful or came home covered in mud.'

'Not so very bad, then,' he murmured against the curve of her neck. Laurel smelled of honeysuckle and the musk of their lovemaking.

'No. Nothing bad at all.' Her voice was ragged now, as ragged as his breathing. 'I loved that boy,' she said as her body convulsed around him.

'Loved—' And then he lost control, went rigid as the pleasure burned through him, a wave of fire, left him shuddering in her embrace.

* * *

'Laurel.'

'Hmm?' He watched her coming back to herself as he always did, marvelling at her total abandonment to pleasure, at the trust she showed in him to care for her.

'Do you remember what you said, just before—?'

'I am not certain I recall which day of the week it is.'

'You were saying that you loved me when I was a boy.' What was he doing, asking that? What did he expect now—that she would say *I still do*?

'Well, yes.' She slid from the desk and began to put herself to rights with precise little feminine dabs and tweaks that made him want to sweep her upstairs and rumple her all over again.

'You were my friend. My best friend. Of course I loved you. I was certain one day that we would be married, although I had no idea what our fathers were scheming about. I had no idea what being married meant, of course.' She was fussing with her hair now, pushing in pins. He couldn't see her face and he had to put his hands behind his back to control the urge to reach out and raise her chin so he could read what was in her eyes.

'All very innocent, although by the time of the…misunderstanding I was old enough to begin having other feelings. I suppose being so used to you as my friend meant that they just never occurred to me as what they were.'

'And after the *misunderstanding* the last thing you wanted was to think of me like that,' he stated flatly.

'It was rather a shock for a somewhat naïve virgin.' She looked up and all he could see was faint, rueful, amusement.

'Yes, it must have been.' That summer afternoon had done more than cause an unholy row and put his life on a new track. It had, he realised, killed what might have been a love match. 'I suppose having the freedom to observe all the neighbouring marriages from the point of view of the spinster daughter gave you a somewhat cynical view of the institution,' he ventured, not at all certain what he was fishing for.

'You mean that I would not have seen much romance in marriage?' Laurel finished putting her hair and clothing to rights and turned to reorganise his desk. 'You would be surprised. My parents' marriage was one. The curate Mr Marriott married Olivia Lawrence, much to everyone's amazement—he being so serious and she being half his age and as flighty as they come—

and that was the sweetest thing. I found them once sitting side by side on the stile into Glebe Meadow and he was making daisy chains for her hair.

'There were others. And there were some where the couple were indifferent, or merely showed liking for one another.' Laurel shrugged, a careless twist of her shoulder. 'But who can tell what goes on behind closed doors? There, that is all your papers smoothed out. There is sealing wax everywhere though. I will ask Downing to send a maid in with a brush.'

'You are going?'

'Why, yes. I only dropped in to tell you I had been successful with Beatriz's mama.' She picked up the pile of post and sorted through it rapidly. 'I will take my letters and let you get back to your labours in peace.'

So, what do we have? Giles wondered as the door closed behind his wife who had left a little trail of crushed sealing wax behind her on the carpet.

It was a friendly marriage, a companionable marriage, a sexually rewarding marriage. They were beyond liking, it seemed to him. But might Laurel love him, find those long-buried feelings she had cherished for the youth he had been?

I hope not, he thought. *I have deceived her, lied to her by omission, forfeited her trust.*

And this time it was no *misunderstanding*. If Laurel ever discovered why he had proposed to her he suspected that her feelings would go beyond the end of love. It might be that she would hate him.

'Beatriz looks very lovely this evening,' Laurel said to Senhora do Cardosa. The Portuguese Embassy was holding a small reception and the rooms were full of a glittering array of military uniforms and men whose clothing seemed laden with orders and medals, as well as the usual throng of the fashionable. 'And she looks calmer. I do hope she is happier.'

'We have a long talk,' the other woman said. 'There were much tears, but now she accepts that Lord Revesby truly is married and that he was never other than kind to her. She is still being foolish about her own marriage, of course.' She heaved a sigh which made emeralds tremble across the tight golden satin sheathing her bosom. 'Your husband is a very handsome man,' she added in a tone of resignation.

Laurel managed not to look at Dom Frederico, who only the most devoted wife could call handsome. 'Yes, he is. He was a most unprepossessing boy—all ears and nose and feet. I did not recognise him when I saw him again after nine years.'

'And yet you loved him from the beginning.' Senhora do Cardosa sighed again.

This was getting uncomfortable. 'Excuse me, I will just go and have a word with Beatriz,' Laurel said, seeing the young woman standing alone for a moment. 'Senhorita Beatriz. How are you?'

'Well, thank you.' She looked at Laurel warily, obviously expecting a lecture. 'I… I am sorry about… You know.'

'I know. Tell me about your fiancé.'

'Dom Ricardo? He is old and he is ugly.' The pout was back, but her lower lip quivered, warning of tears soon enough.

'How old?'

'Thirty-five.'

'That is not so bad. What is he like?'

'He himself? I do not know. He is very stiff— like a soldier—and he does not talk, just one or two words.'

'I expect he is shy,' Laurel suggested.

'Shy? *Tímido?* But he is a man.'

'And he is marrying a lovely young lady whom he does not know, but who frowns at him. Just because he is not good looking does not mean that he is not a good man, does it? What if it was the other way around and he was the good looking one and you were plain? Wouldn't you feel awkward if he looked as though he wanted to burst into tears at the thought of marrying you?'

Beatriz gave a little gasp of laughter.

'You should be kind to him, talk to him—you might find you like him very much. Why not write to him in Portugal, tell him what you are doing, impress him with your observations on England.'

Laurel's attention was claimed by the wife of the Prussian attaché who had heard that she knew Bath and wanted to know if the waters might help with her mother's rheumatism. When she turned back Beatriz was gone, then she saw her across the room, deep in conversation with Giles, both of them looking exceedingly serious.

Oh, Lord. Should I go and rescue him? Or her?

No, her husband looked intense, but not tense, and Beatriz, all her eyelash-fluttering and posturing forgotten, was nodding agreement with what he was saying. She would trust Giles to manage this. In fact, she told herself, she would trust Giles with anything.

'So, was Lady Revesby beautiful when you first knew her?' Beatriz demanded, appearing suddenly at his side and speaking without any preliminaries.

'No.' Giles was startled into honesty. 'She was gawky—that is, thin and not graceful and her face was all eyes and angles. And she was a tomboy—a girl who likes to run wild like a boy—so she was often dirty and her clothes were torn and she was always in trouble.'

'But you liked her?'

'Yes. Very much. She was my friend and she was fun to be with and her imagination was—is—wonderful. And she was loyal and brave. And she still is,' Giles added, looking around the room for her. Yes, there she was, head on one side—so she was thinking hard—and talking earnestly to an elderly diplomat. He found he was smiling.

'So you love her even then, when she is not beautiful?'

'Yes, of course,' he said, still distracted, still watching his wife who was laughing now. Of course he had loved Laurel then, of course he loved her still. He found that he was turning his worry piece over and over in his pocket and drew his hand out, looked down at what he was holding.

'I— Excuse me.' He turned and walked rapidly out of the crowded, hot room into the relative sanctuary of a cross-passage.

I loved the girl, but now I love the woman. I am in love with Laurel.

He wanted, needed, to go to her, take her hand and drag her to the carriage, drive her home, covering her in kisses, carry her over the threshold and shout to the world that this was his wife and he loved her. That he always had.

If he had realised that he loved her before he asked her to marry him, if he had been able to tell her with total truth that his feelings for her were the reason for his proposal, if he had not known about the trust and the legacy until after they were betrothed…then Laurel would have believed him, would have known his motives for asking her to be his wife were honest.

Now what did he say to her? That he hadn't recognised his feelings for her until five minutes ago and that it had taken a chit of a girl to point out to him what had been in his heart for years? He could spare Laurel that insight into his masculine blindness, he supposed, tell her that he loved her, let her assume that the feeling had been growing, developing, through the short days, the long nights, of their marriage. And then hope and pray that she never found out the reason he had asked her in the first place.

Chapter Twenty-One

❦

Something was wrong with Giles. Laurel buttered toast and poured coffee and kept an eye on the supplies of bacon, Giles's favourite for breakfast. And worried. There had been something at the start, when he had stopped being angry about the past and had begun to court her, that had made her uneasy, that she knew he was hiding from her. Then, it seemed, he had relaxed, forgotten it or it had solved itself. Now it was back, that shadow behind those blue eyes. It was not something she had, or had not done, she was certain of that. This was something weighing on Giles's heart.

She could ask him straight out, but he was skilled at the masculine art of the direct answer that was actually no answer at all. He would not lie to her, but to find the truth she had to discover the right question, the one he could not evade, and as she had no idea what the problem was it was impossible to formulate the question.

It was not another woman, that, at least, she was secure about, certain of the impossibility of Giles betraying her in that way. *I love you*, she thought, watching him as he scowled at the latest Parliamentary report in *The Times*.

He looked up and met her gaze. 'What are you smiling about?'

'You, trying to set light to the latest debates with the power of your stare. I am very happy, Giles.'

'You are?' He glanced round. They had the breakfast room to themselves, Downing clearly recognising that newly married couples wanted privacy more than they required attentive footmen. 'I am glad. Laurel, there is something I must tell— Yes, Downing, what is it?'

'An urgent letter, my lord. It has just arrived.'

Laurel eyed the thin folds as she might a coiled snake. Urgent messages that must have come through the night were unlikely to be anything but bad news.

Jamie? But this is for Giles...

She winced at the crack of breaking wax. Whatever it was, Giles read it with one comprehensive glance.

'My father.' He got to his feet, shoving the

chair back, its feet shrieking on the highly polished floor. 'He has had a heavy fall from his horse and it has shaken him badly. They are not certain what caused the fall. It may have been simple error, or the horse stumbled, but he cannot remember and his doctor is worried it might be the result of some other, underlying, problem.'

'Downing, tell Dryden and Binham that we will want them to pack immediately, for a fortnight in the first instance.' Laurel looked at Giles who nodded his agreement. 'And the carriage in two hours.'

'One hour,' Giles said. 'You have no need to come, Laurel. I will be stopping only to change horses. It is likely to be exhausting for you.'

'There are times when the male need to spare us poor feeble females the slightest contact with reality is enough to make one scream,' Laurel remarked conversationally, not sure whether she wanted to hold him or shake him. 'I am coming, too—unless you are telling me that you don't want me with you?'

'Of course I want you with me.' Giles came around the table, his gaze fiercely focused on her, totally ignoring Downing who was still waiting silently for orders. 'Of course I want you. Always. Downing, carriage in an hour and a

half and Dryden and Binham as her ladyship—
Where the devil has he gone?'

'I suspect he is being tactful,' Laurel said, not
trying to free her hands from his grip. 'Do you
have confidence in your father's physician? Perhaps we should send for a London doctor now.'

'He seems a good man, my father always
speaks of him with approval. Laurel, I was away
so long and now I have only just got back.'

*And there may be no more time. What if this
is more serious than a simple fall?*

The words hung unspoken in the air between
them, then Giles sucked air down into his lungs
as though he had just surfaced from under water.
'He knows I will come, just as fast as I can. He
knows that. And he is strong, it was only the gout
laying him up before.'

'Yes, he knows. Now eat—we will both eat
another breakfast, because you will be no use to
him if you are dizzy from hunger.'

*And I will be no use to you and we will not
stop long enough to eat, I am sure.*

Laurel rang the bell and when Peter entered,
sent him to the kitchen to pack a hamper of food
and drink. She looked across at Giles, who had
returned to his seat and was cutting into bacon
he clearly had no appetite for. 'The Marquess

knows you will do anything for him, anything within your power.'

Giles made a sudden, abrupt movement, sending a fork spinning across the cloth to strike the coffee jug. 'Yes, he knows that,' he said, his voice grim. 'I will do anything.'

That was it, that was what was wrong, she realised. He had done something that his father required and he hated it, or hated himself for doing it.

He married me, she thought, choking back the panic. Then, *But he is content with our marriage. Happy. Perhaps it is as straightforward as guilt for having stayed away so long.*

But the Marquess had shown in every way except words how proud he was of Giles and she had seen it in the way he spoke to him, looked at him. He would not have wanted his son back sooner, not when he had discovered that he was taking his part in the fight against the French.

Laurel made herself eat, the toast like sawdust for all the taste it had. Giles had lived an independent life for nine years—now he was an adjunct to the Marquess, the heir. Laurel puzzled that train of thought through. Was he resentful of all the work that would fall on his shoulders? Surely not, not Giles. Or was he dreading the rank and the responsibility that would one day be his? Perhaps already was his, she realised with a sick feeling.

'You have little reason to love my father,' Giles said abruptly as he put down his cup and got to his feet.

'He was a little aloof when we told him of our engagement, but I expect he was embarrassed,' she said, realising it for the first time. 'He had huffed and puffed over you leaving the country and he had persisted in the estrangement between our families and now he had to admit that those provoking children were not so bad after all. I had sixteen years knowing him before everything went wrong and I was always very fond of him. I want to know him better, Giles, for my sake and for yours.'

'Thank you.' He pulled her chair back as she rose, but did not move away, instead pulling her into his arms, one hand flat on her back, the other trailing down her cheek. 'I do not deserve you, Laurel. If you only knew how little I deserve you.'

I love you.

She wanted to say it, but there was something in those murmured words that gave her pause. Would he believe her if she told him now, or would it seem like more reassurance, more support when he was badly in need of it? When she told Giles that she loved him she wanted to do so with his full attention, with nothing to give him cause to doubt her.

So she kissed what she could reach of him, which was the lobe of his left ear. 'I can hear the carriage outside. It is time to go, Giles.'

It took them twelve hours. It should have been just over ten, but malign fate seemed intent on delaying them at every turn. A fire in the high street at Hampton Wick, the bridge blocked at Leatherhead, a horse that went lame just a mile after the change at Guildford and then a fair choking the centre of Winchester, filling the inn yards with carriages and livery horses and cheerfully half-drunk revellers despite it being only five in the afternoon.

'Leave me with the carriage, hire a horse and ride on,' Laurel urged, shouting to make herself heard above the hubbub in the yard that seemed to have the largest stables and the best hope of getting a change.

'I'll not leave you, not in this.' Giles got up on the step of the carriage to block the open door to three countrymen, singing and staggering, ale pots in their hands. 'No, friends, this is not the stage.' He dug in his pocket. 'Here, drink to my health.' They reeled off, shouting their thanks.

'Then get two riding horses and I will come with you. Binham will feel safe with Dryden and your coachman and grooms, won't you, Binham?'

'Yes, my lady,' Binham said faintly, but with a sideways glance at Dryden sitting silent and solemn beside her.

Catching that wedding bouquet had a lot to answer for, Laurel thought, leaning out of the window to talk to Giles.

'It's another twenty miles,' he said.

'I can do that and I can ride in this skirt. If I become tired, we can stop at some respectable inn and I'll take a private parlour, while you go on. I insisted on coming and I am not going to be the cause of you being delayed.' She would never forgive herself if Giles arrived too late.

'I'll see if they have anything—and a side saddle.' Giles gave orders to the grooms who climbed down and stood one at each door, then fought his way across the yard to the long stable range.

Laurel had one of the valises brought down and found stronger gloves and a pair of half-boots. She pushed her small knitted reticule with a few coins into the front of her pelisse and was ready when Giles came back with an ostler behind him leading two horses, one with a battered side saddle.

He tossed her up and checked the girths while she got the skirts of her walking dress and pelisse organised and gathered up the reins. The horse stood placidly despite the uproar around it and she only hoped it did not prove to be a slug, but once they were clear of the congested streets and the racket of the fair with hurdy-gurdies and buskers and stallholders crying their wares, the two horses settled down into a steady canter.

Giles kept his mount level with hers and, despite everything, Laurel had to hide a smile at the way he looked across, studying how she rode, then, with obvious relief, looked forward and quickened the pace. Riding had been her chief recreation during those long years when he had been away and she rather prided herself on her seat.

They rested after an hour at a hamlet just beyond Romsey where an ancient tavern stood on the village green overlooking the stocks and a duck pond. A freckled youth brought out horn mugs of ale to them as they sat in the shade of a beech tree and let the horses stand after a drink in the pond.

'I would enjoy riding with you like this if only

we had no care for the time,' Giles said. He put out his legs, linked his hands above his head and stretched with a groan of relief. 'I am used to days in the saddle, not restrained rides in the parks.'

'Do you miss it? Portugal?' The ale was thin and sour but refreshing and Laurel drank again, watching her husband's long body with a mixture of pride and desire.

'I am glad to be home, but I miss the freedom when I was away from Lisbon. I would be alone, living on my wits, making decisions that might be life and death and yet it felt less onerous than what I am beginning to handle with the estate. The weight of expectation, I suppose.' He shrugged. 'All those ancestors watching me, all those tenants, all those staff.'

'But what you were doing in the Peninsula was life and death for others as well as yourself, surely?' Laurel put down her mug as she twisted on the bench to study his face. 'And you were on missions that would have an impact on the campaign. Those are huge responsibilities.'

'I know. It was the adventure, I suppose. Very shallow of me.'

'No, you were young, you were brave, you had freedom, independence and purpose. Now you are asked to be conventional and sensible and yet you are still a young man.' She smiled at him when he grimaced ruefully. 'There are so many expectations, it must be hard, but I know you will meet every one of them.'

She had hoped her sympathy would cheer him a little, but it only seemed to make his expression grimmer. 'I will help all I can, Giles, you know I will.'

'Yes, I know.' He caught her hand and raised it to his lips. 'You, my dear, are what stops me losing my sense of perspective and becoming buried under piles of estate papers and agricultural reports. I had no idea that marriage could be quite so delightful.'

'And you, my lord, are the most complete courtier. Why, I do declare I have never been so flattered as now, when you express a preference for me over the *Journal of the Society for Agricultural Improvements.*'

As she had hoped, it made him laugh and he was still chuckling when he tossed her up into the saddle again and they rode on.

The tension rose as the landscape became familiar. They splashed across the headwaters of the Ellingbrook, up through the Home Wood and there, in the distance, was Thorne Hall.

'Go,' Laurel urged. 'I'm on familiar ground now.' She held the tired bay mare to a slow canter in Giles's wake, turned from the grass woodland path on to the main carriage drive and strained her eyes to see the front of the house. Were the draperies drawn across the windows and was the huge old iron door knocker draped in black crepe?

'No. Thank God,' she said, reining in to a walk when she was close enough to see. The Marquess was alive.

Giles was at his father's bedside when Laurel climbed the fine Jacobean oak staircase and tapped on the bedchamber door.

'Come in, my dear! Come in. No need for that solemn face, I am suffering from a twisted knee and a lump on my thick skull, that is all.'

'We were anxious.' She approached the big bed and bent to kiss his cheek. 'The doctor was uncertain what had caused the fall.' But her father-in-law looked highly unlikely to be troubling Saint Peter in the near future, she had to admit.

'It was the bang on the head that made me forget what happened. All came back this morning—a deer shot out of the bushes right in front of me, Max shied and I went over the top like some confounded novice. Never been so ashamed of myself in my life. Still, no real harm done.' He sank back on the pillows and beamed at them.

Laurel caught Giles's gaze across the heaped pillows and rolled her eyes. He grinned back. No harm done, just hours of anxiety, an exhausting journey and worry that had dug lines around Giles's eyes.

'You must rest,' she told the older man. 'And I am going to ring for hot water for two baths and then Giles and I will have dinner and leave you to yours. I am certain your doctor wants you to be quiet and have an early night. You and Giles can talk all you want in the morning.'

'Managing, isn't she?' the Marquess remarked.

'Very,' Giles retorted. 'It is just what you need, sir. I will send in your man and will see you after breakfast.'

'Old devil,' he said to Laurel once they were outside.

'I expect he had an unpleasant time of it, especially if his mind was confused after the fall,' she said pacifically. 'He is enjoying having you back.'

'I am enjoying being back,' he said, following her through into their suite and collapsing into an elegant, boneless sprawl on the big bed. 'Ignore all my gloom and complaints earlier. I was tired and worried.'

'And feeling guilty,' Laurel said as she tugged the bell pull.

'What?' Giles sat up abruptly.

'About being away for so long,' Laurel said, surprised by the sharpness of his reaction. 'Giles, this morning, just before the post arrived, you said there was something you had to tell me? Or perhaps it was say to me—I can't quite recall. You were interrupted.'

He flopped back flat again. 'It was the wrong moment. Come here and I will tell you when we have all our clothes off—damnation! Yes? Come in.'

'Hot water and two baths,' Laurel said, with a smile for the footman who had answered the bell and a secret smile for Giles's words. He could not be feeling too exhausted if he wanted to make love.

Giles ordered the two baths to be set together in the middle of the bedchamber and not in the separate dressing rooms where they were kept. Laurel listened to the sound of his voice as he talked to the footman standing in for Dryden who, with Binham, was probably still making his slow way towards them. She was being unlaced by one of the maids, silent with nerves despite Laurel's best efforts to set her at her ease, and the girl was taking what seemed like an age.

Come on, Laurel urged silently.

What was it that Giles wanted to tell her, the thing that would be right to talk about when they were making love? Finally she was out of her clothes and into a robe. She sent the flustered maid scurrying off and waited for her husband to emerge from his dressing room which he did, just as she dropped the robe and stepped into the bath.

'Aphrodite,' Giles said, advancing on her with an obvious intent that became even more obvious when he shrugged off his banyan.

Laurel sank down into the water. 'Bath first. I smell of horse and I am going to be as stiff as a board in the morning if I do not soak now.'

Giles growled, but got into his own tub, scrubbing as though in a race. Laurel soaped and sponged and let herself drift off into an anticipatory daydream involving a clean wet husband and a big bed and— 'Oh, bliss.'

She hadn't heard him climb out of his bath or come over to hers, but he was kneeling behind her, his soapy hands massaging her shoulders, slipping lower, gliding over her breasts and teasing her nipples. Somehow she managed to hold on to some practicality, although goodness knew why she should, she told herself. 'I haven't finished washing.'

'Let me.' He went round to the foot of the tub, water still gleaming on his bare skin, and began to wash her feet, his fingers sliding between her toes, rubbing the arch of her feet, sliding upwards to soap her legs. Then higher.

'Every little crevice.' Giles came up on his knees, bending over her, one hand braced on the edge of the tub, one hand exploring intimately, soaping every crevice, teasing every fold until she was squirming and the water was splashing everywhere.

'Are you clean now, Laurel? Quite clean?' He bent over further, caught her left nipple between his lips.

'*Yes*. Giles! *Oh, yes...*'

Chapter Twenty-Two

Laurel was still disorientated with pleasure when Giles lifted her, slippery and gasping his name, carried her to the bed, pressed her down with his weight and took her with one, long, masterful stroke. And then stopped, quite still above her, raised on his elbows.

'Giles?'

'The thing I was going to say at breakfast.'

'Giles, this is no time for conversation! Will you please—'

'This is not conversation. This is a declaration.' The veins were standing out on his temples and the tendons in his neck were rigid with tension at holding back his body's instinctive movement. 'I love you.' He began to slide within her, slowly, so slowly as she stared up at him, hardly daring to believe what she was hearing.

'I have loved you all my life,' Giles said. 'But

I did not realise that I love you now as a man loves a woman, totally, body and soul. I love you, Laurel.' Then he was driving into her, possessing her, taking her with him as he went over the cliff. She heard his voice as they fell, over and over. 'I love you, Laurel. Love you.'

'Did I dream that?' Laurel asked. She lifted her head from where it had been butted in against Giles's right armpit and peered at the room. It was in virtual darkness.

'If you did, so did I.' Giles heaved himself up against the pillows. 'I love you.'

'Giles, I—'

'You don't have to say it.' He gathered her in against his chest and pulled a sheet over them both. 'It is the truth and I had to tell you, but I do not want you to say things you do not feel.'

'Shhh.' She sat up and twisted round to look at him. 'I love you, too. I always have. I loved you when I was angry with you, I loved you when I tried to tell myself I did not miss you, I loved you when you came back and I was still furious with you. I will always love you,' she said simply and wondered if it was possible to be any happier.

I do not deserve this, it is too perfect.

'Whatever I do?'

'Whatever. You aren't a saint, Giles, let alone

an angel. You are a man, thank goodness. It is highly possible there will be times when I want to strangle you, but nothing will stop me loving you. When did you realise how you felt?' she asked, snuggling down against his long flank again.

'It was something that Beatriz said, of all things. She asked me if I had loved you when you were a girl, before you were beautiful. And I said that of course I had always loved you. And then I realised what that meant.'

'And you said nothing to me?'

'It was only yesterday evening,' he protested. 'I had to pluck up the courage.'

'You were frightened?'

Surely not.

'Terrified. What if you had laughed at me? What if you had been kind and told me that you were *very fond* of me?'

There was self-mocking amusement in his voice, but Laurel shivered. 'Yes, I see. Horrible. Giles, this is wonderful, isn't it?'

'It is heaven and we are going to sleep now and we will wake up and it will still be wonderful.'

She felt his lips in her hair, felt the steady thud of his heart answering hers and slept.

In the morning it was still wonderful, despite two tubs of cold scummy water in the middle of the bedchamber and Dryden and Binham wanting to talk about their slow journey and how long it had taken to escape from Winchester and the faint, residual anxiety about her father-in-law.

The worry subsided after visiting the sickroom and finding the Marquess attempting to get out of bed and generally giving his valet hell for preventing him. He looked fit enough, to Laurel's eyes, to ride in a steeplechase and she said so, making him snort with laughter.

'That's a fine wife you have there, my boy. Listen to her and come and talk to me after breakfast—here, I suppose, if Gibbons is not going to let me out of bed.' He shot the valet a dark look.

'Doctor Harris said I was to hide your breeches if you attempted to rise before he has had a chance to examine you again, my lord,' the valet said calmly and removed himself from the room.

'Blasted doctors. Anyway, there's some problems with the land drains in the lower meadows and I want your views.'

'Certainly, sir.' Giles closed the door on his father and grimaced at Laurel. 'I know nothing about land drains and I want to spend the morning showing you how much I love you, but—'

'You'll have to get a grip on drainage instead. I understand. There was a message from Mrs Finlay asking if I would care to tour the house with her, so we will both do our duty this morning. My love,' she added for the sheer pleasure of hearing the words out loud.

Eating breakfast together should not have seemed fresh and different, but this was the first time they had done something so routine, so normal and domestic and knew themselves to be in love and loved. It was a delicious secret, something to be shared and communicated with a look, a touch, an inflection in the voice asking for marmalade or a fresh cup of coffee.

It even made Laurel smile when Giles went off to talk to the Marquess, grumbling as he went about having to think about drains when there were other, much more important things to talk about. 'And do,' he added, with a look that sent anticipatory heat into places best not thought about in the breakfast parlour.

She resolutely put such thoughts from her head as she accompanied the housekeeper on her tour of the house. 'You will know all the public rooms, of course, my lady, being so familiar from your childhood,' Mrs Finlay observed as she opened the door of the Long Gallery for Laurel to enter. 'And either the Marquess or Lord Revesby themselves will want to show you the portraits. The Marquess's pride and joy, this gal-

lery,' she added as Laurel slowed to look up at
the portraits as they passed.

Those before the early seventeen hundreds
were small and not particularly well painted she
noticed. With the arrival of George I and the
family's elevation they became imposing, large
and considerably better executed. 'Here is Lord
Revesby, my lady, but of course, you will recognise him.' Mrs Finlay stopped before the last
picture in the row, Giles as a young man, serious
and, Laurel suspected, thoroughly uncomfortable
at having to pose.

'The Marquess will be wanting to have your
portraits painted as soon as may be,' the housekeeper added with the confidential air of an old
family servant. 'He is so happy about the marriage, my lady.' She hesitated. 'These last few
years, he's been fretting for Master Giles to
come home, fretting badly. He said to me once,
*"If my boy would only return, he'll make all right
again. I've been a damn fool—"* excuse the language, ma'am *"—and it will break his heart if
I've thrown it all away."* And then he cheered up
and said that Master Giles, I'm sorry, my lady,
Lord Revesby, would make all right. I suppose he
was blaming himself for the quarrel when Lord
Revesby left home.'

'Yes, that must be it,' Laurel said. His heir's

defection would have hit the Marquess hard, because the title and the land were things he was passionate about. Giles felt the same way, she knew. Even as a boy, rebelling in his own stubborn way against his father, she had been aware of his abiding love for this land. Her own father had felt the same deep, visceral tie to the estates and to the land and it had been hard for him to accept that he would not hand them on to his own son.

'Will Lord Revesby be taking luncheon with the Marquess in his room, my lady?' Mrs Finlay asked, jolting her out of her reverie.

'Oh, I did not think to ask. I will go and find out.'

'I will send a footman, my lady.' Mrs Finlay was clearly shocked at the thought of her hurrying off on an errand.

'No, it is quite all right. I have just thought of something I need to say to my husband,' Laurel said. *I love you*, would be that message and it was too tempting to resist delivering it. 'I will meet you in your office for our tour, Mrs Finlay. I won't be a moment.'

I probably look like a lovesick ninny, she thought, hurrying along the corridors. *I probably have a silly smile on my face and Mrs Finlay is having a quiet chuckle to herself. And I do not care because he loves me.*

There was no sign of the valet when she entered the Marquess's sitting room, but the door into the bedchamber was ajar and the sound of male voices was clear. It did not sound as though they were discussing drains, she thought, amused. In fact, the moment they had found themselves alone they had probably started talking about something far more interesting, like hounds or brandy or the war in the Peninsula.

Laurel trod across the deep central carpet and opened her mouth to cough a warning that female ears were approaching.

'…absolutely for the best. I know you had scruples about asking Laurel to marry you and I understand why.'

What?

She closed her mouth and took another silent step forward.

'I am proud of you,' her father-in-law said, his voice disastrously clear. 'You did your duty, you dug me out of a pit of my own making—' His voice broke and there was the sound of him clearing his throat, some low-voiced comment from Giles. 'Palgrave was a stubborn devil and he put you in a damn awkward position, making the land and the debt contingent on the marriage, but all's right in the end.'

What debt? Contingent on the marriage...
Giles married me knowing about the trust and
that I would receive Malden? Is that the land?
But...

'I have never been more glad of anything in my life than that I married Laurel,' Giles's voice was quite clear now and she caught her breath. She had misunderstood, he hadn't proposed for gain. 'But I wish I could have found some way to do it without deceiving her. I never lied, I would never lie to her, but I should have found some way—'

Laurel backed away across the soft silk of the Chinese carpet, one hand to her mouth, the other groping behind her for the door.

'I may have damned myself, but I will—'

Then she was outside, its heavy door panels closing on the sound of her husband calmly discussing deceiving her. Laurel stood and breathed.

In and out. In and out. I will not cry or faint or rush in and shout at him. I love him. I trust him.

But she had just heard, with her own ears, that he had deceived her. At what point did trust become foolishness?

Evidence. You do not throw away what you

have without evidence. You do not condemn without evidence.

Laurel scrubbed the back of her hand across her eyes, although they were dry, she found. How strange, she thought she had been sobbing. There was a footman in the hallway and she smiled at him. It was probably rather thin, but he bowed and hurried forward.

'My lady?'

'Remind me the way to his lordship's study, would you? I have to find some papers for him. And please give Mrs Finlay my apologies and tell her that I must postpone our tour.'

The Marquess, like her father, kept a vast, old-fashioned desk with rows of pigeonholes for documents that could be shut off behind locking doors. And, like her father, he left them unlocked, it seemed.

Of course, the evidence she was looking for might well be with his solicitor, or shut away in the steward's office, but it sounded as though the matter was very much on his mind, something he would want to keep to hand.

Laurel closed the door and sat down at the desk. It was outrageous to be searching someone else's private papers, but it seemed this was a matter that concerned her, to put it mildly. If

Giles and his father were hiding things from her, then she could sink her scruples and pry.

It did not take long to see a large folded document with her father's hand clear on the outside. She pulled it out, flattened it open on the desk and began to read.

She was reading it through for the third time— it was easier to keep reading than to have to think what to do next—when the door opened.

'Laurel?' Giles looked, and sounded, appalled. And he looked as guilty as hell.

'I overheard you talking,' she said. 'So I came to see for myself. Why did you not tell me, Giles?'

'Would you have married me?' He was quite calm, his eyes watchful, only the tic of a nerve in his cheek betrayed feeling.

'No. Not at the beginning. No.'

'So. There is your answer.' It seemed he would not defend himself, or apologise.

'You lied to me.'

'I never lied. Prevaricated, perhaps, avoided answering directly, yes. But I would never lie to you, Laurel, upon my honour.'

'Your *honour*?'

That brought the colour up on his cheekbones, but Giles said steadily, 'That is what this is all about—honour. Do I see my father crippled by shame, do I see our name sink into the obscurity we rose from? Or do I fail to tell a lady the full truth while I offer her the marriage and the position she was destined to have? Where does my duty lie, Laurel? Because my honour depends on me doing my duty, does it not?'

When she did not answer he smiled, a bitter twist of the lips. 'I should never have told you I loved you.'

Laurel folded her father's letter and slid it back carefully into its place, then stood up. She found she had to hold on to the edge of the desk. *How humiliating.* 'I do not think I can talk to you now. I will go and let you get on with whatever you came to do.'

'I came to get that letter and then I intended to take it to you. I have damned myself, I know, and I see no reason why you should believe me, but I could not stand deceiving you any longer,' Giles said.

Liar. The word was almost out of her mouth when she remembered the last words she had heard before she closed the door. *'I may have damned myself, but I will—'*

Laurel sat down again, jarring her spine. 'What do you mean, you have damned yourself?'

'I should have told you about the letter, the

debt, the trust, my father's debts, the reasons I asked you to marry me. Then I should have told you I loved you. Not the other way around.'

Of course I want to marry you. I want nothing more than to marry you...it is the sum total of my ambition to marry you, and only you... Trust. You believed him when he told you he loved you. He had no reason to say it. She had known from the beginning that something was amiss, that Giles was hiding something, was uneasy in his mind. This was it.

For better, for worse... I swore.

'Tell me now.'

Giles told the story as though he was giving evidence in a court of law. The facts, only the facts. It was past the time for emotions or justifications. For pleading.

Laurel sat silently listening to him, that lovely brown gaze wide on his face, giving nothing away. But he knew her and she was hurting, she felt betrayed. She *was* betrayed because he had done what he had judged to be the right thing, the least worst thing.

'I left him for nine years,' he finished. 'Because of my pride and my temper and because I had not seen how much he loved me under all that bluster, how hard it was for a man like him to understand his only son and heir who was so very different from him. I could betray him or I could deceive you by giving you the thing you had always been destined for. And it was not until I realised I was in love with you that I saw it was not only deception, it was another betrayal.'

'I was very angry with you when we met again,' Laurel said, her voice rigidly controlled as though to prevent the tears spilling from her brimming eyes He had put those unshed tears there. 'You were angry with me.'

'And you forgave me when you understood.'

'And you? I was the reason you left the country, after all. Did you forgive me?'

'Yes.' He nodded. 'I desired you and I liked you, and I forgave you—in that order, I suspect.' Was that just the tremor of a smile? 'But I was too wrapped up in the deceit of what I had done to allow myself to understand that I love you.'

Laurel lowered her head and the tears spilled. She made an impatient gesture, brushed the back of her hand across her cheek and he could stand it no longer.

'Laurel. My love.' Giles knelt beside her, dug in his pocket for a handkerchief and began to dry her cheeks.

This was Laurel—the tears stopped immediately and she gave an inelegant, defiant little sniff. 'Don't.'

'Why not?'

'I can't think when you touch me,' she said shakily. 'I need to think. I had worked it all out that all I needed was to trust you this time and it would all be perfect again. I didn't realise that I needed to understand as well.'

'Neither did I.' Giles sat back on his heels to give her distance. Not too far. He was beginning to hope again. 'It wasn't you I needed to understand, it was myself. Why I had left the country like that, why I didn't come back before. Why, when I did, I felt so damn guilty. I am not certain it is all clear now, too much adolescent emotion at the time, too much pride, too much selfishly enjoying myself. I know why I felt guilty about my father and that guilt spilled over into the way I was thinking about you.'

He reached out his hand and she put hers into it, without hesitation. 'I don't know why you should believe a word I say,' he said, holding on to the lifeline of her fingers.

'I always believe you.' It was definitely a smile now. A little shaky, a trifle watery, but a smile. 'I know you never lie to me, I just have to get better at understanding this cunning male skill of avoiding the truth. Cousin Anthony has it, too, now I recall how he told me about Malden.'

'Laurel, come to bed.'

'Now?' The clock struck eleven.

'Now. I want to make love to you and I have something to give you.'

'But—'

'This is part two of the honeymoon. The part where the blushing bride is convinced, quite rightly, that the staff know exactly what is going on every time she and her husband disappear.'

'Idiot,' she said shakily and leaned towards him for his kiss.

Giles locked the door behind them and kissed her. Kissed her while he undressed her, kissed her while he fought off his own clothes, kissed her as they stood, naked in each other's arms.

Laurel began to back towards the bed, but he stopped her, lifted his head. 'I have something to give you. Something of yours to return.'

'Mine?' Intrigued and impatient she followed him to the dresser and watched as he opened the leather box with his studs and pins and rings. A small, grey, crudely shaped lump of metal sat amongst the gems and the gold.

'What is it?' Laurel took it when he held it out, flat on his palm.

'You gave it to me to look after for you, that night at the fair. I've looked after it ever since.'

Laurel rubbed her thumb across it. 'It is the heart, the golden heart I wanted so much and Stepmama refused to buy for me. So you bought it and I realised I couldn't keep it. But, Giles, that was *years* ago.' It had been gold then, all those years ago, gilded with cheap paint that had rubbed off to reveal the pewter beneath.

'You gave me your heart to keep safe and I have.' He took her hand and pressed her fingers to the callouses she had noticed on his right hand. 'I kept it in my pocket, tried to wear it out, but it was too strong for that. I wanted to keep it, but it is right that you have it again. Besides, I have you now, I have your real heart beating against mine.'

There were too many things to say, none of them that she had the words for. He had kept her heart safe.

'Make love to me, Giles.' Her hand closed around the token as he lifted her high against his chest.

His arms felt strong and safe and his weight as he came down over her on the bed was a claiming as positive as his kiss. Giles rested his forehead against hers as they lay, not moving, simply breathing each other in, letting the fear and the anger ebb away and the love and the trust fill them again.

Laurel opened her hand. 'Will you take it back and look after it for me again?'

Giles took the heart, closed his fingers tight on it. 'Shall I have it gilded again? Real gold this time.'

'No.' Laurel looked into the lapis-blue eyes and shook her head. 'That heart is how you shaped it. How I feel about you has shaped me. Neither the heart nor I am perfect, but we are true to you, just as we are.'

'And I have come home,' Giles said as he moved against her, sheathed himself in her. 'Not to a house or an estate or a title. But to you. And to love.'

* * * * *

MILLS & BOON

Coming next month

A NIGHT OF SECRET SURRENDER
Sophia James

'I remember you told me once that you wanted to be a writer.' Shay said.

Celeste breathed out and stood, moving towards the window and looking across the city rooftops.

'You are probably the only person in the world who knows this about me.'

'I kept the story you wrote. The one you gifted me for my eighteenth birthday.'

'A tale of two sisters. One good and one evil. I used to imagine myself as the commendable sister, the one whose life ran along the path of righteousness, but now…' She stopped and placed her palm on the glass. When she took it off the frosted warmth of skin left a mark into which she wrote her initials. C.V.F. Celeste Victoria Fournier. Another thing he remembered about her, the two sides of her heritage.

'I panicked today. I have never done that before and it worries me, because if it happens again it will be too dangerous for the both of us and I would not want…'

He stood and took her hand and the same sense of shock he had felt last night seared through him again.

'The dangers are there anyway, Celeste, crouching and close, no matter what we try to do to lessen them.'

She was soft and unresisting as he drew her in, the

smell of her familiar as he found her upturned mouth and claimed the warmth. Elemental and uncomplicated. Everything was peripheral and far away save for the longing welling up inside.

Slanting the kiss, he came in harder, demanding things she had not surrendered yesterday, the breath of her mixing with his own, a woman who was an enigma and a chameleon.

It was not love he could call on after all these years of separation, he understood that, but what was left was enough.

He'd always been so very careful and correct, but now he was neither. This was undeniable, the roar of something in his blood that he hadn't felt there before, unguarded and heedless.

Copyright © 2018 Sophia James

Continue reading
A NIGHT OF SECRET SURRENDER
Sophia James

Available next month
www.millsandboon.co.uk

LET'S TALK
Romance

For exclusive extracts, competitions
and special offers, find us online:

f facebook.com/millsandboon

◉ @millsandboonuk

🐦 @millsandboon

Or get in touch on 0844 844 1351*

For all the latest titles coming soon, visit
millsandboon.co.uk/nextmonth

*Calls cost 7p per minute plus your phone company's price per minute access charg

Want even more
ROMANCE?

Join our bookclub today!

'Mills & Boon books, the perfect way to escape for an hour or so.'

Miss W. Dyer

'Excellent service, promptly delivered and very good subscription choices.'

Miss A. Pearson

'You get fantastic special offers and the chance to get books before they hit the shops'

Mrs V. Hall

Visit millsandbook.co.uk/Bookclub
and save on brand new books.

MILLS & BOON